THE
Best
Book
IN THE
WORLD

D1101946

PETER STJERNSTRÖM

THE
Best
Book
IN THE
WORLD

*Translated
from the Swedish
by*

Rod Bradbury

nova

Published by Hesperus Nova

Hesperus Press Limited

28 Mortimer Street,

London, W1W 7RD

www.hesperuspress.com

First published by Hesperus Press, 2013.

This edition first published 2013

Peter Stjernström asserts his moral right to be identified
as the author of this work under the Copyright,
Design and Patents Act 1988.

First published by Bailo Kulor Förlag

English translation © Rod Bradbury, 2013

Designed and typeset by Madeline Meckiffe

Printed in Denmark by Nørhaven, Viborg

ISBN: 978-184391-516-4

PART I

In Which the Author Decides Who Decides

*E*nter The Author, *stage left.*

Titus Jensen is going to type the first sentence of his new novel. He has been thinking about the wording all morning.

Enter The Author, *stage left.*

Titus can see the man before him. The Great Author, with his salad days far behind him. He has been granted just a few more occasions to bask in the limelight. Why he has suddenly been given the chance to earn a few more kronor from a public reading, the Great Author hasn't a clue. He hasn't written a book in ages.

Regrettably, he will not be able to read from one of his own books. No, his only chance to gain appreciation and applause is to grab the book that someone hands him the very second he goes up onto the stage. He is placed in front of a microphone and hardly has time to announce the title before the public bursts out laughing.

They are taking the mickey – that he does know. But in a loving way, he convinces himself. He is close to their hearts and that, at least, is better than sitting at home alone in his pad in Stockholm's trendy Söder district. Besides, the booze and the drugs are free. He used to be culture. Now he is just a cult.

Not only can Titus see the author before him: he can sense what the man is thinking, what makes him tick, how he feels and what he is going to say from one second to the next.

What name should he give to the man on the stage? Can he win anything by diluting the fiction with a touch of reality? Titus, who is always sincere and revealingly personal on paper, decides to go the whole way. He is going to lend his own name to the man. He must. He is going to show the readers that he has the courage to put his own name to a man with a harsh and rugged soul. Titus Jensen, that is me, that is him, that is us, Titus thinks. Everything that happens to him happens to me too, in my head. I am the man on the stage. The man with the noose of fate around his neck.

Titus' fingers hover above the keyboard. He is facing one of his most important choices ever. The idea for the book is brilliant. A tripped-out study of hubris. A meta-novel about freedom and dependence. But how do you start an immortal masterpiece?

Enter The Author, *stage left.*

Does he really need to write more than that? Which 'outside' best describes his 'inside'? Is it important to say that the man is wearing a black shirt, black leather trousers and a black jacket? That his face is marked by years of harsh weather in the Stockholm bars? That his scalp shines with sweat under a crew cut? That he is still fairly handsome, despite all the warning bells relentlessly announcing: 'This is an unreliable addict, this is an unreliable addict!'?

Must he describe all appearances down to the tiniest detail? Or will that destroy the experience for the reader? Doesn't the reader have the right to conjure up his own images?

I want to create as many images as there are readers, Titus thinks. It will be just as exclusive as a film that can only be seen by a single spectator, as a painting that can only be viewed by a single person, as a symphony for just one listener.

Enter The Author, *stage left.*

But nevertheless, the reviewer Adrian Throwup had ripped his latest book to pieces, just because the character descriptions were so brief. Which was an absurd criticism considering the almost poetic character of the work. He had written that the 'artistic pretensions do not reach beyond the first page of the book'. What the hell did that creep know about the stringent demands he, Titus, made of himself? Of the sky-high artistic ambitions he had? He had worked for a whole year on the book. Every single day had been filled to the brim with 'artistic ambitions'. That bastard of a reviewer, for his part, had only worked for a couple of hours to skim the book and produced that rotten review. Yet that hatchet job had more readers than Titus' book ever will. It wasn't that Titus' books didn't sell well. But the newspaper was bought by so horribly many more. Would he ever be able to upset the balance of power?

There is no justice, Titus thinks. I want to sell a lot too. I *shall* sell a lot. With or without a hatchet job from that serial killer Adrian Throwup.

But isn't Adrian Throwup a part of the public too? What would he like to read?

Setting: a Swedish summer. A prematurely aged author in his fifties enters the stage under a marquee canopy at a legendary rock festival which takes place every year in an idyllic and rural setting in Värmland, in the west of Sweden. The author's dilated pupils look out over the expectant public. There are about 700 people in the marquee, most of them in their twenties. An eccentric poet of about twenty-five years of age with blue and orange streaks in his hair hands over a leather-bound book to the author, who is dressed for the day in black from top to toe. A rather tipsy youth right up near the

edge of the stage starts to cough uncontrollably. You can
clearly see the remains of a kebab on his white T-shirt.
A strong smell of garlic gusts across the stage.

No, it doesn't work, Titus thinks. That isn't my book, isn't my
story. I can't go on like this. I can't allow my life to be governed
by reviews that stink. I'm an artist. I do what I want. I have
absolute pitch. I am the one who chooses my details, not
Adrian Throwup.

Many women have said that white suits him. Women
who one moment have promised him eternal love, but
the next have slammed the door in his face. So who can
blame him now for only wearing black?

That's got it just right.
Now Titus Jensen is going to be unleashed.

PART II

The Battle for The Best Book in the World

CHAPTER 1
Slam

Enter The Author, *stage left.*

Many women have said that white suits him. Women who one moment have promised him eternal love, but the next have slammed the door in his face. So who can blame him now for only wearing black?

A furious bass drum tears at the public's emotions. The spotlights flash on and off to the beat.

His entrance isn't the most glamorous that mankind has witnessed. Titus Jensen is wheeled onto the middle of the stage on a luggage trolley. There he is tipped off and left erect in front of a microphone stand. The flashing light is turned off after a while but the drumming continues. The public's boots and decrepit trainers create a subdued roar as they stamp rhythmically on the earthen floor.

It is dark for a few seconds before a chalk-white beam of light is turned on above Titus. It is narrow and seems to nail him to the stage. Applause and whistling. Everybody knows what is going to happen.

The young and beautiful romantic poet Eddie X is the host for the evening and amid growing cheers he glides up onto the stage in baby-blue silk pyjamas. Eddie is of Latin American extraction and his body language differs quite a lot from that of northern Europeans. It is perfectly natural for him to flash his smile three inches from somebody's face without worrying about his own or the other person's breath.

Eddie X caresses Titus Jensen with his dark velvety gaze and gives him, first, a rather too long hug and, then, a book. He slowly pulls a strand of orange hair back from his face and puts it in its proper place with the other coloured streaks among his otherwise long and dead straight black hair. He lowers the microphone down to Titus' level, and bends over it.

'My friends!' Eddie hisses with his leisurely northern accent, his mouth sensually close to the microphone. His white teeth glow in the spotlight. 'Dear festival visitors. Look and listen! He is a living legend. The tabloids wrote about his love affairs before most of us were even born. He has written a dozen or so novels about darkness, treachery and evil sudden death. He has a reserved table at the Association Bar. He even has a drink named after him. Now he has come onto our stage and his pupils and senses are wide open! A warm applause for: Titus Jensen – the Great Author!'

The public starts to laugh straight away. Many of them have seen this spectacle before. A couple of extra spotlights are turned on and Titus Jensen blinks in the white light. He sees the public as if in a mist and he hears some bass tones from the rock stage in the neighbouring marquee. He tries to sway in time with the beat. Yes, of course. Now he remembers. He is in the Poetry Slam tent at a rock festival. What happened to the afternoon? Titus can only remember sitting talking with Eddie X backstage. They drank a little, had some fun together and talked about life, literature and love. Then he got high on some unknown drug from one of Eddie's mates in the band. Everything went blank. Well, blank is perhaps not the right word. Everything started spinning like crazy inside his head and suddenly he was covered in black rat fur and was running around inside a fluorescent hamster wheel. He ran and ran, but his thoughts stood completely still. It felt as if several weeks passed while his thoughts only moved forward by one single letter. Then all the lights went out.

But now they have evidently been turned on again, thinks Titus, blinking against the light.

A short roll of the drums announces that it is time. He feels how the presence of the public pushes away the last remnants of his hallucinations and fills him with energy. He picks up the book Eddie has given him, and reads the title loudly and dramatically with his broken bass voice:

'*The Diseases of the Swedish Monarchs, by Wolfram Koch. From Gustavus Vasa to Gustav V.*'

Many members of the audience are already convulsed with laughter. It is senselessly funny entertainment to watch Titus Jensen read weird old books as if they were Greek tragedies. He reads in such an infernally theatrical manner that he could wake the dead.

Titus thumbs through the book at random. Then he catches sight of a picture of the remarkable Karl XIII and makes that his first stop. With a tremble in his voice, he reads a passage:

'It was now apparent that the end was near, and every arrangement was made to quickly promulgate the expected demise. The palace was full of people of all classes who had gathered there to acquire news of the sovereign's condition, bulletins having been posted in the Hall of Pillars. In the last evenings before the sovereign's demise, those people who were waiting there, known as well as unknown persons, were served tea and punch. Only on the final night did an atmosphere of calm evidently pertain, as court function-aries, bodyguards and other royal servants, in a state of exhaustion, fell asleep on *sofas and chairs.*'

Titus spits out the last words in a frenzy. He pauses for effect and looks out over the audience. Many of them are bent double with laughter and have tears in their eyes. They adore him. So he continues his recitation.

'From the autopsy report: the most interesting findings concern the brain and the membranes of the brain which suggest a diffuse senile brain atrophy and senile enlarged leptomeninges. The symptomatology and the autopsy findings indicate minimal old malaceae caused by arteriosclerotic vascular disease in the basal ganglia and pons, thus typical status desintegrationis. The discovery in the lungs ought perhaps to be interpreted as a sign of pneumonia with abscesses. The heart's normal condition appears remarkable, while the thickening of the artery walls with fatty matter seems natural.'

A certain calm spreads among the audience. Occasional giggles. Titus realises that he must find more populist sections to sustain audience interest. But it isn't so damned easy with this hopelessly old book! He thumbs through feverishly. Could this be something? He adopts a pose with his legs apart and puts one hand behind his back. The other hand lifts the book in a sort of gesture of homage. He is Hamlet and the book is a skull.

'About Gustav V!' Titus declaims theatrically. 'I begin with a quote: "The practising of tennis never gives rise to physical injuries. On the contrary, it liberates the body's vigour and vitality in a wonderful manner. The same could hardly be said about a boxing or wrestling match." Well, the King's estimation of tennis as a safe sport was perhaps somewhat exaggerated, which he himself on certain occasions was to experience. But he wished to make light of such interludes. Some tennis accidents may however be mentioned here. The most serious accident on the tennis court affected the King in 1927 when he *slipped on a ball* and hit the back of his head on the floor and dislocated a foot. He was carried out unconscious and remained in that condition a long time. One of the players manipulated the joint back into position before the arrival of C.C. Olin, the royal physician at the time. Mr G., as the King was called when he played tennis, was shocked by the fall and the pain. When he came to his senses he demanded – against the wishes of his doctor – to be taken to the palace at Drottningholm. In the evening he telephoned his fellow players and thanked them for their help, adding that although his foot was very painful he did feel better after a hand of bridge – as we know, King Gustav was a passionate bridge player. The dislocation did, however, prevent him from playing tennis for *no less than three months*!'

Titus gesticulates and waves his arms wildly while he reads the text. The cheers from the young people in the marquee know no bounds. He shifts his voice up a gear to imply the greatest possible drama.

'On one occasion, during the summer tennis season in Båstad in 1932, the King slipped on an old cement court which rain had made slippery, and fell suddenly backwards. He coiled himself up in the fall so he didn't hit his neck but nevertheless took a nasty blow and grazed his legs and hands. The royal physician Hjalmar Casserman, who was present, was afraid that the neck of the femur of his majesty's thigh had been damaged but when he wanted to examine the King, he was told that there was *nothing* wrong with his leg. But *abscesses developed on his hand*, which didn't, however, spoil his joy in playing tennis!'

Now the audience is jumping up and down in step on the earthen floor. They shout and laugh. This whets Titus' appetite and his eye catches details in the text that seem all the crazier. He delivers a lively declamation about Gustavus Vasa's diarrhoea and vomiting on his deathbed, and about Erik XIV's severe schizophrenia after his sojourn in prison. With irrepressible temperament he recounts how Sigismund lost the ability to speak and tells of Karl XI's distended gall bladder.

He rounds off with a preposterous description of Adolf Fredrik's never-ending spa visits to drink the waters, and how his furious vomiting led to even more spa visits which finally threatened to ruin the economy of the entire kingdom.

'...but the mud treatment of the King's head gave good results and Adolf Fredrik no longer needed to change servi-ettes and night cap twice a night!'

Applause and whistling. It seems to Titus that his entire performance is nothing short of a great success. He parodies a courtier and bows deeply sweeping his arm.

'RE-PUB-LIC! RE-PUB-LIC! RE-PUB-LIC!' the audience start shouting in chorus, clapping their hands in time.

Titus Jensen looks around in confusion. Republic? What has that got to do with his artistry? But he bows yet again and leaves the stage just as Eddie enters. When they pass each other, Eddie whispers in Titus' ear to meet him for a drink or two after his own performance.

Eddie X saunters confidently up to the edge of the stage. He throws his long hair back and grabs the microphone. His Latin behaviour combined with his northern Swedish modesty creates a strong field of energy around him.

'That was terrrrific! We thank Titus Jensen for these edifying facts about the honourable history of our kingdom. Now we change subject and tempo. I would like to warmly welcome – The Tourettes!'

The Tourettes are Eddie's sound carpet. A performance from Eddie X and The Tourettes comprises Eddie reading his romantic poetry with incredible ardour and The Tourettes playing improvised and spasmodic music in the background. Lenny, one of Eddie's closest friends, plays the guitar and is the frontman in the band. Lenny suffers from severe tics. His head gives a sudden jerk now and then and the spasms are transmitted through him in the form of a weird enormous blinking. They run down through his shoulders and on towards his knees. But Lenny has chosen to never see himself as a victim; rather he has transformed his awkward syndrome into an advantage, something of which he is actually proud. Tourette's syndrome is a part of him whether he likes it or not, just like his nose or the colour of his eyes. His exceptional musicality, together with his condition, has created a music that has no comparison whatsoever with any other art form. Now and then, The Tourettes perform with Lenny as their singer, which is a strange experience since Lenny has a compulsive urge to utter swearwords as soon as he gets stressed. And since a performance is always associated with a certain tension, the only song that Lenny can articulate is a single long stuttering flow of expletives and four-letter words. It is all quite remarkable.

But today it is Eddie X and his texts that are the centre-piece. Eddie is a warm person and he had a great ability to spread this warmth to all those who read or see him. When he takes part in Poetry-Slam gatherings, his performance is always an entertaining combination of stand-up comedy and poetry. He thumbs through the papers in his little plastic folder containing the evening's poems, which he always takes with him onto the stage. Not that he ever reads from them. He knows his texts off by heart. But the folder gives him security and balance.

'Dear Friends!' he starts off with his warm voice groaningly close to the microphone. 'Have I told you about when I decided to move south to Stockholm?'

The audience starts to hoot and whistle as if Eddie were going to play an old hit. And in some ways that is exactly what he is going to do. Eddie's poems are incredibly popular. A lot of people have heard or read them earlier, with or without the spasmodic sound carpet.

Eddie puts his right hand over his heart and starts to read the poem, or the story, about a tender young boy who comes to the big city:

'*Insecurity* is a vehicle.

'I am eighteen years old.

'I'm a learner driver of all sorts of vehicles.

'I sit behind the wheel on a chair in a bar and watch people circling around.

'Around me.

'I see the *insecurity* in the corners of their eyes and wonder how it works.

'How do they do it?

'How can they cope?

'They are rusty, buckled, scratched and painted over.

'But they hum and purr.

'Dance, laugh, drink, kiss, live.

'They are alive!

'*Insecurity* is a vehicle that can only be driven by flesh and blood.

'Flesh and blood that hates and loves.

'And is alive!

'I finish a glass and wobble out of the depot with a laugh.

'I'm going on to the playing field.

'I'm going to take my driving test.

'Yes, *insecurity* is a vehicle that I can understand.

'I'm going to be a fantastic driver.

'I am alive!'

The audience hums with love for Eddie X – the girls especially. Of course, his texts often verge dizzying on the edge of the precipice of the pathetic. But his youth and his ardour excuse everything. A genuine poet has the right to express what he wants, how he wants, whenever he wants. Every society needs poets and just now the audience at the festival in Sweden need the colourful Eddie X more than ever.

Eddie goes on to read ten or so very candid poem-stories about his life and The Tourettes jerk and shake in the background. There is a great atmosphere in the audience. Everyone is enjoying themselves, hugging each other, laughing and smiling.

They live in the best of worlds.

CHAPTER 2

Battles and Ideas

By the time Eddie gets backstage, Titus has already managed to drink half a bottle of red wine. Eddie sees him sitting alone on a bench at the far end of the beer tent and carefully pushes his way through the partying masses.

The tent is filled to the brim with people, but the seats right next to Titus remain empty. He himself has never been able to decide whether this is due to exaggerated respect or pure and simple distaste. The pattern has pursued him all his life. Do they love him or hate him? Is he appreciated or despised? Pah! Who knows? Whatever, it feels better – and less important – with a bottle of red wine inside him.

But the amiable Eddie, of course, sits down next to Titus. In Eddie's world there is plenty of room for love and all of its synonyms.

'Hi, Titus! Many thanks. You were really funny. You can make great theatre out of anything at all. You are fantastic.'

'Er, thank you very much,' Titus mumbles, embarrassed. 'And how did you get on?'

'Yup,' says Eddie articulating the sound as he breathes in. 'A lovely response this evening. We were close to each other. I love the festival public.'

'Well, that's great then.'

Titus has mixed feelings about what he had experienced earlier in the evening. Of course it's nice to do these improvisations. People appreciate his readings. But it would be even nicer if they just for once were to ask him to read something from his own books.

'Eddie,' says Titus. 'There's something I must ask you about.'

'Yes?'

'I am old enough to be your father. And I don't really understand your generation. When I read… do you think… I mean… everybody laughs so much… do they like me? Or are they making a fool of me? Do you understand what I'm getting at?'

'Titus, Titus, Titus. I'll be completely honest. Perhaps love is too strong a word, I don't know… but they are fascinated by you. You are a living legend. I am quite sure they don't really understand you properly. But they like what you give them. And what you give them is great experiences, that much is for certain. And all those who give something are liked. It's the people who take things from you who aren't liked. The people who take things from you deserve to be despised. You give, Titus. You are one of those who gives.'

Titus raises his eyebrows in surprise. He has never thought of it like that before, that he was generous. Eddie makes him feel good.

'Yeah, right. It's nice of you to say that…'

'No doubt about it, Titus. And royal diseases was the best reading for a long time. Absolutely on a par with when you read *Handbook for a Volvo 245* at the Debaser club last winter. Do you remember that?'

'Well, vaguely. I reckon I had had quite a binge before that reading.'

'I can guarantee it. You *are* popular. And I like you a lot. Can I get you something?'

'A bit of the hard stuff would go down nicely, thanks.'

'Coming up, maestro,' says Eddie, and slips over to the bar.

Eddie has a strong aura which serves as a heat shield when he makes his way through a crowd. He never has to push and shove, or use his elbows to keep his place. Effortlessly he is suddenly standing at the bar and can order a round. He swaps a few artiste coupons for some booze and slips back to Titus.

'Are you dark or light?' Eddie asks, holding a large brown rum and soda in one hand and a smaller vodka and mixer in the other.

'I'll take the brown one, thanks,' says Titus in a somewhat strained voice.

He greedily reaches for the big glass and fills his mouth with such a large gulp that he has to swallow it in two parts so as not to start coughing. His eyes look grimly down into the rest of the liquid. Don't sneak off, you nice drinkie. Stay with daddy.

Eddie sips his light vodka and mixer. He puts the glass down on the table and circles with his index finger around the rim. Titus seems tense; perhaps this isn't really Titus' sort of place, Eddie thinks. But Eddie is extremely good at getting people to feel at ease, almost to the point of being compliant. He always says that there is no greater challenge than getting a fellow human being to feel good.

He wonders what they could talk about that would make Titus relax. Eddie is a good judge of character and knows very well that a conversation partner thinks and acts according to three rules of human intercourse: it is boring to talk about you; it is okay to talk about other people; but the best of all options is to only talk about me.

'Where did you actually learn how to read with such fantastic insight? You've been to drama school, haven't you?'

'Uh, no. But I usually read my texts aloud so that they are as close to everyday spoken language as possible. It makes it more lively. Perhaps that has given me a bit of experience. And of course I've done lots of these book improvisations now.'

'Is that right? You haven't been to drama school? Your voice sounds so trained! So incredibly experienced!'

'Oh, I don't know about that. In that case it must be Philip Morris who has trained my voice,' says Titus and laughs. 'And Macallan and Absolut and Aquavit. Yeah, Jesus, those are quite some schools, haha…'

Eddie smiles when he sees that Titus has finally relaxed.

'So what project are you busy with now?'

'Well, it's been a while since I wrote anything. Anything that really hung together. But I've got lots of fragments.'

'That sounds exciting,' says Eddie and lets his gaze stray outside the tent.

'Um, in some ways. They are pretty good texts I think. Perhaps. I don't know. It feels a bit straggly. But it doesn't sell very well unless you can package the texts in a genre, does it? Who's going to buy a book called *Fragments* by Titus Jensen? How many copies does an experimental book sell?'

'No, you are quite right about that!' shouts Eddie.

Sales figures are a subject that really gets Eddie going, even though economics and money are normally not topics you would associate with romantic poets. But nobody can eat poems, not even Eddie X.

'It's just crazy,' he goes on. 'You simply *must* have a suitable label if you're going to sell. I mean, I hardly sell anything either. I don't get much in royalties each year. I live almost exclusively on what I earn when I perform. And all the T-shirts with my aphorisms of course. It's just crazy when you think about it.'

'Yeah right, you're bloody right! You have to fit in under a label to sell! One ought to write… hell, one really ought to write a bestseller…' says Titus dreamily, and takes a big slurp of his rum.

'Precisely! Exactly. That's what a bloke should do!' Eddie chips in, and takes a hefty gulp too. 'Let's drink to that,

Titus! One really should write a proper bestseller. That's the bottom line!'

'Umm, nothing more nor less. A smash hit. That'll sell like ice cream during a heat wave! One of those books that people will talk about for years. That top the lists year after year!'

'Yes, let's drink to that!'

'A book that'll be translated into lots of different languages!'

'A book that will win prizes!'

'A book that will be turned into a film!'

'That'll be put on the stage!'

'That'll start a new trend!'

'It will indeed!'

'Exactly!'

'Cheers!

'Cheers!'

Both authors are touchingly in agreement. One ought to write a bestseller. Precisely. Exactly. But how? What sort of book is it that one ought really to write? They sit there in silence for a few moments and concentrate on their drinks. Eddie, of course, is the first to start talking again. He points at Titus' empty glass.

'Another of the same? I've got lots of coupons.'

'Yes please, that would be nice.'

'But meanwhile you can reflect upon what the book should be about,' says Eddie with a warm smile. 'Okay?'

'Haha… yep… yeah, err…' mumbles Titus, who is starting to feel a bit the worse for wear.

Eddie surfs through the crowd and parks himself by the bar. He is immediately seen by the barman, who responds as if he is physically struck by Eddie's charisma.

Titus sees that parts of The Tourettes are making their way through the backstage area to the beer tent. He knows all about them. Lenny is an institution in Sweden, always praised by the pop-culture elite. Having a severe compulsive disorder and still making great art makes him untouchable. Everybody loves Lenny.

The Tourettes jerk and twitch in various ways, all of them. Lenny is worst with his weird whole-body blinks. It's most difficult for him to control this when he is on stage, where he sways like a field of rye in a hard wind. But the others are not far behind. One has severe facial tics, another takes long steps to avoid stepping on lines, one suddenly sticks his arm right out as if in a spasmodic salute. It is untidy and noisy.

Weird really, so many different types united in a single band, thinks Titus. By themselves they are nothing, but together they are something great.

Titus' musings come to a halt.

By themselves they are nothing, but together they are something great. Fragments and pieces of a jigsaw puzzle. A bit like his texts.

Eddie is soon back with more booze.

'Titus Jensen, future bestseller! How are you getting on? Have you come up with a brilliant idea?'

'No, but, well…' croaks Titus, slurring a little, but all the more enthusiastic. 'I've got a sort of idea, I think. If I put it like this: "One at a time they are nothing, but together they are something great." What does that make you think of?'

'Yeah… no, I don't know…'

'Well, my idea… would it be possible… couldn't you combine a whole lot of different types of books and make them into one single book? Write in lots of different styles and genres at the same time, sort of?'

'How do you mean? The only book you need, like? A combination book?' Eddie wonders.

'Yeah… perhaps… or yes. That's it exactly! A single book that is all the other books at the same time.'

'Gosh! Brilliant! Let's drink to that! Jesus, just think how that would sell!'

'Cheers! Yes, indeed, it would be a hell of a success. A single book which is a bestseller in lots of different categories! Crime, cookbooks, diet books, management literature, DIY books, self-help, how to be happy, everything all at once!'

'The works!' shouts Eddie.

'It'd be the best book in the world!' remarks Titus and takes a large gulp.

'Easily!'

'It's going to be translated into lots of different languages!'

'And win prizes!'

'Be made into a film!'

'Into a play!'

'Start a new trend!'

'Indeed it will!'

'Exactly!'

'Let's drink to that!'

'Cheers!'

Once again they are touchingly in agreement. They look at each other in a moment of real earnest. Is this just a fun drunken idea? Yes, perhaps, but just now it feels as if it is of decisive importance. To write a book that fills every single bestseller category at the same time – that would put the author on the map forever. But to make an attempt that fails would, in turn, guarantee a prominent position in the encyclopedia of misfits. The risks are great. Horrible.

What have they got to lose?

Quite a lot, in fact.

Being the first, for example.

They both think that thought at the same time. You've got to be first. First, first, first! Otherwise you've had it. Oh dear, now it's a matter of playing it cool. Now there is suddenly an awful lot at stake. Their gaze wanders and they look a little askance at each other.

Silence.

Wandering eyes.

Eddie, who always takes responsibility for social situations, is the first to speak up.

'Yeah, well, Titus, that was a really fun idea. Somebody ought to write a book like that. But it's probably impossible to put all those different bits together into something that works, don't you think?'

'Right… yes, absolutely. If it could work, then somebody would already have done it. That's for certain. But it is a fun idea.'

'Yeah…'

'Um…'

'Shall I get some more booze?'

'Yeah, sure. Then perhaps we can come up with some even better ideas, don't you think?' says Titus, and laughs somewhat forcedly.

'Right. That's the attitude, Titus. Now let's forget this and have a bit of a party! I'll get some drinks and tell Lenny and the boys to come over. Nobody can party like The Tourettes!'

Eddie goes to fetch the spirits and his mates. The night is long and is filled with conversations, laughter and facial twitches.

Neither Titus nor Eddie mentions the book idea again.

Both of them know what this is about.

The Best Book in the World can give eternal life.

But only to one of them.

CHAPTER 3

A Star Publisher Enthuses

Titus wakes up in the back seat of his car in the festival parking area. He is dripping with sweat. The sun is already high in the sky and you could fry an egg on the car bonnet. It is stuffy. He opens the car door and falls out into the cool Swedish summer morning. The birds are chirping and all around him he sees misted-up windows of cars full of other festival-goers. He goes to the shower building, which is still fairly quiet. He stands under a jet and lets his head clear, gulping water to try and flush out his body.

The idea still feels good. Almost even better. This is exactly what he needs. A big project into which he can channel all his energy.

He buys a squashed cheese roll from a stall and goes towards his car. Wonder where Eddie got to? They had been drinking a long time and then Eddie had suddenly just disappeared. Somebody said that he thought that Eddie had got a lift home to Stockholm already, in the middle of the night.

Titus gets behind the wheel and bounces out from the field that has become a temporary parking place during the festival. When he is back on the road, he picks up his telephone and rings his editor at Winchester Publishing.

'Umm, hello? Astra Larsson here.'

'Hi, Astra, it's Titus. Sorry to phone you so early on a Sunday.'

'Oh, it's you. Hi, Titus. And yes, I am feeling a bit groggy. I was out dancing until three last night. We had a girls' dinner which became… well, something completely different…'

'Sounds like fun. Astra, I have had a great idea that we have to talk about. When can you see me?'

'Err, I don't know. I don't exactly keep my diary with me in bed. Sometime next week?'

'No, no, no! It is much more urgent than that. You've got to hear this. Can I come over this evening?'

'No, I don't know. I'm going to dinner at Evita Winchester's. The will of the boss is law, you know. She has invited all her editors so that we can talk about next year's list.'

'Well then, that's perfect!' Titus shouts. 'I can get to you before the dinner! What time are you due there?'

'Five,' says Astra. 'You are making me really curious, Titus. What has happened?'

'Let's talk it about later. I'll be at your place by four o'clock latest. Then I'll give you a lift to the Winchester Villa on Djurgården. Okay?'

'Okay, let's do that.'

'Thanks, Astra. Thanks.'

'See you.'

CHAPTER 4

Chez Astra

At three o'clock Titus rings the bell by Astra's door. He has never liked using lifts, so he has lumbered up the stairs to Astra's flat. He is a bit out of breath and sweaty when Astra opens the door.

'Hi, Titus, are you already here? Nice to see you. You look… you look as if you've been having fun… or something,' says Astra, who looks just as beautiful and freshly showered as usual.

'Hi,' Titus pants. 'Everything okay?'

'How did you get on at the festival? What did they hand you this time?'

'*The Diseases of the Swedish Monarchs.* It was a great success.'

'Yes, well. I'm glad to hear it. Congratulations, I suppose one should say then.'

'You sound ironic…'

'Yes, but you know what I think about all that. It might be fun and so on, but I don't think it does much for your brand image as an author.'

'My brand image?' says Titus, irritated. 'I get a fee, damn it! *Money* is good for my brand image. But perhaps you are thinking of raising my royalty rate? Are you?'

'Sorry, Titus, sorry. I should have kept my mouth shut. Come in, now.'

Titus enters the flat and kicks his shoes off in the hall. They are in good company. Astra has at least twenty pairs of shoes there. Light airy shoes that look very expensive. Shoes that go perfectly with Astra's young, glowing and slim legs.

Astra is already in the kitchen. She pokes about behind the counter.

'What can I offer you, Titus?' she calls out to Titus when he walks through the living room. 'Espresso? Latte? A beer?'

'Yeah, that'd be good. A beer would go down nicely.'

'I've only got medium-strong beer. But it's cold and good!'

'That'll do fine.'

Astra gets out a beer and Titus sits on the other side of the counter. He strokes his crew-cut scalp with one hand and opens the beer can with the other. He looks pretty rugged, to put it politely. Then he empties about half of the contents of the can in a few large gulps. Astra looks at him at first with surprise, but her forehead and eyebrows stretch further for every gulp he takes. That doesn't look as though it's good for him, she seems to be thinking.

She knows very well what it is about. When she 'inherited' Titus Jensen a few years earlier, she had been warned about the way Titus burned his candle at both ends. His former editor couldn't cope any longer with his empty talk and continuous binge drinking. Astra, who had built up a reputation at work for her strong will and her literary sense, got to take him over and had the task of trying to steer his work. But since his writing hadn't gone anywhere for a long time, there was nothing to steer. Titus just went round and round.

But now it seemed as if the embers were about to flare up in Titus. Astra feels a mix of hope and worry.

'Well, was there a bit of a party yesterday, then?' she asks.

'Err, yes. Sure. Really great. Eddie X was MC-ing. And he performed with Lenny, you know, and those other Tourette guys. I think Lenny and Eddie have known each other since they were kids. Lenny is bonkers. We were partying together all night and in the end Lenny could only say "c-c-cock in your ear!" "C-c-cock in your e-e-e-ar." Over and over again.

33

Just sat there and twitched and said "cock in your ear". Completely out of it.'

'There is medicine for that.'

'Yeah, but he doesn't want to take any. He says it would numb his mind.'

'Who knows. I would like to have my mind numbed a bit if the only thing I could say was "cock in your ear". Well, anyway…'

'Whatever,' says Titus, who is in a hurry to talk about his book idea. 'I was livened up by that party. And an incredibly good idea suddenly popped up. Listen to this.'

With sweeping gestures, Titus starts to describe the book that is going to top all the lists in all categories at the same time. He has already got quite far with the actual plot. The protagonist is an overweight chief inspector whose career ambitions in the police force have stalled. But by being able to make fantastic dishes with special ingredients he starts slowly but surely to lose weight. It transpires that the weight loss is permanent. The slimming soon gives him energy and the self-confidence to set new targets for his life and his work. One thing after the other suddenly starts to run smoothly. His new way of looking at the world makes him question the methods used by the police. The unorthodox style of detective work he initiates soon bears fruit and a number of unsolved serial murders finally look as if they would find resolution, if it weren't for his boss, the unsympathetic chief superintendent, who is keen on team spirit and 'the way the police have always worked'. The hero of the book, the chief inspector who is now a normal weight, sets off a grass-roots revolution and a radical organisational transformation begins. It is a development story of great proportions. Criminal elements will be cowering.

Astra listens to Titus with growing interest. She has never seen Titus so enthusiastic before.

'Do you get it?' Titus croaks on. 'Are you on board? With this framework I can fill in with wisdom, recipes and DIY tips at length. I can write any amount!'

'I believe you,' answers Astra slowly. 'I really do.'

'So what do you think? Shall I get going?'

You can hear Astra think. On the one hand she thinks it a good idea. A really good idea. Brilliant, quite simply. She knows that Titus writes superbly, and presumably a change of genre would be just the thing his writing needs. On the other hand, it is a crazy project. To let loose a more-or-less alcoholic author on the task of writing a bestseller can never end well. It is impossible to know in advance which books will sell, that much she does know. To give Titus false hopes might douse his flame for good. And how should she present the project at Winchester's? If she says she is intending to turn Titus into a worldwide success, everybody is going to laugh at her. There is no way she is going to take that risk. But sometimes you've got to chance it, haven't you? What the hell should she do?

She must give this more thought. At the same time, Titus deserves a response. Support and encouragement are a publisher's most important contributions. Except for the advance on royalties, of course.

'It's a brilliant idea, Titus. It really is. The best I've heard for years, in fact. Besides, I think the book could be extremely well received if you are the person behind the project. You've got no "tainted record", quite simply.'

'Tainted record?'

'You would be able to get good reviews. Nobody is going to believe that you are doing this just to be commercial. If you were a crime writer then they would make mincemeat of you. Or even worse a dietician, chef, cleric or management guru. But you are Titus Jensen, the heavyweight novelist.'

'Umm… could I have another beer?'

'Weren't you going to drive me to the Winchester Villa afterwards?'

'But it's only medium-strong, damn it!'

'Okay, okay…' says Astra resignedly, and gets a beer out of the fridge.

'So what do you think?'

'I will be totally honest, Titus. The idea is superb. At the same time I do see a whole lot of risks involved. For you, for me and for Winchester's. I'll talk to Evita this evening, I promise. I'll ask for a mandate to do this as a secret project that only you, me and she will know about. If she says yes, then the advance is in the post. If she says no, then I don't know… What do you say, shall we let her make the decision? I promise to present the idea as positively as possible.'

'Should I wait outside in the car, or what? Can't I present the idea to Evita myself? I've written books for Winchester's for years. You must have earned… well, a bit from me, at any rate.'

'Trust me, Titus. And now I'm being totally honest again. Evita is a tough bird, you know that. You don't exactly inspire confidence with the way you look now. And your breath is not the sweetest I have come across. I promise you, you don't want to meet her today. I'll phone you tomorrow. Is that okay?'

'Okay…'

Titus is satisfied with that for now. What else could he do?

They talk a bit more about the book and which elements it can be filled with. The more they go into the plot, the better it feels.

They are happy and buoyant when Titus drives Astra to Evita Winchester. Titus then drives home to Söder and parks his car. He is happy, tired and needs a well-deserved rest after a hard working weekend and tough negotiations with his editor. Perhaps it would do him good to take a bracing evening walk before going to bed early.

Ten minutes later he is sitting and smoking at his regular table at the Association Bar.

It was a bracing walk.

CHAPTER 5

Evita's Conditions

A doorbell rings inside Titus' head. First a short ring. And then one more. Then a couple that are a bit angrier. The sound of the flap of a letterbox being opened. There's a creaking inside his head. A voice calling out 'helloooo' in a can. A long extended ringing sound vibrates inside his head. Riiiing… creak… hello… riiiing… screech… helloooo…

Stop it…

Stop it!

Titus wakes up. Somebody is ringing his doorbell, he realises. Since he is already dressed he hobbles across to the door and opens it.

Astra. And she doesn't look pleased when she sees Titus' appearance. His eyes are red and he smells like a smoking room due for demolition.

'Oh my God, Titus. What in heaven's name are you doing?'

'Err… I had a little celebration at the Association yesterday.'

'Celebration? Why?'

'Um… well… didn't we have a nice conversation yesterday? I thought so. I was thinking about the book and celebrated with a couple of glasses. But I've got such a dreadful cold, so it hit me harder than it usually does.'

'Yeah, sure, skip the excuses please.'

'Er… but why are you here? How did things go with Evita yesterday?

'That's why I'm here.'

'Oh, right…'

'And I had to see it with my own eyes,' says Astra and points into Titus' flat.

The flat isn't much bigger than what you can see with a single turn of your head. But if you were to go through and sort everything, it would take a couple of weeks. Books, magazines, dirty clothes, unwashed dishes and bits and pieces. Titus' home is simply crammed full of rubbish from floor to ceiling.

'You what? What's with the "see with my own eyes" thing?' Titus yawns.

'How you live, of course.'

'Are you working for Social Services today? What the hell is this about?' croaks Titus sourly when he understands that his lifestyle is under scrutiny. 'Would you like a coffee?'

'Yes, please.'

Titus goes into the kitchen alcove, takes the old coffee filter out of the machine, throws it into the bin and puts in a new one. He opens a cupboard and pulls out some crisp bread and a squeezed-out tube of fish paté.

'A little Danish sandwich, perhaps?' he asks ironically when he sees Astra turn her nose up.

'Thanks, but don't bother,' answers Astra, smiling.

'So, what did she say?'

Astra sits down on a kitchen chair and takes a deep breath.

'Evita says two things. First, that it is the best idea she's heard for years. With the right author it can be a worldwide bestseller.'

'Really, you don't say! That makes me really happy!' exclaims Titus and starts laughing.

'Hang on a moment, Titus. The second thing she says is a bit tougher. She says… that you aren't the right author.'

Titus coughs up the gulp of coffee he just swallowed, spraying it over the kitchen table and his crisp bread sandwich. He dries his chin with the sleeve of his jumper.

'What the hell are you saying? Is she out of her senses? This is my book and nobody else's.'

'Titus, we had a really long conversation, me and Evita. She means what she says. She knows how you live. And what she says is: Titus Jensen is not the right author for *The Best Book in the World*. But he could be! He – could – become it.'

'What?'

'You could *become* the right author! I mean, both you and I know that you are the only person who can pull this off, quality-wise. But to get Winchester's to publish this and to pay an advance, you must go along with some conditions.'

'Oh indeed…?'

'Number one: you must sober up.'

'What utter rubbish! As if I was some sort of wino. What the fuck? There's a hell of a difference between having a really good time now and then, and being a down-and-out wino. I like partying, but I'm not a bloody drunkard.'

'No, of course. But either way, you've got to be sober. You mustn't drink a drop of alcohol while you are writing this book.'

'That's just sick…' he protests lamely, but bides his time before mounting any more indignant protests.

'Number two: you must rein in your material. This book could run to three thousand pages, just like that. You've got to agree to condense the material into two hundred and fifty typed pages – max. The idea is based on gathering together many genres in a single book, and the only way to prove that you've really succeeded is to make the book slim.'

Titus looks at Astra and nods slowly. She seems resolute. She's thought it through. A short manuscript is a lot more difficult, he thinks. But the book is going to be a first-class product, a masterpiece. He wants that, Astra wants that, and so does Evita. They all want it. Condition number two is good, he realises. Damned good.

'A slim book. That's okay,' he says, with earnestness in his voice.

'The third condition is that your work process must be one hundred per cent professional. For example, there's got to be total confidentiality. Only you, me and Evita are going to know about this. You'll write the book this summer and autumn. You and I will meet at regular intervals so that I can see how your work is progressing. We'll never use email. Never, ever. And if you are sober and keep working away at it, we will pay the advance a bit at a time.'

'A bit at a time! Then it isn't an advance!'

'Yes, the book won't be published until next spring. We're keeping a spot for it in the spring catalogue and we'll book the printers for the week after New Year.'

'That's a bit tight…' murmurs Titus.

'Not if you work eight hours a day, five days a week!'

'But I can relax at the weekends?'

'Go boozing, you mean?'

'Cut it out. But perhaps have a glass or two of wine on Friday and Saturday?'

'No. You must be completely teetotal. Are you up for that or not?'

'That condition is totally sick… how can you write a best-seller in six months if you can't relax between working bouts?'

'It shouldn't be difficult, should it? You say you aren't an alcoholic.'

'No, I'm not!' says Titus emphatically.

'Well then, then there are no problems, are there? Are we in agreement?'

Titus sees from Astra's demeanour that there is no room for negotiation. Besides, he knows Evita Winchester's methods very well. She is the one who sets up the rules of the game. Astra is just a pawn, albeit one made from the hardest marble.

'Let's go for it,' says Titus quietly.

'Sign here!' says Astra and hands over a contract. Titus sees both Evita's and Astra's signatures at the bottom of the paper. He signs his own name next to theirs.

At last, Titus is writing again.

CHAPTER 6

Deadlock

Astra has barely left the flat before the doorbell rings again. Titus has just opened the fridge to see if there is a very last beer to be found there. Cold and refreshing, a farewell that must quench his thirst for a long time to come. It would be a waste to pour it away. But the fridge is empty. Damn it! He slams the fridge door and goes and opens the front door instead.

Astra again.

'Hello Titus. I forgot to give you a couple of important things!'

'Oh, right…'

'You'll have to start by reading this book. It's called *Cleaning*. It is brilliant. You'll get a completely new attitude to cleaning when you've read this, I promise you. You'll start to feel comfortable at home. You're worth it.'

'Yes, well…'

'And in this bag is the tool you'll need to cope with the project. A laptop.'

'But I've already got a computer…'

'Read the contract and you'll see that you must write the book on the computer supplied by the publisher.'

'Oh, really! For what reason?'

'It has the security features that we deem necessary. Your own computer looks extremely unreliable. This new machine has a memory that can only be opened and read if you have the right codes. The hard drive makes automatic back-ups to the memory stick which you put in here on the side. As you see, there are several extra sticks. When we want to check on your progress, you simply give me a memory stick so that I can read the manuscript. But most important of all: this computer has a BAC lock... in other words, a breathalyser. You must blow into a tube and the computer will only start if you are stone cold sober.'

'A breathalyser! What the fuck? Don't you trust me? Haven't I already agreed to far too much? This is totally sick!'

'Alcoholism *is* an illness.'

'But I am *not* an alcoholic, I've told you!' Titus shouts.

'No, of course not,' Astra snaps back. 'That's fine. Then there'll be no problems with logging in on the computer either.'

'This is just bloody fucking unbelievable!'

'Take it or leave it.'

'*Okay, okay. Yes!*'

'Right you are, be seeing you, then. Good luck!'

Titus says goodbye to Astra, looks for an empty surface and opens the lid of the laptop. As he does so, a plastic tube pokes up from where the start button is usually found. Titus stares at the tube sticking out expectantly. Should he degrade himself and blow into the device? Does he have any choice? He puts his mouth round the tube and blows.

After a couple of seconds the screen lights up and a text box appears:

Welcome Titus! For the time being you cannot access me. It is estimated that you will require eight hours to metabolise the alcohol in your blood. You are very welcome to return after 7 p.m. Have a nice day!

The screen goes blank.

He feels deeply offended. Degraded. At the same time, he feels a bit shaken. Sure, he has sometimes asked himself whether he has the wrong attitude to drugs and alcohol. It feels like he has overdone it thousands of times. But he loves partying. That's almost the only thing he is good at nowadays.

Nobody has ever said that he is an alcoholic. At least, not to his face. Somebody might have said that he 'should calm down a bit' or 'be a little kinder to yourself' and that sort of thing. But from there to being accused of being an alcoholic is quite a big step. This doesn't feel comfortable.

How many people have actually been going around thinking that Titus is an old drunk? To hear Astra it sounded as if the whole world thought it. At any rate, everybody at Winchester Publishing. Is that why people laugh at him when he does his improvised book readings? Is he just a pathetic pisshead who says funny things as soon as you fill him with spirits and drugs? How would he himself regard somebody like him – if he hadn't been Titus Jensen himself, of course… completely 'objectively' that is…

The insight hits him like a baseball bat. He falls onto the sofa and remains seated a long while, with an absent stare.

He *is* a pisshead. Once he was an intellectual author who had something to say. Now he is a joke. A pathetic nutter of an author dressed in black who loves alcohol and drugs of every type. He stinks like a skunk. He looks like an old rag. When did it go wrong? When did the partying become more important than everything else?

Can he manoeuvre his hull back into the shipping lanes? He must. If he doesn't succeed in writing *The Best Book in the World*, then he's finished. This project is more important than anything else. It's time to choose now, Titus Jensen. Are you a man or a mouse? An author or an alkie?

Yes, *The Best Book in the World* is his last chance. He can feel that with every nerve in his body. This is the turning point for which he has waited so long.

A sense of calm gradually takes over his brain. Lots of small doors of worry and desire are slammed shut. He is well aware that the only chance of keeping them shut is to let the energy from *The Best Book in the World* fill him. Every minute must be filled with energy. And when a new, completely empty minute approaches, he must take charge immediately. Get that minute to work. And the next minute, hour, day and week. Better to be obsessed than dependent, he thinks.

With the help of the cleaning book he starts to clear the mess in his flat in a wild frenzy. He fills binbag after binbag with the remnants of his old life. He vacuums, scrubs and sweeps. Runs back and forth to the laundry room in the cellar. Irons his shirts. Mangles sheets. He can do it! He wants to do it! His forehead drips with sweat and his skin steams with the poisons leaving his body.

Better to be obsessed than dependent, he repeats time after time to himself.

Better to be obsessed than dependent.

CHAPTER 7

Learning for Life

It's evening. The flat smells clean. Titus has showered and made the bed with clean sheets. He is drunk and high. But not from the usual old drugs. This evening he is drunk on new promises and high on the desire to write.

Titus blows into the tube and peers at the screen. A pop-up box soon smirks at him:

> Hi, Titus! Is it time to start working? You are welcome. After six hours I will shut down and save your work. If you want to continue after a two-hour break, you only have to blow into the tube and then you can go on writing. But remember this: if you don't blow-start me for three days then all your files will be deleted and you will have to start from scratch. Good luck!

Bloody monster, Titus thinks. But he isn't in the slightest bit angry. On the contrary. He realises that he has to surround himself with routines and 'musts' to bring this off.

First of all he must write down a checklist. He is going to jot down some fundamental human elements that he must learn more about.

> LOVE. Everything about relationships, women, men, intimacy, sex and erotic life. From small talk and air kisses to conversations and fucking.

PSYCHOLOGY. Human driving forces, leadership and various forms of therapy in practice and theory. Gender theory and mental illnesses. Who wins, who disappears?

CRIME. Offender profiles, reckless violence, financial motives and other driving forces. Perhaps something about racial tensions and class struggle too. Court trials and sentencing practices.

FOOD. Nutrition, food history, tastes, cuisines, cooking and recipe techniques. How to slaughter and skin animals, and cut up into joints. And everything about herring! Herring is tasty!

He looks at what he has written in his list. He can't think of anything else just now. Wasn't there more to it than this? Is that all the knowledge he needs to acquire to write *The Best Book in the World*? Pah! A piece of cake.

Now all he needs is a method of working. The book must be ready in six months. It will take at least three months to put together a rough manuscript. But he can't collect knowledge for three months and save all the writing to the end, that would be taking too much of a risk. No, he must stake out some guidelines first, so that he knows what to look for when he does his research.

Everything he writes must be kept brief. Every paragraph must be just as full of information as a DIY manual. Every page must have a life of its own. If he digresses even a little, he will be abusing the very soul of the book. *The Best Book in the World* should, quite simply, be filled to the brim with emotion, plot and facts. Yes, he's got it there, that's the heart of the matter, and in just three words! 'EMOTION', 'PLOT', 'FACTS', he writes under the list of everything he must learn more about. To achieve his goal, he must be prepared to slaughter sacred cows, to reduce explanations to a minimum and to cut out all the dead meat in the text. 'SHORT AND CONCISE', he writes last of all. He is going to cut it to a minimum; this is going to be trimmer than trim, he thinks, saving the document as 'Manifesto for *The Best Book in the World*'.

He leans back and looks at the screen. A good and encouraging day's work. He deserves a reward. Something really fancy and nice.

It is fairly late and he suddenly feels violently hungry, thirsty and in need of a cigarette all at once. Ah, how quickly the craving came back! Now it was a question of finding a formula to survive the evening. He must have food and water, otherwise he'll die. But there would be no more cigarettes or alcohol. Because if he smokes then he'll crave beer or wine. And if he starts drinking beer or wine – then there'll be no stopping.

He realises that his heart is completely programmed according to old and far too generous reward systems. Tired or miserable? Have a glass! Really, you have done something good? Have a fag! Feeling down and misunderstood? Have a glass and a fag! A mistake? A success? Have two, they are so little!

No, if he is going to succeed, then he'll have to re-program his brain. Program it back to how it was, so that it will work like it did when he was a child, before his brain had learnt that it was fun to smoke and drink. It is not about being brainwashed – quite the opposite. His skull has been brainwashed time and time again for far too long. Rinsed and soaked in alcohol and nicotine, his mind has become frayed and bleached. But now his brain will have to manage entirely without washing powder and become a self-supporting ecological system. Every time he feels the craving, he must focus on good thoughts instead of on spirits and ciggies. Good thoughts, good pictures. Models.

He tries to find good pictures that he can produce quickly to block the pathways where his brain starts to wander in the wrong direction. He flips through the slides of threat and reward images inside his head for a few minutes, picks the best and discards the rest. Finally he settles for two that he will use as and when required.

In one of the pictures, he is an adult man the size of a baby. He is lying on his mother's bosom in what looks like a delivery room. His beard stubble has grazed one of her breasts so that it is pink under his chin. In his mouth he has a cigarette, and in his hand a large glass of whisky. His mother is crying violently and holding her nose.

In the other picture Titus is about twelve years old and as yet with no beard growth. He is lying with his head on the exposed bosom of a young woman, holding a book. You can't see the young woman's face but her nipples are stiff and goose-pimpled. Who is she? Titus has a white milk moustache on his lip and he is looking straight into the eyes of the observer, that is, Titus himself.

He switches between the two pictures. His craving diminishes. More and more details appear each time he pulls them out. Distinct or far too distinct? Who cares, Titus thinks. Cerebral images work. They must work! Work, work, work!

Better to be obsessed than dependent. Better to be obsessed than dependent. Better to be obsessed than dependent.

CHAPTER 8

A Divine Pizza

Food. Food, food, food. *Food*! I'm hungry! Please, somebody, I must surely be allowed something to eat at least? FOOD, FOOD, FOOD!

Titus' brain gets up speed. He charges out from the flat, runs down the stairs and out onto the street. Fresh air! A deep breath. Food! I must have some food! He looks around. Pizza! He rushes into the pizzeria on the corner and reads the menu. No specials now, Titus, it takes too long!

'A Quattro, please!'

'That'll be fifteen minutes.'

'It usually takes only ten!'

'Okay, ten.'

'Great, thanks.'

'Eat here or take away?'

'Eat here. Here and now.'

'Help yourself to salad over there. Something to drink?'

'A weak beer, please. No, no, no, not that! Water. I'll have some water.'

Titus takes a helping of oily grated cabbage salad and sits at the bar counter in front of the pizza baker's worktop. A little sheet of glass separates him from the various bowls with ingredients. He looks at the pizza guy, who whirls the round dough in the air. Pizza is tasty. In a sense, pizza is the mother of all cooked food. Tasty newly baked bread and various small yummy dishes on top. A portable smorgasbord in a hot portion-pack. Elegant and refined. Pizza must absolutely be given a star role in *The Best Book in the World*! Especially Quattro Stagioni, the Rolls-Royce of pizzas. He must, quite simply, get hold of the perfect recipe for a Quattro and give it pride of place in the book. Perhaps the pizza recipe is the only recipe he needs to make the cookery book perfect? Let's be honest, a cookery book doesn't get any better just because it has lots of long and boring recipes, does it? Surely, it is the quality that counts. What more could you need than a single perfect recipe? And you can eat pizza for lunch as well as for dinner! And breakfast, if you've got some leftovers from your takeaway pizza. Isn't that right? Exactly!

The Quattro can be the main character's favourite dish, the one the master detective conjures up for his dinner guests and seduces long-legged ladies with. The cunning detective chief inspector's Quattro is famed far and wide and now the secret recipe will be revealed once and for all in *The Best Book in the World*. The mother of all culinary dishes in the mother of all books!

Titus must immediately learn more about this wonderful dish! He turns to the pizza guy and asks: 'Hello, is it true that Quattro Stagioni is named after Antonio Vivaldi's piece?'

'I don't know, mister. Where does he work? Is that the Antonio at Melini on Kungsgatan? I wonder about that, you know he has only been in Sweden about fifteen years. I think Quattro was here before him. Long before. But I know it's tasty, his Quattro, he uses real mozzarella from Palermo. That's why it's tasty. Mozzarella is tasty. And expensive. They charge forty-nine kronor for a Quattro there.'

'No, I mean was it named after the Four Seasons, Vivaldi's piece for violins?'

'What do you mean, named? It is called Quattro Stagioni. That means the four seasons. It's Italian. Pizza is Italian.'

Titus decides to drop the Vivaldi line of enquiry. There are other things to find out about. Lots of things. Who knows where the road leads when you get on with your research? When you have an unencumbered mind, you'll discover things. I am unencumbered! Titus thinks. Obsessed, possibly, but above all unencumbered. He looks at the pizza guy who scatters small prawns over a quarter of the pizza.

'Which season is that?' says Titus, pointing at the prawns.

'What?' says the pizza guy, and their eyes meet for a second. What is this guy's problem?

'Yes, which season are the prawns?'

'I don't know,' says the pizza guy, and thinks for a moment. 'The summer, perhaps.'

'Why?' Titus wonders, surprised.

'You know, summer and swimming in salt water and all that. There are, like, more prawns in the summer.'

'Have you ever seen a prawn when you've been swimming?'

'No, but why not? What do you think?'

'I think prawns is autumn. Look how they twitch. They twist into themselves, sort of turn themselves off. As if they were suffering from an autumn depression. Suddenly an all-powerful being throws these sea creatures into an oven and dries them, slowly but surely. Just like us humans in the autumn. We are shut up inside our houses with boiling hot radiators that pour out regulated heat while we wither up and whimper. Yes, prawns could very well be autumn.'

'All right, then, if prawns are autumn, then what are mushrooms?' the pizza guy goes on, having now joined the match. 'Mushrooms must be autumn, surely. Wild mushrooms are picked in the autumn. Not by me, I mean, but by people who pick mushrooms.'

'Yes, damn it, of course you're right about that,' says Titus and puts his hand thoughtfully on his chin. 'Okay, mushrooms are autumn and prawns are summer. But what about the ham and mussels?'

The pizza guy laughs as he slides the peel under the pizza and loads it into the oven. 'You are a funny one, mister. I have never thought about that before.'

'So, what do you think? Aren't mushrooms just as much summer as prawns?'

'No, no. Mussels are women. Women are spring. When life awakens in the spring, it's full of women. I know, we Italians love mussels. They open up in the spring. Like flowers that produce buds and then come into bloom, you know. Mussels are spring. The best season, that's obvious'

'Then ham must be winter. And that goes with Christmas ham and so on.'

'Yes, perfect! We have solved the pizza mystery, mister.'

'Have we? Are you sure?'

'Absolutely. It was easy!'

'But we haven't finished. The artichoke in the middle. What's that then? It can't be a fifth season. Is it the sun, perhaps?'

'No, not the sun. It's grey. A bit brownish, sort of. That's no sun. The sun is yellow. Then there would have been a pepper.'

'But what is it then?' Titus wonders, sincerely worried by the mystery.

'God, perhaps?' the pizza guy hazards, and makes the sign of the cross on his white shirt.

'Greyish-brown... yes, perhaps,' says Titus, almost to himself. 'An elderly man with a beard. Like in the pictures of God at primary school. Yes, perhaps it is God... who watches over the world...'

'You know, not all pizza bakers have artichokes in their Quattros.'

'No? Why not?'

'I don't know. I haven't thought about it. Perhaps they think it's a tastier pizza without it.'

'Deism. Deism-baker. God has left the world,' says Titus thoughtfully and looks into the oven. 'He is no longer a part of the pizza. He only watches it from a distance.'

The surface of the pizza bubbles a bit. It begins to turn nice and brown. A little part of the rim of the pizza is even burnt. God is certainly still on this pizza. The planet is in flames and he sits like a Buddha in the middle, his arms crossed, without so much as lifting a leaf of his artichoke overcoat. He is seemingly completely unperturbed and still has the same nuance that he had when he first came to the pizza. Why doesn't he do anything? What's he waiting for? The Big Bang?

The pizza guy takes the beautiful newly baked Quattro out of the oven. He puts it on a large plate, shakes a little oregano over it and slides it over to Titus.

'*Bon appétit!*'

Titus devoutly tucks into the part with the prawns. But hang on a minute. You must surely start eating a Quattro in the middle of winter, after New Year? The seasons can't begin in the middle of summer. There must be some damned order, even on a pizza. That means that you must begin about one third of the way into the ham. Then you eat your way clockwise with the mussels, the prawns and the mushrooms, ending with the ham again.

Titus starts afresh. He turns the plate round and puts the knife into the New Year's night of the ham.

Then he discovers something horrific. The prawns come after the ham! The seasons come in the wrong order! This was bad news, very bad news. But he makes up his mind not to say anything to the pizza guy. Why trouble him with it? He has been friendly and helped Titus to sort out all the difficult Quattro concepts. It would not be right to burden him with this. The pizza costs only thirty-nine kronor after all.

Titus bears his cross and eats the pizza in the correct order, despite the confusion on the plate. It looks a bit strange with the pizza bits on either side of the plate. But what would that matter in a hundred years?

The calories calm him down, and with his self-control secure, he can eat the pizza with a degree of devotion. He thinks that *The Best Book in the World* and the pizza should have the very best of ingredients. Genuine mozzarella, mushrooms from the market, the day's catch of prawns and genuine Parma ham. But should it have artichokes or not? Which philosophy would suit the heroic detective best?

Titus is energised by the delicious season-pizza. For once, he has had a reward without poisoning himself with alcohol and nicotine. He is on the right path. He's going to like this.

There is writing to be done!

CHAPTER 9

Foreword

Dear Reader,
This book is short. But it contains more than you can imagine. I would ask you to read slowly and with reflection so that you miss as little as possible. The book only contains one repetition and that occurs in the Foreword, here and now: I would ask you to read slowly and with reflection.

Perhaps that is a tad arrogant, Titus thinks. But if the book is to be a success then he must establish a contract with his readers. Everybody involved must be in agreement about making the experience as magnificent as possible. Should he write a special foreword for the reviewers too? Ask them to try to experience something positive instead of wrecking and looking for faults…?

Esteemed reviewer! There are moments in life when we must open ourselves to the world around us. Moments when we need to come to a halt in order to be able to comprehend the significance of what is new. In all epochs, mankind has been afraid of novelties. Think of the many doomsday prophets who have incorrectly proclaimed the end of the world! Think of the many commentators who have criticised technical advances that have later turned out to be faithful tools in the service of mankind!

Think of the critics who have dismissed artists and
works of art that have later won the genuine love of
modern man! And how often has a reviewer won the
heart of his public? I only wonder.

Titus soon loses his benevolent intent and launches into
an irate harangue for several pages. He gives examples of
historical mistakes committed by reviewers, and directs his
anger at cowardly publisher's editors while he is at it. He
writes and writes. The embers flame up into burning hatred.

...and now I demand of you, you pathetic clown
of a reviewer, that you read this magnificent book
with the most open attitude that your withered and
poisoned brain is capable of. May you burn in hell if
you are incapable of appreciating the magnificence
of this innovative work of literature.

Titus leans back contentedly on his office chair and enters
the command to preview the text. Four pages of compact
lines appear on the screen. A word bomb!

He is forced to swallow a nasty-tasting lump which rushes
towards his throat when he realises his mistake. He can have
just 250 pages of text, and he has used four of them for the
foreword!

Talk about addictive behaviour, he thinks. I need my head
seeing to! I'm an idiot! This is never going to work. Delete!
Damn...

He is a useless author and an even worse person. Titus
is suddenly swamped by a strong impulse to eat, drink and
smoke. Indeed, to do anything that will take him away
from here. But he tries to calm himself a little by pulling
out of his brain the reward image with boy-Titus and the

milk moustache. He shuts his eyes and concentrates on his picture therapy. But what's happening? The boy is naked! And one half of his bottom is far too long! It's supported on a crutch, like a tired giant penis. And on top of the half-bottom there's a piece of bloody meat. The boy is wearing a cap with a peak that is also too long. That too is supported on a crutch!

Titus' thoughts become clearer. He has seen that picture before, in reality! It is a painting by the surrealist Salvador Dali. The painting is called *The Enigma of Wilhelm Tell* and it hangs at Moderna Museet in Stockholm. This is a sign of some sort. He must go there! Has he found a main thread with which he can weave the book? His own Da Vinci code... the Dali code? Eureka!

Next stop Moderna Museet!

CHAPTER 10

The Bottom on the Crutch

Titus stands before *The Enigma of Wilhelm Tell*. He has more-or-less run all the way from his little flat in Söder. He breathes heavily and he doesn't get any calmer when he sees the painting before him. He must gasp for breath to get any air down into his lungs at all.

It's an enormous painting. Enormous in size, and enormous in the way it blows your mind. Titus has a memory from the first time he saw it. He is five years old and on a Sunday family outing to the museum. He runs around amidst all the happenings and paintings at his own speed and without really having to keep an eye on mum and dad. Then suddenly he finds himself in front of the big Salvador Dali painting. He doesn't know how long he stands there staring at the painting. Perhaps time has stopped. Every detail is etched into his retina, for all eternity it feels like. Even though he is only five years old, Titus knows that he is having a great art experience. These few minutes will haunt him for the rest of his life. His senses are wide open and filled to the brim with experiences just as if somebody had stood there and poured adventures into him from a bucket. Suddenly, after a few minutes' staring from his five-year-old worm's eye view, he sees his dad's grey trouser legs flap past in front of him. He stretches out for dad's hand to make sure that dad sees the painting too. They must share this great art experience. Look dad! Can you see the bottom? He gets hold of the hand. Holds it firmly. Lifts the linked hands towards the picture to point and show it to dad. There! Can you see it? Dad doesn't answer. So Titus must look away from the picture to see what dad thinks. What? A complete stranger is standing there holding his hand! A totally alien dad who gives him a friendly but wondering smile. Shame washes over Titus. He has got hold of the wrong hand. Wrong dad. Titus can't understand that the man just thinks that he is a cute boy. He can't understand that this is the sort of thing that five-year-olds do all the time. Get me out of here! He lets go of the man's hand with a start, and looks up at the picture again. Staring intently, he loses himself in the only thing that feels safe just now.

The work of art.

It is just as fantastic now as it was then, Titus realises. A man is half-kneeling in front of a marble plinth on a brown floor. You can't see his facial expression because it is shaded by a peak cap with a peak that must be more than one metre long. The peak hangs over the whole of the left side of the picture and rests on a crutch so as not to droop. The man has turned his side and most of his back to Titus. On a marble plinth between the crutch and the man there is a little clock that is sort of melting towards the man. Or is it time that is oozing from him? It's hard to say. On the foot closest to Titus, the man has a grotesque sandal and large knotted toes. On the further leg, which is kneeling on the ground, he has a grey-black sock with a tight garter round his leg just beneath the knee. He is not wearing underpants. His shirt hangs down like a heavy long scrotum between his legs. His further bottom-half is far too long. It is enormously long! That too is supported on a crutch, almost at the very far right-hand side of the picture. It is inconceivable (at least for Titus) that the bottom could represent anything other than a giant penis. Does it need help to be able to support its weight, or to retain its stiffness? Whatever, the bottom-cum-penis sticks out about half a metre from the crutch like a glans inside foreskin without an opening. Gosh, what happens if he has to pee? Titus wonders. On the extended buttock, between the actual crack in his bottom and the crutch, hangs a bloody steak. And on one of the man's sleeves there is another sort of beef steak, a sort of tennis-ball steak with a lid. Like a secretive meat cream bun, Titus thinks. The man's other sleeve is just a sharp cone, a shirt spear which points backwards, into the black background of the picture. Under the bottom-cum-penis and the beef steak, some sweet little birds are pecking at the brown floor. Are they licking up the drops of blood from the beef, do you think? Meat-eating birds?

Titus has felt an affinity with Dali ever since that first acquaintance. As an artist, you can hardly be more obsessed than Dali. Dali knew what was what. Better to be obsessed than dependent. Me and Salvador, we are kindred spirits, Titus thinks. I must be just as merciless towards the surrounding world as he was. The world's best painting must be related to *The Best Book in the World*.

Suddenly, Titus is surrounded by a group of school-children who look about ten to twelve years old, together with a female museum guide in her thirties. You can see from far off that this is a guide who takes her job seriously. She touches the children and bends down to them when they ask questions. And most important of all: she laughs and smiles at their eyes.

'This, dear children, this is *The Enigma of Wilhelm Tell*. An enigma means a mystery. This is one of the most famous paintings in the museum, a painting that actually contains lots of paintings and stories. It was painted in 1933 by a Spanish artist called Salvador Dali. What do you think about when you see this painting?'

'He's got his prick on his back!' a boy calls out.

'Yes… perhaps… what else do you think?'

'He's spooky,' says a girl who giggles, slightly embarrassed. 'I think he's funny!'

Several children think the same. They giggle, laugh and shout 'yuck' and 'urgh how horrid' in turn. But they are without doubt more amused than worried.

'What is it meant to be?' another girl asks.

'There is no simple answer,' says the guide. 'Shall I tell you a little about it?'

'Yeees!' all shout.

'One of Salvador Dali's aims with his life was to become a living legend. A celeb. For example, he twisted his moustaches so that they reached all the way out here,' says the guide and shows with her fingers how they stretched across the cheeks. 'This is how he started his autobiography: "When I was six years old I wanted to be a chef. When I was seven I wanted to be Napoleon. And, since then, my ambition has grown all the time." That was quite something, wasn't it?'

'Who was Napoleon?' a thin voice calls out from the very back of the group.

'He was the emperor of France. A warrior who conquered lots of countries which he wanted to make part of France.'

'Was Salvador a warrior too?'

'No, he was an artist. But he was just as mad as Napoleon, perhaps. Shall I tell you about *The Enigma of Wilhelm Tell?*'

'Yeees!'

'Well, Salvador Dali wanted people to be able to interpret his paintings in lots of different ways. His paintings could include almost anything: reality and things which only happen in dreams. There was room for it all. So this is what I think: this man in the painting can be all the gods, fathers and sons in the world, in one and the same person. The whole of mankind perhaps. And all the dreadful oppression in the world too. You can see how mutilated and imprisoned he is. He is stuck there, he is bent, you can't see his face, and so on. Yes, he is dreadfully oppressed. Probably the painting is also about when dads treat their sons badly, because Salvador's dad was almost always horrid to Salvador. Although he was a bit proud that Salvador was clever at drawing, he always thought that Salvador was silly and weird. He questioned everything that Salvador did, from what Salvador wanted to work with to what he was like as a lover. That alone should be enough for a whole life as an artist! Don't you think?'

The children don't really know what a lover does. Nor do they know what is necessary to be an artist. And round about now, the guide loses contact with the children for a few moments. What started as an exciting story soon gets lost in psychological explanations and incomprehensible references to Freud, Schiller and Nietzsche. She slowly notices that the children have dropped out, realises her mistake and gets back in line.

'…but the people who have studied which things influenced Dali during this period say that *The Enigma* is also about political oppression and class conflicts. Workers and peasants against the growing middle class. There was a lot of anger in the world too. Do you think Salvador was an angry uncle?'

Some children nod. What else can they do? The group starts to break up at the edges and some kids sneak away to explore the surroundings on their own. A girl who is leaning against the wall looks dead. Suddenly she shows signs of life by blowing a big bubble with her chewing gum. Pop! The bubble bursts, and she is once again as stiff as a corpse. But the guide continues unabashed:

'As I said, Salvador Dali had decided already when he was young that he would become a myth. An extremely complicated and totally fantastic myth that the world would never forget. He even lived in his own museum with giant eggs on the roof. He would NEVER be satisfied with a painting unless it had lots of different levels. Now listen to this: in Dali's family there were several people who had suffered from mental illness – paranoia, schizophrenia, manic depression, indeed the whole works. But nobody was allowed to talk about it. So Salvador decided to both live and paint those behaviours that were forbidden. For example: when Salvador was going to ask Gala to marry him, he smeared himself with goat poop so that she wouldn't choose him just because of his appearance! And she actually said yes.'

That saved the situation for the guide. Now the children wake up again, the few who are left. Poop works in every case and some of the kids even start to laugh out loud. Titus observes the spectacle with increasing amazement. The guide feels the wind in her sails and throws in more:

'But his marriage became extremely weird even though they always loved each other. Perhaps Salvador's dad was right when he said that his son was a rotten lover. It was said that his wife, Gala, who had a house in a little fishing village on the Costa Brava, welcomed the fishermen when they came home every day after their day's fishing. She made love to them all, wildly and beautifully, every day. She was a nymphomaniac of grand proportions. Do any of you know what a nymphomaniac is?'

The museum guide looks at the children. They shake their heads. A vacant look on their faces. Now she has them where she wants them. They are wide open. They will remember this moment for the rest of their lives.

'If you think this sounds weird, it's nothing compared to what's going to come. Right: we have learnt that *The Enigma of Wilhelm Tell* is about Salvador Dali's wish to get revenge on his dad and on narrow-minded middle-class attitudes. But we're not going to have it as easy as that. *The Enigma of Wilhelm Tell* is perhaps most of all about the darkest side of human behaviour. Our uncontrolled desire to eat and – *cannibalism*! Who knows what cannibalism is?'

A little boy sticks his hand up.

'I have seen *The Silence of the Lambs*…'

Others have seen it too. Titus, who is watching the performance from the sidelines, can't believe his eyes and ears. That film is X-rated! These children have seen *The Silence of the Lambs* but have never heard of Napoleon.

'Bravo!' the guide shouts. 'The film is about the same thing! People who suffer, people who are afraid to die, people who force themselves to do horrible deeds because of their guilt about their own inadequacies. Do you remember the mass-murder boy in the cellar? The one who sews clothes from the skin of his victims? He could just as well be the boy at the bottom on the crutch. Both of them suffer from an extreme inferiority complex. Just like Napoleon did! And Salvador Dali with his stupid dad! Do you get it? Everybody has an inferiority complex at some time. Everybody has the same feelings deep inside. We are all like Salvador! All of us have our bottoms on a crutch!'

The children look at each other with wrinkled foreheads and puckered noses. They don't have their bottoms in crutches, do they? What does she mean?

'Now we'll move along! Can you see the goat with a car tyre around its tummy over there?'

The group of children disappears as quickly as it turned up.

Titus remains standing in front of *The Enigma of Wilhelm Tell* for a few more moments. He is on the right track, his mind is in overdrive. The bottom on the crutch, the bottom on the crutch… then he suddenly gets it. Yes, of course!

The serial killer in *The Best Book in the World* must naturally hang up the body parts of his victims on crutches. As a protest against his dad, the brusque middle-class dad who never let him come into full bloom. Who, on the contrary, belittled him and ill-treated him mentally and physically. And when the heroic detective eventually gets on his track then the arch villain is of course given the nickname Salvador, or perhaps even Serial Salvador. And Serial Salvador leaves clues that demand that you must analyse Dali's paintings according to a new pattern in order to trace him. In that way, *The Best Book in the World* will be a revolutionary book about art history too! Perfect! Now all Titus has to do is read lots of books about Dali and then he'll have cracked it.

Just what the doctor ordered, Titus thinks, satisfied. A good title for a book too, *The Bottom on the Crutch*… must go to the café and write it down!

He just has time to turn towards the exit when somebody grabs hold of his earlobe, pulls Titus' head towards him and screams right into his ear:

'COCK IN YOUR EAR!'

CHAPTER 11

The Start of the Hunt

Is there any limit to how quickly you can think? Sound travels at 340 metres a second in ordinary air. The fibres of your body transport nerve impulses almost as quickly.

Since the screaming mouth is as good as inside Titus' ear, it is only a question of a hundredth of a second before the sound is transformed into an impulse which is sent to the brain along half a metre of winding fibres inside Titus' skull. So it takes a second or so before he is aware of what is happening. The scream paralyses him in the meanwhile. During the second that passes, some traumatic episodes of Titus' life are screened before his eyes, like a condensed and nasty near-death experience. An unpleasant situation flashes past, like a frozen memory image for a tenth of a second, before it disappears again.

He is in school, fifteen years old. Two boys in the class with downy beard growth have him in their grip. He can see their teeth. They smell of cigarettes, and beer: Pripps Blue. Titus starts to panic. They are going to hack their pencils into his hands. They are going smash him to bits. He writes too much. They hate that. They won't let him be good at anything. They hate him because he does something they don't understand. Poems are for homos. Only queers read novels. But writing is the only thing he can do! Writing is the only thing he wants to do, and they are going to take that away from him. He must flee. He must get away. Fight or die. Help, where is his reward image?

Ah, plop, there it is! Suddenly he is lying on the woman's bosom again. He licks away his milk moustache. He breathes easily. He becomes calm.

One second has passed since the scream in his ear to self-control and calm. One second that proves to Titus that anything is possible. His technique works. Whatever the situation he finds himself in, he has only to resort to his threat or reward images. It takes less than a second. He is strong now. Titus turns toward the loudmouth.

'Lenny... nice to see you,' he says without conviction, and touches his ear as a sign that he intends to protect it from further aggressive trespassing.

'M-me too. I mean... the same. Sorry that I screamed in your ear. Can't help it. It just happens. Tourette's syndrome, you know. As soon as I get the slightest bit excited or surprised, then it comes. I was happy to see you.'

'Yes, but I know, Lenny. It's cool. It's okay.'

'Thanks, Titus. Well, what are you doing here?'

'I'm just sort of scouting around, you could say. Got a new project going and I need a bit of inspiration. And you?'

'M-my girlfriend works in the museum café. Malin – have you met her?'

Titus shakes his head.

'Well, she works in the restaurant here. Shall we scrounge something tasty?'

'Okay.'

Titus gets in the queue for the cashier behind a couple of cultured ladies dressed in black. They smile at him and nod very discreetly, as if they knew him. Or had known him a long time ago and now wanted to make themselves known so as to avoid any embarrassment. Has he slept with one of them? Or both? Nothing is impossible, Titus realises, and nods back almost as discreetly before looking away.

The counter is filled with enormous ciabatta sandwiches and cakes and biscuits that are as big as small plates. The sarnies are a bit rustic and look as if somebody had scattered too much flour onto them before they were put in the oven. Houmous, brie, salami, some fancy cabbage leaves and sun-dried tomatoes, the contents are overflowing on all sides.

The giant biscuits have extremely uneven edges. Titus thinks that the person who has baked them must have been a little child or somebody with a serious disability. It's a very good thing that they employ disabled people at Moderna Museet! The cultural upper class can be in need of a bit of grim reality. To be forced to cope with your own or somebody else's handicap is an everyday occurrence for many people. It doesn't really matter what the biscuits look like; it's the contents and the taste that counts. And the contents are extremely visible since the biscuits are very buckled. Here and there, bits of chocolate, raisins and nuts stick out. Besides, not all the biscuits have been baked properly; some are even burnt at the edges. Titus takes a handicap biscuit and fills a large cup with coffee. He pushes his tray towards the cash register.

'That will be fifty-nine kronor, please,' says the cashier and gives him a friendly smile.

'What, I took one of the failed biscuits! Look, it is almost burnt. Isn't there a price reduction for these?'

'Very funny!' the cashier laughs. 'No, they are meant to be like that. These are Jamie Oliver's biscuits. They are really tasty, I promise. We sell his biscuit and cake book in the shop.'

Now Lenny comes up to the cash register. On his tray he has a portion of cake that is the size of a little flowerpot. He leans over Titus and makes a kissing sound with his lips.

'He-hello, Malin.'

'Hello, Lenny.'

'H-he is with me. This is the Titus Jensen that I told you about. The festival, you know.'

'Oh yeah! Eddie's mate. Right. Hi, Titus.'

Cashier Malin glances at the queue behind Lenny. Some young mothers stand pointing and deciding among the various biscuits and pastries. Their indecision has created a little gap after Lenny and Titus. Malin lowers her voice and gives them a sly look.

'Okay, coffee and cakes are on me today. Enjoy yourselves. See you!'

'Oh, thank you very much,' says Titus, and rather regrets not taking a giant sarnie instead. But they looked so expensive and he hadn't really trusted in Lenny's being able to get one for free.

He takes his tray and aims for a couple of empty chairs beside the window facing towards the Vasa Museum. Today, Stockholm is in its very best mood, Titus thinks, when he sees all the people walking in the sunshine on Strandvägen on the other side of the bay. Somebody has just lit a grill on the afterdeck of one of the houseboats moored below the museum. The smoke rises straight as an arrow up into the sky. Even the sea breeze seems to have gone on holiday.

Lenny stays for a while and talks to Malin. Lenny is tall and lanky. His body looks nervous, despite a confident go-to-hell-I-am-a-rockstar attitude when it comes to clothes. A lot of black, a lot of studs. Malin, too, looks like a rock girl with all her rings and her unruly hair, even though today she is disguised in the black and white uniform of the restaurant. Now and then, they look in Titus' direction.

The two cultured ladies are sitting a few tables away. They, too, look at Titus now and then. Titus pretends to be staring straight ahead. Over the years he has acquired a certain ability to look from the corners of his eyes. He is never able to fathom whether people stare at him with admiration or contempt.

Lenny gives Malin a kiss and strolls across the limestone floor. The sole of one of his canvas shoes has loosened and when he gets close to the table Titus can hear the squelching sound. Even though Titus' financial situation is more often than not somewhat precarious, he does at least always have decent shoes. His dad went on about that when he was little. 'As long as you have decent and polished shoes, you'll stand firmly on this Earth.' It was easy for his dad to say that, he was a shoemaker with his own hole-in-the-wall shop on Skånegatan. The shoe repair shop was open six days a week. His dad never did anything other than repair and polish boots and shoes. He had done it since he was fifteen years old. When he became a pensioner, he sold the premises to a paper shop for 15,000 kronor. Then he sat in his kitchen for two months before his heart said stop. He died with his eyes open and his forehead on the kitchen table right next to a cup of coffee, his chewing tobacco and his pools coupons. Death was no sadder that anything else in his quiet life.

'W-what's the biscuit like?' Lenny wonders when he sits down opposite Titus.

Lenny evidently feels comfortable and relaxed. His twitching and stammering is much calmer now than when he and Titus met at the festival.

'Quite all right,' Titus answers.

'M-me, I took a great big cake. Like a lunch in itself.'

'It's a muffin.'

'What?'

'It's a muffin, not just a cake.'

'You're taking the piss!'

'No, I am not.'

'B-but muffin sounds like an insult. "You bloody muffin!" type of thing…'

'Yeah, I agree it sounds a bit daft. But it is still called a muffin, a sweet muffin.'

They sit in silence for a few moments. Whether it is just a cake or a muffin is hardly a subject of conversation to get people relaxed. Titus feels a gust of anxiety. What was the point of saying what he did? Must he be such a damned know-all? Fuck, now a large cold beer would taste really good instead. His hand trembles a little when he lifts the cup to his mouth. Pull your socks up, Titus, damn it! Better to be obsessed than dependent, he thinks.

'Did you have fun at the festival?' Titus wonders in an attempt to jump-start a conversation.

Lenny blows some air out of the corner of his mouth as if he was trying to blow his fringe away from his face. Pfff. Pfff. Twice in quick succession. But his fringe doesn't move an inch. It never does when Lenny blows air out of the corner of his mouth. Titus realises that Lenny's tics are more a case of twitches on account of his Tourettes than on account of the irritating fringe.

'Y-yeah, man. It was a fucking success. It's always great to play with Eddie. The atmosphere is far out. You can almost touch the love in the air. And touch the heat too. I love playing in a marquee. It's a bit like lying down and making out with the entire audience in a hot midsummer tent. Everybody sleeping with everybody else, but in a good way. Do you get what I mean?'

Titus looks at Lenny. He doesn't get it all. It sounds absolutely revolting to sleep in a hot tent and make out with hundreds of teenagers. At the same time, he must keep his end up and be a little accommodating. Lenny has fixed a free café visit after all.

'Yeah, I think I get it. I agree, there is a special atmosphere around Eddie. I remember the first time I saw him. It was when Stockholm was the Cultural Capital of Europe. They arranged a culture marathon out by the gasometers at Ropsten. A whole week, day and night, with actors, writers and artists who took turns reading classics and newly written works that in one way or another were about love. I was there one night when it was hot, full of people and a really brilliant atmosphere. Then Eddie read *I Adore Love*. There was only just him and a guy with a double bass. Eddie was wearing a white silk suit, as big as a shift, with the arms rolled up, and he was barefoot. He had feathers in his hair, he looked like a Sitting Bull on a bathing holiday by the Riviera. There must have been five hundred people in there sitting on the floor around him. It was like he had an aura, and he looked bloody handsome too. I'm not usually easy to impress but even I thought it was a bit magical.'

'F-fuck, bloody great. *I Adore Love* is brilliant. Was that the time he read the whole book?'

'I suppose so. It took half the night. He was slower in those days, sort of more northern and reflective. It was as if people were in a trance. It sounds like a cliché but I really think that the world gets a little better with nights like that. Even I felt happy for hours afterwards.'

'What do you mean "even you"? Aren't you human like everybody else?' Lenny wonders, and takes a big mouthful of his mega-cake. Or rather, mega-muffin.

'Sure, but mass experiences are a hell of a problem for me. I become suspicious, I think that somebody is trying to sell happiness to me. You can't buy happiness. You can't give it away either. Happiness is, if anything, an absurd way of regarding the world. I mean, sometimes happiness occurs, even for me. But it is not because I have hunted for it, rather the opposite. It is not until you stop hunting it all the time that it can come. At the same time, it is almost impossible *not* to try to hunt happiness. Hunting happiness is probably the most human activity one can imagine. Animals can be satisfied without happiness, but not us humans. We need more, always something more.'

'M-me, I'm not so fucking sure about that. Are you hunting happiness just because you go to a concert reading by Eddie X? Can't you just take it easy and have a cosy time? Just be, sort of, fairly content?'

'Yeah, of course. And that's what I mean. The world gets a bit better from that sort of thing. But if it is happiness or not, that I don't know.'

'Does it make any difference what you call it?' says Lenny, and blows with the corner of his mouth: pfff, pfff.

'No, you're probably right about that.'

Titus glances at the cultured ladies. Are they still there? Yes, they are, they're sitting and breaking small pieces of their enormous biscuits, popping the crumbs into their mouths like beautiful small birds. Giggling and glistening with their nice teeth. They look rather expensive from a distance, with their highlighted hair in fancy coiffures. Something has definitely happened with cultured ladies in recent years, Titus thinks. Just a few years ago, most of them had hair that was dyed red, preferably with an uncombed look and set up with a colourful hair ribbon. Sensible shoes and multi-coloured clothes. Now they are more discreet and stylistically pure: high heels and tight skirts, pretty as models, almost regardless of age. You can no longer distinguish between culture girls and upper class chicks. That sort of hairdo must cost at least a thousand kronor. What has happened? Have wages gone up in the culture sector? Not in Titus' sector at any rate, he is quite certain about that. Although when he thinks about all the glass and brushed steel he saw in Astra's flat he becomes uncertain again. She is pretty in that way too. Not sexy pretty, but expensive pretty. Fuck, I'm way behind, he thinks. I want money too! But not so that I can look like an expensive upper-class chap. I just want the freedom.

'And what are you working on at the moment then?' Lenny wonders. 'A new book under way? I've read *Storm Clouds* and *Treacherous Charades*. Quite a lot of pain and blackness. Perfect reads for a grim week on Gotland in November. Is there more in that style coming along? Pfff. Pfff.'

Titus is taken unawares by the question even though over the years he has learnt to never talk about a book he is working on. It gives the whole project bad karma. Expectations are every author's worst enemy, so you should never try to describe a book yourself. Not when it's finished, and even less before it has been written. When the book is ready, it must manage on its own.

'Yeah, well, I'm busy working on a synopsis for some things. Talking a bit to the publishers and that.'

Titus feels uncomfortable. This is no good. It is simply crazy to be sitting drinking coffee with a guy who sits there making small weird blowing sounds all the time. He ought to be working instead of wasting time. The days pass and he must actually catch a mad serial killer. And bearing in mind that he has never been anywhere near writing a crime novel, it's high time to get on with it.

'W-will it be g-good, then?' Lenny asks.

'What?'

'Y-your b-book, of course.'

'Book? Oh, we'll see how it turns out,' says Titus and tries to prevent his eyes from going all over the place. He doesn't like Lenny prying about the book. Which book? Titus' book is nothing that is any concern of Lenny's.

'You know, Lenny, I must be getting along. Work calls.'

'Oh my God. You too. I'm so impressed by you all.'

'Us?'

'Yes, I only know two authors. And both of you work as if you were possessed, it seems.'

Titus feels that in his solar plexus. What does he mean? *Who* does he mean?

'Who else do you mean?' says Titus slowly although he knows very well who Lenny means.

'Eddie X. He is working like a madman too. I have hardly seen him since the festival.'

When Titus hears the three syllables of Eddie X's name, he feels the blood draining away from his head. He is forced to hold the table with both hands so as not to fall off his chair.

'Oh really… Eddie,' he says, but silently thinks to himself: fuck, fuck, fuck. Then it's true, his worst suspicion is confirmed.

'H-he doesn't p-poke his nose outside the door. Just works, works, works. Day and night.'

'With what?' Titus hears himself asking.

He feels paralysed. If Eddie X has started working on his version of *The Best Book in the World*, then Titus has been robbed of his victory. People love everything that Eddie touches. Sure, Titus is a living legend too. Respected on the arts pages. Hunted by the gossip press. But Eddie X is much more than that. He is a saint. The day he stops writing poems and starts writing novels, he'll get millions of readers and become a millionaire without even trying. Titus must know. Have the judge pronounce sentence. What is Eddie working on?

'H-he says he is working on his summer radio programme. It's being broadcast next week. But I don't know, he doesn't usually take that radio stuff so seriously. It's the third time he has done the summer programme and he didn't work especially hard even on the first one. He's got it all inside his head. He only has to turn on the tap. But, of course, perhaps it takes time to choose the music.'

The beloved Eddie X is slaving away like an animal with a project that is probably going to make him immortal. Meanwhile, the soot-black has-been Titus Jensen is sitting here drinking in a café with a spasmodic blowfish.

If there is any justice at all in this world, then it is high time it starts doing its job.

CHAPTER 12

The ABC Method

Competition is not a whip that usually cracks behind Titus. But when it does finally sing through the air in Titus' flat, it sends his adrenaline levels sky high.

Now it is a matter of ping-pong. There is no time to play tactically and plan in detail. No, what he must do is smash every ball that comes his way. Since he has a good overview of the plot of the book in his head, he can allow himself to churn out the various chapters in any order. Then he can cut and paste.

He blow-starts the computer and savours a brilliant idea:

The ABC Method.

The very thought of the perfect slimming method made Chief Inspector Håkan Rink's body so exalted that he burnt 100 calories. Never before had anyone packaged slimming tricks in such a smart and concise manner as he had done. Never ever had the advice been so simple and candid. And besides, he himself was living proof that the system worked. In only five weeks, he had lost ten kilograms. And he had just passed the 'ogling threshold', the magical eighty-two-kilo boundary. The ogling threshold was the perfect measure of a person's ideal weight, and it was much more reliable than the tired old BMI value which only measures the relationship between weight and height. Weight and height are of no interest to mankind in the long term. The only thing that counts is if and when you can mate. And BMI has no say in that. The ogling threshold, however, puts the focus on more natural instincts.

Eighty-two kilograms: that was the boundary when women yet again started to meet Håkan Rink's eye. They hadn't done that for ten years. Before, when he weighed more than ninety kilograms, there wasn't a single soul who eyed him up. But now that he weighed a little below eighty-two, at least one or two gave him an appreciative smile. In the reflection in a shop window, he had even noticed how a girl raised her sunglasses and sneaked a look at his arse. To be objectified – that was a wonderful feeling that Håkan Rink wanted to experience more often. Besides, people had started to listen to him at work in a new way. They took him seriously again. Now he was competent as a mating partner and transporter of human genes. As such, that made him credible as the leader of the flock.

The ABC Method

A: Abstain from all food in the evenings
B: Brown carbohydrates only
C: Crisps and sweets forbidden at all times

It wasn't any harder than that, Håkan Rink thought. He could see the straight and narrow (or slim) path that lay wide open before him. He would now achieve miracles. Now he would catch Serial Salvador. Now perhaps he would even be able to lose his nickname.

He was sick to his back teeth with being called
Detective Hockey-Rink.

Is he good, or is he good? Thousands of slimming books can go to hell. Millions of magazine and newspaper articles can go and hide in the corner. The ABC-method, the best slimming method in the world, fits on a postcard, Titus thinks quietly, and closes the lid of the laptop.

He wonders about Eddie X. How far has he got? Can that man really write about anything other than love?

Titus is reminded of an article about positive and negative energy that he read some years ago. A team of scientists had compared the ability of people to solve difficult problems. One group that was studied comprised people who used positive thinking and liked to work with target images. Those people saw the final reward as the best way to provide motivation for success. When you know *why* you should succeed, then you *will* succeed. This positive method is often used by athletes. The other group was the pessimists. As soon as they were given a task they became grumpy and started looking for problems. What were the obstacles that would prevent them from succeeding? When was the most likely time the whole thing would get screwed up? In their workplaces they were often called whiners. For the pessimists, it was completely rational to think about failure from the very first. It was a matter of mapping out and evaluating the problems before they started work. The results of the study were very interesting. Both groups succeeded well with their tasks. It transpired that optimists and pessimists were just as good at achieving good results. The important thing was to find the method that best suited one's character. An optimist gets terrified if you talk about problems instead of faith, hope and love; a pessimist is suspicious of anything not based on facts.

Titus remembers how liberating he thought this study was. There was just as much hope for the coal-black prophets of woe as there was for the warbling optimists. At the same time, it was tiring to think about how well these ridiculous self-help books sold, and how much all the optimist consultants earned. Why was that so? Who had even heard of a multi-millionaire who had got rich by claiming that everything gets screwed up? It must be because the optimists have access to the media, and that the pessimists are discriminated against. At a guess, the pessimists earn a fraction of the salary of the optimists even though they do just as good a job. Equal wages for unequal mouths! That should be the slogan.

Titus is determined to do everything in his power to confirm the study. He is going to be literature's Cathy Freeman: a feted pessimist at the kernel of optimism. The aboriginal and asthmatic runner from Australia dominated the 400-metre tracks around the turn of the century, and harvested lots of Olympic and World Championship medals. She belonged to the indigenous population that had been declared incapable of running their own country and had been cowed by the white colonial optimists for hundreds of years. Every time she won, she looked a bit uncomfortable because the next time she would probably screw it up. Why celebrate with the public now? At the next competition, all those white teeth would scornfully laugh when she lost. But perhaps, perhaps, she could nevertheless be able to try again. If only she prepared a bit better, trained a bit more intensively, a bit longer, a bit more often.

Preparation and facts make for proficiency. Since I am basically a gloomy pessimist, I must devote myself to facts, Titus thinks. *The Best Book in the World* shall be written with the best research in the world.

The boy at the woman's bosom may well be a positive and fine image to quickly counter the craving for poison.

But if the sceptic didn't get more nourishment, it would all get screwed up.

CHAPTER 13

At the Library

When the city library opens in the morning, Titus is the first to enter. He has slept well, and almost runs up the long steps.

Behind the counter stands an erect and correct man with a rather strange appearance. He has all the necessary requirements to be strikingly handsome: thick brown back-combed hair, clear-cut features with distinct and forceful cheekbones and young-looking skin, almost a little rose-coloured. He has a relaxed smile but there is a trace of shyness in his eyes. If only he had spent a little more time outside the library, he would have been handsomely furrowed. If only he had eaten something other than salads in the lunchroom, he would have looked forceful. Now he sticks out a bit with his pointed face and his thin wrists, like a prototype of a good-looking man that never left the dream factory. He is *almost* beautiful.

Titus is familiar with the prototype. He has met him at book fairs and various writers' gatherings. His name is Christer Hermansson and he divides his life between the books he has written himself and books that others have written. In his role as a librarian, he is also one of Sweden's most influential innovators and debaters in the subject. Titus doesn't know much about libraries, but is a great admirer of the warped humour in Christer's books.

'Christer! Hi, what are you doing here?' says Titus, and is genuinely pleased to see him.

'*Ich bin ein bibliothekar!*' says Hermansson and stands to attention, knocking the soles of his Birkenstock sandals together.

Ich bin ein bibliothekar is also the title of one of his books. This is quite clearly a man who takes the expression 'live your life like a book' seriously.

'Ha, ha,' Titus laughs. 'I know, but I thought you worked in Södertälje.'

'My boss, Eva Larsson, carried out an excellent reorganisation of the entire region. Now I've been posted here for a year to replace the legendary librarian Oliver C. Johansson! The C stands for Cromwell. For the time being, Oliver is the acting head of department of cultural services in Strängness. The general impression is that he won't be there very long. There is talk of malign narcissism. He has evidently used dubious methods to try to buy out the entire library services in the Mälardal region with the help of venture capitalists. According to their slogan, they're going to offer "wide-ranging experiences for the people". But, whatever – I am the acting director of the library! Here and now!'

'I see... congratulations are in order then,' says Titus, who is slightly surprised by the formal tone and the long explanation.

Outside the library walls, Christer is a totally different person who likes to boast about his tennis skills and his literary successes: 'The critics loooooove me.' But at work he is evidently down-to-earth and irreproachable.

'And how can I help you, Titus? Something about the rise and fall of the Roman Empire?'

'No thank you,' says Titus, and curses his parents for calling him Titus. Always these jokes about emperors and the Roman Empire.

'I'm working on an essay about reading habits and need some help with something special. First I need to get hold of all the copies of *The Swedish Bookseller* magazine from the last five years. Then I want to borrow all the books that have been on their various bestseller of the month lists for the same period.'

'Aha! Glad to hear it – you have come to the right place. We love tasks like that. We'll fix it. If you go and have a cup of coffee, it will be ready in about fifteen minutes. The Dan Brown books might be out on loan. They usually are.'

'It doesn't matter,' says Titus, and breaks into a smile. He had envisaged having to run around the shelves himself to pick up the books. What service!

When he walks towards the café, he sees Christer Hermansson gather several colleagues and gives them orders. Wonderful people, these library types, Titus thinks. They really do a great job on the quiet.

The library gradually starts to fill with people, mainly students and pensioners who graze among the newspapers and the books. The silence is pleasant. In the same way that voice volumes are turned down, the visitors move around slowly, as if a sudden movement would be just as disturbing as a loud noise. I must come here more often, thinks Titus.

En route to the café, he passes a lecture hall and some small reading rooms. The door to one of the rooms is ajar. At the far end of the room sits a student with a hairstyle that is almost as brilliantly coloured as that of Eddie X. He is studying and the desk is cluttered with books. His face is buried in his hands.

Ah, there's the café, over there. Or, to be more exact, the coffee machine. Titus puts in a few coins and presses the button for ordinary black coffee. The café is fairly empty and there are plenty of free tables. Titus sits on a chair right in the corner and thinks for a while. He already knows quite well what is going to happen in *The Best Book in the World*. Perhaps it is a bit over-the-top to be doing all this thorough research?

What he really ought to be doing is sitting and writing. After twenty novels, he has mastered the form of the novel, so the actual structure isn't going to be a problem. Above all, what he needs to improve is the non-fiction genre. Facts, facts, facts. He must, amongst other things, get hold of the best pizza recipe in the world, humour to knock you over, and a management book that promises salvation. He has already dealt with the slimming thing with the ABC method. And he has also got quite a long way with giving up smoking and drinking thanks to the threat and reward images. He can easily include them in the chief inspector's life. You can't have too much sex, so he will have to read up on that. Not to mention therapy. He must absolutely be the best at therapy.

His thoughts are suddenly interrupted by his mobile ringing. He sees on the display that it is from a withheld number. He retreats as far as he can into his corner so that he won't disturb those around him when he answers in as quiet a voice as possible.

'Yes, this is Titus Jensen.'

'Hello, Titus, hello. My name is Fabian Nadersson. Can you spare a moment?'

'Er, well, I suppose so. What's it about?'

'Well, Titus, I am ringing on behalf of Mensa. They have a special offer just for you, Titus.'

'What? Mensa? You mean that club that only admits intelligent people?'

'Yes, exactly, Titus. Now you can buy an interactive training package for only two hundred and ninety-nine kronor, you see. With this package you will be able to improve your IQ. Then you can apply for membership of Mensa.'

'What do you mean? Should I buy an intelligence test for two hundred and ninety-nine kronor? And why would I want to join Mensa?'

'Mensa is a worldwide network. You can gain great advantage from being a member of Mensa.'

'In what way?'

'Well, you can meet people of a like mind. Other gifted people that you can share experiences with. That's exactly what it's about, Titus! Yes, indeed. Shall I sign you up for a training package?'

'If I am smart enough to be in Mensa, is it people like you that I will come across if I wanted to become a member?'

'No, unfortunately. I am only an agent for their online courses. I am not a member myself.'

'So you haven't gone on the course?'

'Yes, but I am not a member…'

'You mean you didn't pass the test?'

'Er… I have a mate who bought the training package. It took him two weeks and then he became a full member.'

'But answer my question! Would you yourself want to be a member of Mensa?'

'Yes, of course. Everybody would, surely? Does a training package sound interesting? Only two hundred and ninety-nine kronor if you order it now, during the summer.'

'No, I don't think so. I don't understand why people with a certain IQ would have anything in common. You might just as well start clubs for people with a particular skin colour. And no thank you, we've seen enough of that sort of club in history.'

'So you want me to book you down for a training package?'

'*No!* Do you have difficulties in understanding?'

'Okay, Titus. Thank you anyway. Have a nice day!'

Titus shakes his head. Intelligence is an uninteresting measure of a person's gifts. It is like trying to pick out the best colour in a painting. It's the composition and the combination of colours that determine whether a painting is good, not how many litres of paint have been used. Besides, intelligence is far too abstract a concept. It is almost impossible to conceive of a life with a different intelligence than the one you are equipped with yourself. Ask anyone at all if they want to change their appearance or get a higher IQ and they are guaranteed to choose bigger breasts, a smaller tummy, fuller lips or a super-equipped cock.

When Titus returns to the lending counter, Christer Hermansson looks grim.

'Sorry, Titus. I have bad news.'

'What has happened?'

'The books are already out on loan.'

Inside Titus's corduroy jacket, his heart goes sour.

'All of them?'

'Every single one,' says Christer Hermansson and twitches his head a couple of degrees backwards and upwards. He blinks slightly nervously.

'To whom?' Titus hisses.

'We can't, of course, say that. We are very strict about library confidentiality.'

'What damned library confidentiality?' Titus shouts. 'Just tell me who has borrowed my books!'

'Now, shall we calm down a little? To start with, they are not your books. They are the library's books. We stock them in order to lend them to the public. And now they have been borrowed. By a member of the public. Or several. The books you have asked for are in fact very popular. That's how it is.'

Curses! Titus realises that it is Eddie X of course who has borrowed the books. It isn't enough that he has stolen Titus' basic idea of writing *The Best Book in the World*. He has also pinched Titus' working method!

Another piece drops into place. The student with the same hairdo as Eddie X, up there in the reading room that he went past just a few minutes ago, is of course not a student. It is Eddie X! He's sitting here, in the middle of Stockholm, at the City Library, and writing my book!

Titus rushes down the stairs and off down the corridor that leads to the lecture halls and the reading rooms. Which one was it? He tears open door after door. Empty. Nobody there. No Eddie, anyway. Has he imagined it all? When he reaches the last door, he stops and catches his breath for a moment. What shall he actually say to Eddie?

He grabs the doorknob. Locked! He knocks on the door. No answer. He knocks harder and puts his mouth against the keyhole.

'Hello, is somebody in there?'

Not a sound. He bangs the underside of his fist against the door. Hard, time after time.

'Hello!'

Suddenly he hears the sound of a chair being moved across the floor. Somebody's there!

'Open the door!'

'Hello?' says a weak voice from inside. 'Yes, what do you want?'

'Open the door, I want to talk to you!'

There is silence for a few moments. Then the key is turned on the inside. The door is slowly pushed ajar. Eddie's brown teddy-bear eyes peep out through the chink. Titus tries to push the door further open, but Eddie has evidently put something against it. It won't give an inch. Eddie breaks into a smile inside the little opening.

'Hi, Titus! Great to see you!'

'What are you doing, Eddie? What on earth are you doing?'

'Haha,' Eddie gives a friendly laugh. 'Are you working for the police now, what's got into you? You look stressed, Titus. You must take more care of yourself.'

Always this pleasant tone. It really gets on Titus' nerves. Can't you even get into a raging fury without that damn love poet starting to behave like a saint? But Eddie's calm does its work. It always does, for everything and on everybody. Even on Titus – his pulse slows down a little.

'Yes, well, I walked past here earlier. And then, after a long while, something clicked inside my head. It must have been Eddie sitting in there, I thought. So I went back, but then the door was locked.'

'Oh, right, good thing you came back. It is really great to see you again!'

'Er, yeah, same here…'

'Are you here to borrow books?'

'Yeah, right. That was the idea.'

'Anything particular you're looking for?'

'No, not really, just scouting round a little…'

How do some people always have the ability to steer a conversation in the direction they want? Sometimes it doesn't seem to make any difference however strong your intentions are. Sometimes there is a cat in hell's chance of getting your way. Titus feels that the situation is running through his fingers. How can he confront Eddie with what he knows? Er… *knows*? He doesn't actually *know* anything. He hasn't really got a clue as to what Eddie is doing. Perhaps the whole thing is just a figment of Titus' imagination. A phantom image of a horrible crime that says 'pop' and goes up in smoke as soon as you turn the light on.

But nevertheless. No smoke without fire.

Damn it, I'm stone-cold sober and 100 per cent compos mentis, Titus thinks. Of course I must be able to rely on my intuition!

'And you, Eddie, what are you doing?'

Eddie brushes away a blue lock of hair from his eyes and loosens his colourful silk scarf, which is wrapped several times around his neck. A very solemn look spreads across his face.

'I'm writing.'

'Oh, yeah…?' says Titus, and wants to hear more.

'I'm writing something I am forced to write.'

'Umm… I can believe that,' Titus mumbles to himself and sees that a confession is close. He knows Eddie and realises that he isn't bad deep inside. The guy can't keep a secret. If he is writing *The Best Book in the World*, he's going to say so.

'Yeah, well, I have been prowling around this project and not been able to take the plunge. I can't wait any longer.'

'No?'

'It's about my dad.'

'What? Your dad?'

'Yes, I'm trying to find out what actually happened when I was a child. You know, Titus, I regard myself as a fairly happy person. Yet there is an unpleasant darkness some-where which sometimes drags me down. I suspect that it is my childhood that is behind it all.'

'So now you're going to write a book about your dad?'

'No, no, I'm working on my summer programme. On the radio, you know. They're broadcasting it next week, there'll be millions of listeners. I've had to rethink it completely; at first I'd planned to do a programme of reminiscences inter-woven with my favourite music, from when I was little up to the present day. A delightful document of the times, with lots of nostalgic touchdowns. First time I made out, the first festival, stuff like that. But then I got hooked on a Peter LeMarc song that I heard him play live long before his stage fright got the upper hand. *Blue Light.* Have you heard it?'

'I don't know…'

'It goes something like this: "I was born under a blue light. Grew up in a blue house. Lived in a blue binge. But now I

92

realise that there is another Sweden. I have seen that there are other colours.'"

'Yeah, right, I think I've heard that.'

'I started thinking about what the lyrics could mean to me. And then it struck me. I too grew up in a blue house. Metaphorically speaking. My dad was a nutter.'

'A nutter?'

'A paranoid schizophrenic,' says Eddie. 'He suffered from severe delusions and was often deeply depressed. He got the idea that evil people climbed into his soul and stole his goodness.'

'Oh dear,' says Titus. He can't help wondering how he got here, in a heart-to-heart conversation about Eddie's dad through a chink in the door at the City Library.

'Sad pictures pop up out of my memory. But I don't want to apportion guilt. I simply must find out more. So I have borrowed loads of books about this, other people's stories about what it is like to live close to a mental illness. I have been forced to re-do the whole programme. There won't be any laughing and kidding. I am going to turn my heart inside out instead. It will be a one-and-a-half-hour blue summer.'

Titus breathes out. In a sense, it is a relief to hear that Eddie had a rotten childhood. It means that he won't have time to think about *The Best Book in the World*. I hope he'll dig really deep into the shit, Titus thinks maliciously. After the light comes darkness. Eddie is on his way into a tunnel. Hope it will be long and narrow. Now I am the one who sees the light!

But, in that case, who the hell has borrowed all the books? Is there another rival? Or is it all just another figment of his imagination?

Titus realises that he has gone down the wrong track. It is ridiculous to try to follow other people's recipes to create a bestseller. He could read all the bestselling books in the world without being able to find a pattern. No, he must find *The Best Book in the World* within himself.

Now he is the little boy at the woman's bosom again. He licks away his milk moustache and waves goodbye to Eddie and his crazy dad.

Quick recap. What has he got?

He has an overweight and charismatic detective chief inspector who has cracked an important slimming code and will soon change the world's view of leadership. On top of that, he has a polished serial killer, a frightfully tasty pizza and the best artist in the world throughout the ages, his soul mate Salvador Dali. Plus lots of good ideas and a synopsis that will soon overflow from his brain. Wonderful.

Time to go to work.

CHAPTER 14

Serial Salvador

Serial Salvador. He had seen the name on the placards for several weeks now. It was repulsive. A way of simplifying and uglifying. His task was much more beautiful than that. His art would not fit on a newspaper placard. His art would not fit in a museum or an art hall. They would get to see. They would feel it.

Sure, there had been artists before him who had worked in his spirit. The American photographer Andres Serrano, for example: his photos of dead people in mortuaries were dazzlingly beautiful. Murdered gang members and innocent mugging victims. Naked, broken, bloody and seductive. Serrano's pictures were hated by some, loved by others. But was it art? Wasn't it simply documentation of the art works of others? Somebody had killed another person deliberately, perhaps for revenge or some other desire.

It must surely be the person who triggers the experience who is the artist, not the one who experiences it, looks at it or just consumes it? Serrano portrayed experiences, he didn't create them. Did that make him an artist? Or was he just a tool in the service of the murderers? A paintbrush, a canvas, a palette with paint. Yes, it must have been the murderers who were the real originators.

Serial Salvador. He sniffed at the name. No, he would once and for all rub out the boundary between moral and immoral, between art and reality. When the crime-scene technicians from the police took pictures of his installations, those works of art became eternal. The police became Serrano-clones, obedient tools in his service. Without understanding it themselves, they became artists, public and critics at one and the same time. Shocked and in despair, they stood there and lit up his installations with their camera flashes. Dead and mutilated bodies hung up on weird crutches in the strangest of places. Men, women and children, nobody escaped. When the photos were subsequently spread between colleagues, prosecutors and media leaks, the whole world became his art hall. The guardians of morality became the foremost apostles of immorality. His art was spread at the speed of light via TV, radio, the Internet and newspapers.

The person who spread it most and best of all was that slimmed-down Håkan Rink, who presided over press conferences and theorised about his offender profiles. It was repulsive. Repulsively delightful.

The days pass in the sign of mass murder. Titus has full sail. He is relaxed and writes at a furious pace.

Better to be obsessed than dependent.

Serial Salvador hangs people up on crutches.

Chief Inspector Håkan Rink is right on his tail.

CHAPTER 15

The Return of Fabian Nadersson

Sometimes Titus has to take a rest from his writing. Not because he wants to, but because the computer turns itself off at regular intervals. Astra has decided that Titus must rest now and then. Besides, he must stay sober as he has to use the BAC lock every time he wants to start working again.

Yes, Astra is a wise editor. The alcohol lock ensures that Titus slaves away at the computer when it is turned on. Each session lasts for exactly six hours. When the computer turns itself off, he can't start it up again for two hours. As if out of respect for the computer and its sleep mode, Titus always puts the lid down and says 'Sleep tight!' During the breaks Titus manages to eat, rest and communicate with the outside world. He turns his mobile on and checks whether he has any messages. He rarely does.

Today the fridge is desolate. A half-eaten pizza tries to make itself look interesting through its transparent and greasy plastic container. It is unsuccessful. Titus sighs deeply and looks at the clock. Yes, he's just got time to get down to the shop if he hurries.

Then the telephone rings. He answers angrily:

'Yes? Titus Jensen here.'

'Hello, Titus. This is Fabian Nadersson! Can you spare a minute?'

'Hello... er, no, I'm just about to go shopping. What is it about? Wasn't it you who tried to sell Mensa courses to me a while back?'

'That's right, Titus! We had a really nice offer there.'

'Fabian Nadersson... what sort of name is that actually?'

'It's my name, Titus.'

'But I mean Nadersson. Never heard it before.'

'Exactly. I used to be called Andersson. Now I'm called Nadersson. A bit more personal. I feel very comfortable with it. That's how it is, Titus. Can I tell you what is on my mind today?'

'Do I have any choice?'

'Haha. Of course you do, Titus. Obviously you have a choice. Today I'm phoning on behalf of the Multi-therapy Association.'

'What did you say it was called? Multivitamin Association?'

'Multi-therapy, Titus. Multi-therapy Association.'

'And what on earth is that?'

'Well, thank you for asking, Titus. I'll tell you. The Multi-therapy Association offers solutions for motor-skill and mental blocks. The pedagogy assumes that all problems can be solved. Does that sound good?'

'Good? It sounds ridiculous. What do you mean "all problems can be solved"? Can they go and do my shopping, the people in this association? I need milk and bread. And eggs. And quick as hell.'

'Haha, nice one. No, multi-therapy is a form of treatment that deals with – for example – obsessive-compulsive disorder. What I can offer is an open house at a multi-therapist near you. On Saturday, the association has open house across the country. It is free to get information, and if you want you can then buy a test consultation which costs only four hundred and ninety-nine kronor for the first hour. Since you live in Stockholm, I can warmly recommend a visit to Dr Rolf on Valhallavägen. He has a very good reputation.'

'What, is it free?'

'Yes, the actual information is free. And the first hour is at the giveaway price of four hundred and ninety-nine kronor, as I said. Does that sound interesting?'

'What do you mean? You don't want to sell me anything, here and now?'

'This conversation is a part of a national telemarketing campaign that the Multi-therapy Association is carrying out. You don't need to buy anything. Shall I book you in for a free session now on Saturday? Shall we say at 10 o'clock at Valhallavägen 1?'

'I'm not sure about that. Are you certain it won't cost anything?'

'Not an öre. Thank you, Titus, then that's settled. You are booked in to see Dr Rolf on Saturday at 10 o'clock, Valhallavägen 1. Good luck!'

Titus shakes his head. Multi-therapy sounds New Age. If there's anything that Titus dislikes, then it is incense and new spiritual things. At the same time, it will do him no harm to leave the flat for a couple of hours and gather some new impressions. He knows, too, that spiritual things sell like hotcakes, regardless of whether they are new or old. Who knows, perhaps he can get some ideas that Håkan Rink can use in his hunt for Serial Salvador. A good chief inspector must be an expert on relationships and therapy, he has always thought that. Now he'll have the chance to learn some more.

CHAPTER 16

Meeting about Alchemists

The view of the Old Town and Riddarfjärden bay is enchanting. The grey-toned glass from floor to ceiling lets you see both the blue water of Lake Mälaren and the cumulus clouds over the parliament building. Of course there aren't any curtains or furniture to obscure the view of the beautiful summer day. There is a gigantic walnut desk and a lime green suite from Italy in the room – that is all. On the desk is a chalk-white laptop on a large leather writing pad in the same shade as the sofas. Otherwise, the desk is empty, except for a large flat screen with a white frame. Although this is a room at a publishing house, there isn't a single bookshelf in it. That is most unusual. Most of the other rooms at Winchester's are packed from floor to ceiling with books, manuscripts, newspapers and catalogues.

Astra Larsson sits on the sofa in Evita Winchester's room and waits for Evita to finish talking on the telephone. It is irritating that Evita never turns her phone off when they have a meeting. Evita is always available and her contact network is red-hot.

Evita Winchester has had a unique career. During the twenty-five years she has been working, she has done a stint as an arts reporter for *Dagbladet*, been editor-in-chief in Swedish Radio's Culture Hour, head of the arts section at the *Evening Post* and director of programmes at Swedish TV. It was, of course, always on the cards that she would eventually end up as boss of the family's own publishing house, but she has always emphasised over the years how important it is that all the companies in the group are run on a commercial basis and not by nepotism. And nobody thinks Evita Winchester got the job just because she's called Winchester. In just a few years, she has made Winchester's the most profitable publishing house in Sweden. She herself is most proud of having realised at an early stage just how important it was to control the new distribution channels. With the help of lots of money and skilful manoeuvring, Winchester's now owns large segments of the electronic book trade and the distribution companies that have long-term contracts to supply books to the major retail and super-market chains.

Evita is one of those people it is impossible find irritating once you meet them. All grudges and bother are forgotten as soon as you see her face to face. Those green eyes are lively, and her lips – always just as red – seem to move at the speed of light. Her energy and presence are extremely contagious. As soon as Evita puts down the phone, Astra feels her mood improving.

'Sorry, Astra! I had to take that call,' says Evita and runs her fingers through her short jet-black hair. She sits on the sofa beside Astra.

'It's okay. Don't worry.'

'Goodness, what beautiful legs! Do you wax them?'

'Yes…'

'I mean, do you do it yourself or go to a parlour?'

'I do it myself…'

'Goodness, you're so clever! How do you find the time? You look gorgeous, Astra. Really,' says Evita in admiration with a gaze that devours Astra from top to toe.

'Thank you… you too,' says Astra in an attempt to reciprocate.

'What have we got today?'

'Well, to start with I want you to know how Titus is doing, and then I need a little help with Veronica Fuentes.'

'The Bitch in Barcelona?'

'Precisely.'

'Oh dear, are we there again? Well, well, let's get on with it! How are things going for our dear Titus?'

'They're going well. You were quite right to force him to pledge temperance. He is in really good shape now and is slaving away.'

'Is it going to be good, then?'

'I haven't seen anything yet. He wants to get a bit further before he shows me anything. But from just looking at him, it's going to be good. At first he was a nervous wreck, but now he seems calmer.'

'Great news. Yes, without doubt he is one of our best. If only it wasn't for the booze, he would be a national treasure. Just imagine if he could be sober for real! Then he would have the whole country at his feet. At any rate us women, haha! There's something of a merciless animal about him that is extremely attractive.'

'You think so?' says Astra surprised. She has never ever thought of Titus in that way.

'Yes, absolutely. He can be dead good-looking. He is completely uncompromising. I like that. Don't you remember those author portraits that Ulla took of him for *Baroque in their Blood*? Of course, it's a long time ago. But in those days he was drop-dead gorgeous! Shaved head, sun tan, and his shirt unbuttoned down to his navel. Yummy!'

'Yes, well… perhaps. Whatever. It seems to be really going well for him. He has even started going to the gym. I think he sneaks off to a solarium too sometimes, but I haven't dared ask him, haha,' laughs Astra.

'Is that true? God, men get so silly when they approach their fifties. Haha, it's wonderful! Let me know when he is getting close to finishing and I'll invite him to dinner. I can gobble him up in one gulp, don't you think?' says Evita with a loud and lively laugh.

'I promise. I'll bring him along on a leash. Grrr!'

'Super. But seriously, Astra. You've done a fantastic job. You're going to pull this off. It'll be fun to read when the time comes. Just make sure you follow up regularly. You can never trust an addict one hundred per cent, even if he has become a teetotaler. Don't forget that.'

'No, I won't forget,' says Astra and uses the serious note that turned up after the laughs. 'This means everything to Titus. He knows it, and he knows that we know it too. I think we can strike gold here, I really do.'

'Good. In that case we shall print a huge run straight off and prepare the market thoroughly.'

'I'm going to meet him the day after tomorrow. We'll see how far he has come.'

'Good. That's settled then. Have you got new worries with BB?' Evita wonders, giving her head an anxious tilt.

BB means the Bitch in Barcelona. That is the name that the people at Winchester's use for the literary agent Veronica Fuentes in Barcelona. BB runs an extremely successful agency which only has a single client, the bestselling Mexican New Age author Pablo Blando. Blando writes self-help books about how to find the right path on your journey through life, how to accept your sexuality and see the spirituality in everyday situations. He often bases his stories on old tales and legends that he polishes up and fills with poetic one-liners. He has millions of readers, most of them women. Winchester's launched him successfully in Sweden about ten years ago and since then he has had a regular spot on the bestseller lists.

But the more you have, the more you want. The bitch in Barcelona is never satisfied. She and her bitchy staff bombard Blando's publishers across the world with daily demands for follow-ups and reports on what has been done on the PR front. BB doesn't trust anybody, despite the fact that the publishers have bought the rights for astronomical sums and ought to be interested in making a good job of it. The Barcelona bitches always unleash their mail-bomb missives at night, which makes publishers fear a new list of demands in their inboxes when they come to work in the morning.

'Now it's worse than ever,' sighs Astra, who has been landed with BB and Blando since she is exceptionally tough and is a rising star at Winchester's.

'What's new?'

'There are several things. Above all is that business with the Nobel Prize.'

'Oh no, not again!' Evita exclaims and rolls her eyes.

'Yep, she is quite bonkers. She demands that I write a report on the strategy we have to get him on the Academy's shortlist this autumn.'

'But that's impossible! He'll never get the Nobel Prize. Never ever. Not in this life, and not in the next. He writes quasi-philosophical soft porn chicklit. Boring rubbish. I don't suppose they have ever even considered opening one of his books!'

'I know, Evita, but I can't say that to BB. Besides, I haven't time to write reports for her. It doesn't say anything about reports in the contract for the rights, does it?'

'No, of course it doesn't.'

'The thing is that she's got Pablo to believe that he is in the running for a prize already this year. So now he wants to come to the Gothenburg book fair in September to show his interest. He thinks that the more often he comes to Sweden, the more delighted the Swedish Academy will be with him.'

'No, no, no! Absolutely not! The fair is in just a couple of months. No way. Everything is already planned. It isn't possible to arrange a seminar or anything good now. No, he can't come. He is *not* allowed to come.'

Pablo Blando has already visited the annual fair in Gothenburg several times. Although he is about seventy, he still has an exceptional ability to attract women. There is always a long queue when he signs his books, and he pays most attention to the very youngest women. During a four-day visit he usually invites at least as many young girls up to his hotel room to spend the night with special Latin treatment. And in addition, he doesn't refrain from picking out the most beautiful one and taking her to the big banquets arranged by the fair and the publishing houses. 'This evening you are my wife!' he usually whispers chivalrously, and kisses her hand until she blushes. What he likes best of all is to feed her little bits of cheese on cocktail sticks – in public. Everybody there thinks it's terribly embarrassing, but what won't people do to rub shoulders with a bestselling author and his never-ending ability to make gold from gravel. Astra has seen it and can sometimes be disgusted with herself for being a part of the word-alchemist's senile circus act.

'The bitch knows there isn't much time,' she says. 'That's why she wants Pablo to come to Gothenburg incognito. It's just sick. Like when a king travels abroad without it being a formal state visit. Secret, but nevertheless she wants lots of media coverage. Why not? She regards him as royalty. But you know what the worst thing is?'

'No, what? Must there be some Viagra waiting in the room as usual?'

'Listen to this. She wants to arrange a lunch for the Swedish Academy with Pablo as the host. He is a member of the Mexican Literary Academy and the social occasion would strengthen the ties between the two countries, she thinks. Pablo would be able to help introduce more Swedish authors in the Latin American market. She is very enthusiastic and thinks it's a brilliant idea. You get it? You scratch my back, I'll scratch yours,…'

'Is she out of her mind?' exclaims Evita her hand on her forehead. 'To ask to get the Nobel Prize is like pouring a bucket of shit over yourself in a public square. Nobody forgets such a faux pas, never ever.'

'Actually, I don't think she does get it,' says Astra with a resigned sigh. 'I've tried to tell her in a nice way, but it just doesn't sink in. I'm going on holiday soon and must sort this out pretty quick. Have you any good ideas?'

'Okay. Lets do it like this. I'll write a very clear letter to Veronica and say that it would be a total disaster to even show yourself in Sweden if you ever want to get the Nobel Prize. I can ask the cultural attaché in Barcelona to deliver it to her in person. That ought to have an effect, I think. Then we'll not run the risk of seeing Pablo at the book fair for at least the next two years…'

CHAPTER 17

A Worthwhile Art Round

It wasn't the first time this week that Detective Chief Inspector Håkan Rink had stood in front of the large noticeboard in the incident room. It was almost entirely covered with little bits of paper in various colours. Each colour represented a different type of 'note' as it is called in police jargon: crime scenes, clues, testimony and so on.

It was late evening and the team had gathered together to listen to an art historian tell them more about Salvador Dali's driving forces. The crime scenes contained increasingly obvious signs that the serial killer was inspired by the surrealist twentieth-century painter.

'Thank you for not going home to your dear families just this evening,' Håkan Rink started off. 'When we capture Serial Salvador, not only your own families will thank you – the whole country will show its gratitude. Sweden is cowering in terror. We see how the fear acquires new and nastier ways, such as bomb threats against museums with avant-garde exhibitions and the persecution of experimental authors and contemporary artists. Indeed, people vent their anger at culture in general as if it was culture that was to blame for how society has become harder. But I am still convinced that culture is a mirror of society – not the other way round. Let me welcome

Alf Linde, one of Sweden's foremost experts on the surrealist movement.'

The ten or so police officers in Rink's team gave Linde a short but friendly round of applause. Linde was very old and looked as if he himself could have been around when the Dadaists were transformed into surrealists under the fanatical command of the author André Breton in the early 1920s. When he spoke, there was a quiver under his chin like that of a turkey.

'Thank you, Håkan. Yes, in this case it does rather look as if the murderer is busy creating a reality mirror of art. Very strange. To the best of my knowledge, this is the first time a murderer has copied an innocent artist. I am therefore also convinced that if you are ever to catch him you must become deeply familiar with Dali's art. Understand it with your subconscious mind.'

The colleagues in the team nodded gravely at each other. That seemed sensible. They already know something about Dali, but definitely needed to learn more.

Now he must be concise, Titus thinks, and puts the brakes on his frenzy for a while. It would be a piece of cake to spew out thirty pages about Dali. His enormous waxed moustaches alone were worth a couple of pages. Did Serial Salvador have the same? No, that would be too simple.

Alf Linde handed out copies of a hand-written page and chuckled aloud to himself: 'Here's Dali in a nutshell; here's Dali in a surrealist nutshell.'

Against the simple	For the compound
Against uniformity	For differentiation
Against equality	For rank
Against collectivism	For individualism
Against politics	For metaphysics
Against nature	For aesthetics
Against progress	For permanency
Against mechanisation	For dreams
Against youth fanaticism	For mature Machiavellian
Against spinach	For snails
Against film	For theatre
Against Buddha	For Marquis de Sade
Against the Orient	For the Occident
Against the sun	For the moon
Against revolution	For tradition
Against Michelangelo	For Raphael
Against Rembrandt	For Vermeer
Against primitive objects	For over-cultivated objects
Against philosophy	For religion
Against medicine	For magic
Against mountain regions	For coast
Against figments of the brain	For ghosts
Against women	For Gaia
Against men	For me
Against time	For soft clocks

Then Alf Linde talked for just over an hour about Dali and his art. Why he distanced himself from the other surrealists, how he became so extremely successful commercially, and how he eventually buried first his wife Gala and then himself in the cellar of his surrealist mansion in the middle of the

Catalonian town of Figueres. It became a museum of his life's work and one of the most remarkable tourist destinations in the world. Naturally with sky-high entrance fees.

'In conclusion, I must tell you something about his inventions. Before Salvador Dali made his breakthrough as an artist, he sketched a number of innovations to earn his living. He carried out a bitter struggle and was regarded as an idiot by those to whom he tried to sell his ideas. Here are a few examples: dresses with false insertions around the hips and bosom to distract men's erotic fantasies; false nails with mirrors; water-filled transparent mannequins with swimming goldfish inside to illustrate blood circulation; kaleidoscopic spectacles for motorists for when the surrounding landscape got too boring; tactile film where cinema-goers could touch the settings in the film. And so on, and so on. About one hundred of Dali's inventions are well documented. What we can see today is that many of them have become reality in one way or another: the push-up bra; virtual reality spectacles; 4D cinemas, et cetera. Perhaps he wasn't mad, just terribly before his time. But listen carefully now. The invention to which he devoted the greater part of his energy was the rotating pork sculpture. He bought large amounts of meat at the butcher's and hung it on crutches that he placed on electric rotating tables. Nobody knows what he wanted to achieve with the rotating pork. What do you think? Was he as mad as a hatter, or was he simply a misunderstood inventor?'

Truth and knowledge were the keys to Håkan Rink's leadership. No frenzy to find positive images à la sporting clubs. No group-dynamic exercises fashionable for team-think in the commercial sector.

His police colleagues looked at each other, suddenly struck by the insight. They must search for Serial Salvador among inventor circles. Go through rejected applications at the Patent Office. Investigate misunderstood entrepreneurs and devoted enthusiasts who have not been given their credit. Dig among people labelled with odd combinations of letters to find those that have lost their footing. That is where they would find him!

Håkan Rink smiled contentedly to himself. Yet again, his simple and direct methods had borne fruit.

This time it was the FFI Method: FACTS are the FATHER of IMAGINATION.

CHAPTER 18

The Best Pizza Recipe in the World

After the evening meeting, the chief inspector treated his colleagues to some sustaining night food at the police station.

Håkan Rink's Quattro Stagione, the pizza with four 'seasons'.

Pizza dough

½ packet of fresh yeast: crumble the yeast into a large bowl

Add 200 ml lukewarm water and dissolve the yeast in the water

Add 500 ml wheat flour

Add 3 tablespoons of olive oil

Mix the ingredients into a pizza dough. Grease a roasting pan with olive oil. Cover the bottom of the pan with the dough pushing it out to the edges with your fingers. Cover the pan with a tea towel and leave it to rise for about 20 minutes while you prepare the sauce and the various toppings. Turn the oven to 250°c.

Pizza sauce

1 tin of chopped tomatoes
2 tablespoons of tomato purée
2 teaspoons of white pepper and black pepper
A few drops of Tabasco
1 teaspoon of oregano
1 teaspoon of salt
1 crushed garlic clove

Mix all the ingredients for the pizza sauce, and taste. By all means sprinkle a little vinegar, sugar and pepper onto the mixture. Experiment a little! Let the sauce simmer a long time.

Pizza toppings

Prepare the toppings while the dough is rising.

Fresh, newly peeled prawns
Fresh, finely sliced mushrooms
Air-dried Italian ham
Mussels pickled in water
Pickled artichoke

Cut and grate the cheese: equal amounts of mozzarella, emmental and parmesan

When the dough base has risen for 20 minutes, spread the sauce over it and start with a layer of cheese.

Divide the pizza into quarters and add the topping in the following order: from '12 o'clock' on the pizza and clockwise: ham is winter, mussels are spring, prawns are summer and mushrooms are autumn. If you believe in God, stick an artichoke in the middle. Push the topping gently into the sauce with your hand.

Bake in the oven for 15–20 minutes at 250°c.

If you have used an artichoke, say a prayer.

Take a break from the ABC Method, and enjoy the best pizza in the world!

CHAPTER 19

White Coat

Titus is sitting on the exercise bicycle at the gym. The sweat is running down the inside of his old bleached T-shirt with the Einstürzende Neubauten print that he bought in Berlin in 1983.

He has started to appreciate these two-hour breaks all the more. When Astra had turned up with a gym membership card, he had just snorted at her. But she evidently knew what she was doing. Titus has a feeling that she always knows what she is doing. An alpha woman. Young, attractive, clever, independent and with just the right amount of pushiness. He couldn't have a better editor. He has been lucky in that respect.

Titus likes his new life. It's been going on a few weeks now. Not since his teens has he had such a long period without any alcohol at all. Sure, he pulls out his reward image now and then, but it's more to keep it alive than because he really needs it. Like an amusing joke, a pleasant memory. For the time being, another form of energy keeps him away from spirits and cigarettes.

The book.

Writing gives him energy. He's rattling along and he knows it's going to be good. The book is easily accessible in its style, but heavy as lead in its themes. He throws in so many references that critics will be kept busy for decades trying to analyse his intentions. The characters around Håkan Rink are built up in such a deliberately slow and refined manner that the reader should feel obliged to read on. The breakthrough and unexpected turning points are planned down to the tiniest detail. At the same time, Titus is careful not to reveal too much to readers. That would be an insult to their intelligence. Too many details are for nerds and bores. My readers are here making history with me, Titus thinks. It is my readers who will fill the characters with flesh and blood. It is my readers who will create the details in the room. It is they who will get involved, who will let themselves be amused and worried. My readers are the cleverest and the best, he says to himself, and pedals away for all he is worth on the exercise bike.

Titus doesn't like the suburbs. He has lived all his life in the centre of the city and likes crowds and asphalt. The few times he has been on holiday abroad, it has only been to other big cities. There, he never runs the risk of suddenly finding himself without a bar within easy reach.

Of course, he has been in the countryside – but only in the safe context of a boozy midsummer party or similar event. Titus has always felt that nature shows off a bit, that as soon as he comes along it spruces itself up to an incredible degree and tries to seduce him with its birdsong and its smells, although what it really wants to do is entice him into the mud in a dirty forest pond. And suddenly he has been conned. He sinks slowly under the surface while the pixies scornfully laugh at him with the blue midsummer night sky in the background. No, the countryside is hell. Out there, you must be on your guard. Or very drunk.

The suburbs are not the slightest improvement on the countryside. People in the suburbs are farmers. Instead of tractors, they drive around in enormous estate cars. All they talk about is the weather, sports news and lotteries. The only difference from real farmers is that the suburban people have cheap blue suits instead of cheap blue overalls.

Now, Titus is forced to visit the suburbs. Well, forced is perhaps not strictly accurate. He has been given a chance to learn about therapy for free. It would be an abuse of his professional responsibility not to profit from the chances that pass his way.

FF, as Håkan Rink would have labelled it. Follow the Flow.

When Titus gets off the bus he is on the very edge of Stockholm. Beyond the roundabouts and viaducts he can just make out the thousands of detached houses, terraced houses, the blocks of flats, the playing fields with artificial grass, and the shopping centres. He shudders and thanks his lucky stars that he only had to go as far as no-man's land and not the whole way, deep into suburban hell. Valhallavägen 1 and the roundabout at Roslagstull are without doubt Stockholm's precipice – another couple of metres and he would have risked falling over the edge and that would be the end of it.

Instead he presses the bell down by the entrance. It just says Dr Rolf. Strange that there isn't any surname. What sort of doctor only has a first name? Has he come to a children's hospital?

'Yes, hello!' a voice shouts over the intercom, loud enough to drown the roar from the roundabout which catapults the big silver-coloured suburban cars northwards.

'Yes, hello!' Titus shouts back into the microphone. 'I have a free appointment for multi-therapy at 10 o'clock!'

'Come inside, I've nothing to hide! Fifth floor. There's a lift on the left!'

A short buzz signals that the door can be pushed open. Titus enters and approaches the lift. When the door shuts behind him, he finds himself in total silence. The feeling of being in the suburbs soon fades. This is going to be exciting, he thinks, and overcomes his aversion to lifts.

When he reaches the fifth floor, the door to one of the flats is already open. He sees a hall that could well belong to a therapy clinic.

'Next!'

A large and jovial man in a white coat suddenly appears from nowhere. He stretches his hand out towards Titus.

'Hahaha! Titus Jensen, I presume.'

'Quite right.'

'I am Doctor Rolf. Ralf Rolf.'

'Ralf Rolf?' wonders Titus, who thinks that Ralf Rolf sounds more like a dog barking than a name.

'Exactly! Ralf Rolf. But you can call me Ralf. Doctor Ralf Rolf or just Ralf, that's me. Welcome!'

Titus looks around in the waiting room. Along one wall there are open chests full of theatre clothes and strange props all jumbled up together. Police uniforms, loose noses, wigs, dresses, coats of mail, theatre masks, fake boobs, and enormous Tyrolean short trousers. In the corner next to the chests is a room divider with an arrow and sign that says: Get changed here.

On the walls, Titus sees enormous framed poster-like images with black one-liners against a white background:

Hmm, thinks Titus, what a good idea. One-liners are philosophy in a concentrated form. An idea what won't fit in a one-liner can never be understood by the masses. Naturally, *The Best Book in the World* must have the best one-liners in the world. He has already touched on that subconsciously, but can throw in even more into Håkan Rink's dialogue. Ingenious abbreviations and one-liners, that'll be what characterises the chief inspector's language. A person who talks with abbreviations and one-liners wins Respect with a capital R.

And a capital R is something that is always on Håkan Rink's mind.

'Do you like them? I found them on Internet. On my own homepage, hahaha!' chuckles Doctor Rolf with loud joviality, and puts his arm around Titus. He leads him into the consulting room.

'Take a seat! But don't take it home with you, haha!'

Titus finds them rather trying, people who are implacably jolly. It is as if they have a monopoly on good cheer. They smother everybody else's attempt to be cheerful. Doctor Rolf is most certainly one of those people who starts a party by reeling off four or five funny stories, Titus thinks. It is so damned twentieth century to tell funny stories. And without a doubt he'll be an expert on dirty stories too. Dirty stories are the worst sort of all funny stories.

Doctor Rolf sits down behind his large desk that is full of folders, prescription blocks, pens and a keyboard that looks a bit sticky. A plate with a half-eaten Danish pastry explains that. Doctor Rolf is one of those people who munches away and makes a mess while surfing or working. Since all his attention is directed towards the screen, he doesn't notice when he spills something on the keyboard.

Titus sits in the visitor's chair on the other side of the desk. It is a bit low in relation to the desk top, and Titus feels small.

Besides, the armrest is too high. And the armrests are too close to each other for it to be comfortable to have your arms inside them. It's too cramped; he feels like a fatty in a doll's chair. So he puts his arms on the armrests even though it makes his shoulders almost shoot up towards his ears. His fingers turn white as he firmly grasps the front of the armrests.

He does not feel at all comfortable with this visit. Doctor Rolf doesn't seem a hundred per cent serious. Rather the opposite, in fact.

'Yes, well indeed. Welcome, one might well say.'

'Thank you.'

'Right, you wanted to know a little about multi-therapy, is that correct?'

'Yes.'

'How much do you know?'

'Nothing.'

'Oh, I see,' says Doctor Rolf, and indicates his serious intentions by pulling a little on the collar of his white coat.

'Let me start from scratch. What is your problem? I mean, why were you curious about coming here?'

'I don't have any problems. I came because I got curious after a telephone salesman phoned me,' said Titus, in a friendly tone.

'Excellent! That is a good basic attitude. "I don't have any problems." One might think so. It is not entirely correct, but I won't say that it is entirely wrong.'

'No?'

'Multi-therapy is based on an ancient philosophy. Everything that you understand as life and "the world" consists of events that are processed by your brain. Your brain is unique, so your picture of the world is unique too. What you perceive as green may be seen as red by somebody else. What you see as right is wrong for another person.

120

When you think *"nemas problemas"*, your fellow man may regard the situation as terrible.'

'Mmm, yes…'

'Experiences are nothing more than chemical reactions. Take what people call love, for example. Falling in love is about a bundle of hormones rushing around inside your body. There is no rational explanation for why a certain person attracts another. But what we do know is that we can influence the selection processes through conscious acts. By, for example, following norms and changes of fashion, our ability to attract increases. Adaptation is considered attractive because the opposite party understands that we have enough imagination to manage to support our offspring. Thus: our actions affect our hormones. A pair of modern jeans on a perfectly ordinary bottom gets more hormones going than does a pair of old-fashioned jeans on the same bottom. The act sets off a chemical reaction that creates the experience of love. It isn't the bottom that gets the hormones going, it is the act. The choice of the correct pair of jeans, that is. The act itself is everything. Do you understand?'

'Yes, I think so…'

'Well, life is chemistry. You are a chemistry set. I am another.'

Doctor Rolf leans back and looks at Titus. Titus wonders where they are going. Doctor Rolf puts one hand on the back of his head and slowly pushes it through his hair down towards his brow. His fingers drip slowly down his forehead. The hand stops when it reaches his eyebrows. It rests there a while. Then he tugs a little at the skin of his forehead. His eyebrows go up and down, up and down. Then he suddenly lets go of his own head and continues:

'You say that you don't have any problems, don't you?'

'Yes…'

121

'That is an interesting attitude. Most people who come here think they have problems. Serious ones, even. I usually tell them that they do *not*. But now the opposite would seem to be the case. Here is somebody who says he is without any problems.'

When Doctor Rolf says 'without any problems', he makes it sound like the exact opposite, like a condition that is very serious, indeed mortal. Doctor Rolf closes his eyes and emits a short snoring sound. Titus gives a start and tries to seem like an ordinary person.

'Yes, well, without any problems – what does it mean: without any problems? I do of course struggle with some problems. Or have done in the past, one might say. But I don't have any mental afflictions, if that is what you mean.'

'No, of course not. I understand. "No mental afflictions."' Doctor Rolf pronounces his diagnosis slowly. Then he quickly gets up from his chair.

'Yes, Titus. In that case, there is nothing I can do for you. Regrettably.'

'Are we already finished?' wonders Titus.

'No, by no means! But if you don't have any problems, I will then have to exhibit some of mine. You wanted to find out more about multi-therapy and so you will.'

'Thank you, but I don't know if that is necessary…'

'Oh, but yes. Don't be silly,' says Doctor Rolf and turns on his best lecturer voice. 'First, I shall tell you what it is about. Then I shall demonstrate how it can work. Thus: life is chemistry. Everything you perceive depends upon your chemical make-up. Everything you perceive *wrongly* also depends upon your chemical make-up. All qualities or singularities you have that can be interpreted as abnormal in the eyes of others can be altered with the help of chemical reactions. It is, for example, quite common that people take medicines containing chemicals if they feel excessively persecuted. People who are too happy may take medicine made from the chemical element lithium to deal with that affliction. And people who feel extremely unhappy may also take lithium. With enough lithium in your body, we will all feel good and be like each other. That is what they want. Or what their relatives want. Be that as it may: chemicals are far too clumsy according to us multi-therapists.'

Titus nods cautiously. He is of course curious as to what Doctor Rolf has to say. At the same time, he has a feeling that one shouldn't stimulate him too much with one's interest. Doctor Rolf rolls all the time between apathy and frenzy. One moment, he looks as if he is falling asleep. The next, there is lightning in his eyes.

'Adding chemicals from outside can create more imbalances. Multi-therapy sees it all from the other side. We ensure that the body starts to produce the chemicals it needs. Since everything you experience depends on the chemistry in your brain, all your life is in a sense imagined. It follows from this that your illnesses and problems are imagined too. They are quite simply figments of your imagination concocted by the chemistry in your brain!'

'So you mean that paranoid schizophrenia, for example, is purely a figment of someone's imagination?'

'Exactly!' shouts Doctor Rolf. 'That is indeed the case! Split personality is an *idée fixe* and there are some excellent therapies to deal with that. It is simply a question of tailoring a therapy that works specially for you. That is multi-therapy in a nutshell. If there is a problem – there is a therapy!'

'It sounds extremely simple…'

'Simple! On the contrary, it can be incredibly difficult to find the right therapy. Imaginary illnesses are often very deeply embedded in people's brains. You might have to test hundreds of placebo therapies before one works.'

'Placebo therapies!' says Titus, who is having a hard time keeping up.

'Like sugar-coated pills! The patient thinks that the medicine works and is healed because of that. Even though the only active ingredient is sugar. That is exactly how it is with multi-therapy. As long as you think you are being healed, it will work. When you finally realise that you have an imaginary illness, you will search high and low for an imaginary therapy that works. You will stop seeing yourself as a victim of unfortunate circumstances, genes, childhood environment, or whatever it is you blame. When you get your willpower back, you will blow the whistle and the factory starts working again. Your brain and body will suddenly start producing the chemicals that are needed for you to function properly again. Thus: when you *want* to be cured – you *will* be cured. That's how it is! Now I think you have twigged how it all works, yes?'

'What I regard as my life, you can actually govern with this placebo therapy?'

'Ha! You are clever!'

'Umm, I wonder if I believe this,' says Titus doubtfully. 'Can you give me some examples? What can you cure?'

'Everything! I can cure anything at all. Everything, everything, everything! Paranoia, schizophrenia, agoraphobia, snake phobias, fear of flying. You name it! The whole caboodle! From Münchausen by proxy to Tourette's syndrome.'

Then something clicks inside Titus' head. He thinks about Lenny.

'What, can you cure Tourette's?'

'Yes indeed! Yep. Tourette's is straightforward imagination. A malicious trick of the brain, pure and simple. There is no good reason why people should go around twitching and saying stupid things. No, they do it purely because their brains think they must. For imaginary illness there is only one remedy. And that is…' puffs Doctor Rolf and moves his hand in a circle so that Titus finishes for him.

'…imaginary therapy.'

'Bravo, Titus! Imaginary therapy, placebo therapy, multi-therapy. We have many names for what we love.'

'But how do you go about it, then? I mean, how can you cure somebody with Tourette's, for example?'

'Hard to generalise. But it is almost always a matter of going to extremes. Of going beyond every possible boundary. And then taking one more step, over the precipice. It is about putting people in a context that is so ridiculously exaggerated that they realise their own behaviour is trivial and of no consequence in a larger context. Then one continues to reduce and reduce their problems until they disappear completely. For a Tourette's patient, for example, it might involve forcing the person to be extremely spasmodic and shout out dirty words for hours at a time during each therapy session. Perhaps dressed up as a clown, or something similar. It can be extremely tough going for all involved. My theory is that Tourette's cases have a certain number of spasms inside them. If they try to curb their excesses, the effect is simply that they keep the larder well stocked with terrible things. In the worst cases, the larder will keep them supplied all their lives. No, it is better to hunt down the Tourette's like mad dogs, and force all the shit out of them in a short period. Ride them in like wild horses at a rodeo. In the end, they tire of all the nonsense. We quite simply empty them of their spasms and expletives. But it can take three months. Years in the worst cases.'

'Oh, stop it. That sounds sick. Don't you think it is an extremely degrading approach?'

'So it might seem. And that is why it takes place within sealed rooms at an authorised multi-therapist's. We have signed an oath of confidentiality,' says Doctor Rolf, and smothers a yawn.

How can he be tired now, wonders Titus. He was going on overdrive just thirty seconds ago, when he described Tourette's sufferers as mad dogs.

'If it's as good as you say, then how come multi-therapy isn't better known?' snorts Titus.

He thinks the whole thing sounds like a joke. It is too simple. Genuine traumas must be deeper than simply dressing like an idiot and exaggerating your problems to make them disappear. It would be like trying to lose weight by binge eating.

'Better known?' Doctor Rolf continues to rant. 'It comes with the territory. Who wants to be an ambassador for us multi-therapists, do you think? A person with paranoia that we have forced to go around spying on people 24/7, wearing a trench coat and sunglasses? A schizophrenic who is forced to live in dozens of identities, although he only feels at home in two? Some poor guy who is afraid of pigeons and who has to spend the entire summer in the Piazza San Marco in Venice? The thing is, once they have been cured we never see a trace of them again. By then, we have completely tired them out. When they think about what we have put them through, they feel ashamed like cats that have had a drenching. In a way, I can understand them. Granted, these treatments can be really hard going, but that is roughly as far as the science of placebo treatment has come. Anyway, who complains about brutal chemotherapy as long as it knocks out the cancer? The main point is that the treatment saves lives. And there are a lot of people out there who have us multi-therapists to thank for their being able to function in society, I promise you. Or, as we like to say: wherever in the world you may go, you will see lots of friends of placebo!'

'Oh, right…'

'Besides, it's an extremely tough profession being a multi-therapist. It wears you down.'

'Oh, yes…?'

'Yes, you see. We must test all therapies before we try them out clinically on people. That is one of our ethical rules. There are a lot of therapies. Just as many as there are people, or so sometimes feels.'

'Oh, right…'

'Take somnambulism, for example. That has affected my life fundamentally. I have cured hundreds of patients who have walked in their sleep and not been able to distinguish between dreams and being awake. A sleepwalker can fall asleep anywhere. When they dream, they think that what is happening in the dream is taking place in reality. They have no idea what is a dream and what is for real. You might think that sounds unbelievably ridiculous and silly, but in fact it is very difficult to cure. For them, an effective placebo therapy is like the sleep-and-food alarm clock that the absent-minded professor has to have in the children's cartoon story. I am convinced that the professor is actually a somnambulist and that he has found a method of setting limits for himself. His sleep-and-food clock tells him when he should eat, when he should go to bed, when he should wake up. Damn it, it tells him when he should shit and piss too. So I give all my waking-dream patients a little bell. Every time they are going to do something, they must give the bell a ding-a-ling and say aloud what they are going to do. The slightest thing, and they must give a ding-a-ling. "Now I must yawn, ding-a-ling." "Now I want to talk, ding-a-ling." Everything they do must be preceded by a ding-a-ling of the bell. Everything, every single thing. And they can only go ding-a-ling when they are awake, can't they? The sound becomes a conditioned reflex. Ding-a-ling means that they are awake. Silence means reward and sleep. Eventually, they can take the bell away and just pretend to go Ding-a-ling. They keep track of themselves. The Ding-a-ling becomes a cognitive brake in their life.'

'Does it really work?'

'Oh yes, indeed it does! Look at this!'

Doctor Rolf stretches across the desk and digs out a little bell from among his papers.

'Somnambulist, indeed! Now I want to sleep!'

He goes ding-a-ling with the bell. Then he flops down with a crash in a heap over his desk. He isn't a doctor any longer. Now he just looks like a big heavy sack of flour. He is, however, still breathing, deeply and slowly. Doctor Rolf sleeps like a newly felled fir tree in the forest. A tiny sliver of saliva-like resin runs out of the corner of his mouth and down onto the sticky computer keyboard.

Titus leans over Doctor Rolf and gives him a little careful shake. He tries a 'Hello?' and a 'Doctor Rolf?' but the only answer is a deep wheeze.

Jesus, that was one hell of a chemistry set, Titus thinks, and sneaks out of Doctor Rolf's consulting room, never to return.

Research can be a pain. The more you dig, the bigger the hole. And how should you judge your discoveries?

What is stupid today can be gospel tomorrow.

CHAPTER 20

The Calm of Stockholm

When Titus leaves Doctor Rolf's building, the air is still. He realises that there is no longer a promising early summer feeling that meets him. It is the middle of July and the very height of the summer. He feels a bit out of sorts and needs to clear his head after the strange visit to Doctor Rolf. He decides to walk all the way from this northern edge of the city down to Söder.

He walks via the Observatory Park up behind the City Library so that he can follow Drottninggatan from its beginning right down to the Old Town. The trees in the lower reaches of Observatory Park groan under the merciless rays of the sun and fight with the grassy banks for the last drops of water in ground. You can almost hear the sucking and slurping. The green of the grass is sometimes broken by brownish patches. The leaves in the park droop humbly in a prayer for a little rain.

He loves the Strindberg quotes that have been inserted into the centre line of Drottninggatan after the bottom of the hill. The street is still picturesque with cosy cafés and middling restaurants. The buildings are low enough to allow the sun to reach the pavement tables. This part of the street crawls with hip teenagers trying to break a record in drinking lattes as slowly as possible. Then, closer to the Old Town, the street is transformed into a bustling shopping Mecca for all the usual high street brands: H&M, Intersport, Stadium, Zara, Clas Ohlson, McDonalds and so on.

Families with children dominate here. They rush between the escalators and swing doors with dripping ice creams at the ready and enormous plastic carrier bags under their arms. Woe betide you if you don't look happy. Damn you if you don't look rich. After Sergels Torg and the House of Culture, Drottninggatan dissolves into an icy cold corridor in the shadow of government departments in tall and ugly buildings. The only people to be seen are the odd middle-aged civil servant and occasional flocks of tourists that have probably gone astray. Weird shops sell elk motifs on T-shirts and Dala horses of every possible size. Who buys Dala horses? wonders Titus. What can you do with them? Perhaps there are bus trips directly to the souvenir shops, because they seem to be crammed with short and happy Japanese tourists. They compete to grab at the Dala horses. They obviously know something that others don't know. Dala horses are good for potency. You crush them and mix the result with saké. A clunk of that and you get a magnificent swaying mid-summer pole from the Swedish Dalecarlia.

Stockholm in summer is like nowhere else, Titus thinks. If you ignore the completely re-built area around Klara and the southern part of Drottninggatan, Stockholm is objectively the most beautiful summer city in the world, of any kind. No doubt about that; it must be considered as proven.

The sound of the city is different in the summer, too. Birdsong that is almost painful in May and early June sounds like normal and pleasant interval music now. The cars are not in such a hurry between end-of-term celebrations, overtime work and suburban shopping. Instead, they roll slowly along the streets in a sort of proud parade to manifest what every genuine Stockholmer feels: Stockholm is best in the summer. That's when the hundreds of thousands of 'newer' Stockholmers travel home to their provincial roots and are seen as rich and successful 'homecomers' for a few weeks. While there, they can subject their old cottages to an extreme makeover, they can push up the prices at local knick-knack auctions, grill Flintstone pork steaks and piss in the water at public bathing beaches to their hearts' content. And the permanent local residents can moan and grumble about the people from the capital. Indeed, country folk need their images of the 'Stockholmers'. That they are in actual fact mirror images of each other is of lesser importance.

When Titus reaches the Old Town, he decides that he deserves a cup of coffee. He needs to think. He walks up to Stortorget and goes into the café in the Grillska building. With a cup of coffee and a cinnamon bun on his tray, Titus sits at a window table and looks out onto the square and the old Stock Exchange.

The last few weeks have been eventful. For starters, he has written a copious amount. Most of it has been top-notch stuff. He knows that when he reads through the material in a week or two, it will be easy to decide what is up to standard. He has absolute pitch. When it comes to text, he can trust himself 100 per cent.

The Best Book in the World is beginning to acquire a structure that he really likes. The variation of a thriller with elements of fact works better than he could have imagined. The bits with Håkan Rink's hunt for Serial Salvador are snappy and hard-boiled. They always end with an exciting cliffhanger. The sections with facts occupy at most one or two pages each time, and serve as comfortable resting places in the midst of the action. He has already managed to incorporate the most common subjects that the bestselling non-fiction and reference works usually deal with: from crash slimming to self-help. The language is almost impertinent in its accessibility. Sometimes he wonders if it really can be so lucid and easy to read when the theme is so intellectual. You can't help but go on reading and reading, to keep finding out what happens next. Titus is pleased with himself: this is exactly what he wants to achieve. Language is communication, not an art form in itself. The work of art is that which remains inside the reader's head. A unique picture that only exists in a single copy.

But best of all is nevertheless that Astra forced him to sober up. He feels bright and energetic. The poison has left his body. In a purely chemical sense, I have conquered the abuse, he thinks. His body no longer screams for poisons. What remains are figments of his imagination: he can still find himself looking in the fridge for a beer or feeling in his pocket for a fag. The force of habit is powerful, but these remnants are no worse than he can brush aside with the help of another figment of his imagination: the reward image where he is lying there enjoying life on a warm young female body. Better to be obsessed than dependent.

He feels the calm returning to his body. It has been quite a while since he has been away from his computer for such a long time. It doesn't feel totally wrong to be out on the city streets again. Cafés. People-watching. Relaxing.

That unpleasant Doctor-Rolf feeling is losing its grip. What an idiot. What a pathetic life. What a repulsive attitude towards people. At the same time, it was quite interesting to hear what he had said about Tourette's syndrome being just an imaginary illness.

What if he was right? What would that mean in Lenny's case?

CHAPTER 21

Dark Clouds Appear

When he steps out of the lift and in through the door to his flat, Titus immediately gets an unpleasant sensation of somebody having been there. Hard to say why. Does it smell funny? Or is it simply that a neighbour is making weird food and the smell is spreading through the ventilation system?

No, somebody has definitely been here. Titus looks around. Since it is a one-room flat with a kitchen alcove he doesn't even have to leave the hall to see everything. Besides, nowadays it is well cleaned. He bends down to look under the sofa-bed. No uninvited guest there, anyway.

He opens the flat door again to check the stairs, and hears someone running down them. The entrance door slams shut with a smothered heavy sound and silence falls again. Who the hell was that? Titus rushes to the window to try to see. Not a soul outside the front door. A long and shambling figure is just going round the corner. Black jeans. A studded belt glistens. Lenny? Gone. Titus could have sworn it was Lenny.

He jerks the window open and shouts out:

'Lenny! Lenny! Come back, damn it! What the hell are you playing at?'

A white-haired lady on a balcony shakes her head and takes a slurp from a dainty coffee cup. Oh, it's him again. That drunken writer. All he can do is booze and take drugs. But keep the laundry room in the cellar clean? Not a chance! Yes, that's him.

Titus charges down the stairs to try to catch up with Lenny. When he gets round the corner where Lenny disappeared, he sees a completely empty street before him. He has disappeared into thin air.

Although he has started to feel that he is in fairly good condition from all the spinning at the gym, Titus is seriously out of breath after that short sprint. He leans against the wall and pants heavily.

What the hell…? Was it Lenny? Or was he seeing things? But surely it had been Lenny? Fuck! What was he after?

Titus runs up to the flat again to check if anything has been stolen. He can't find anything amiss. There isn't much to steal. Who wants a pile of pizza boxes? At the same time, that unpleasant sensation is still evident. Somebody has been there.

Then he sees it.

Oh, shit! He was right after all!

The desk by the window. The computer. The lid has been opened. He never leaves the lid up when he has a rest. That is something that has been imprinted since he was a little boy. A lid should always be put down again after use, and that's that. He might have been something of a careless fellow for the greater part of his life. But lids? No, he has put them down as far back as he can remember.

So Lenny has been there sneaking around. Has he got inside the computer? Has he managed to get past the breathalyser lock?

Titus blows into the tube and waits for the computer to start up. A message appears on the screen:

Hello Titus! A little while ago, you or someone else started me incorrectly. This means hibernation for a further one hour, twenty-two minutes and forty-three seconds. Please come back a little later!

The figures flick past on the counter. After a few moments, the screen goes blank.

What the fucking hell, thinks Titus. Lenny has tried to force his way into my computer! That can only mean one thing: he is after my manuscript!

But how has Lenny found out about *The Best Book in the World*? There are only four people in the whole world who know about the idea: Titus himself, Astra, Evita Winchester and Eddie X. Who talked? It could hardly be Astra or Evita – they have everything to lose from revealing something. They would never jeopardise good sales. He himself has hardly met a soul for weeks. Besides, he has been stone cold sober.

So it must be Eddie. But why would Eddie tell Lenny about the idea? Wouldn't it be better in that case to do what Titus has done: just shut himself in his room and write the book without talking to a soul about it? Besides, Eddie X is too kind-hearted to sell out Titus. No, it doesn't seem likely. Not Eddie.

The only reasonable explanation that Titus can come up with is that Lenny must have eavesdropped on his and Eddie's drunken ramblings at the festival, when they thought up the whole idea. Then, when Lenny and Titus happened to meet at Moderna Museet and sat in the café, well… Lenny must have put two and two together. He saw that I was sober and on the ball, thinks Titus. Must have thought that I seemed to be back in the real world again. Like hell he did – he must have realised that I'm busy with something big when he twigged that I wasn't boozing any more. What could have got Titus back on the straight and narrow? And then he got curious. Why didn't I think of this earlier? I can't go around looking like a new person until all this is over. Everybody is going to wonder what's got into me. And then the speculation will get going. A new book, a new woman, what the hell could it be? No, not until the book is finished can I let people see me sober, thinks Titus.

He grabs the telephone and punches in Astra's number. He lets it ring a while. Lots of rings. Finally, she answers.

'Hi, Titus! How are things?'

'Truth is, it's all fucked up.'

He tells her everything that has happened. About the message on the computer screen and who he suspects, about their meeting at Moderna Museet. He hadn't uttered a word about the book to Lenny, who nevertheless clearly seemed to be on his case. This is much worse than industrial espionage. Cultural espionage – this threatens our entire democracy. Threatens our very existence. Titus is at full steam ahead now, blurting out all his worries.

Astra is a model of calm. She wouldn't be a star publisher if she couldn't cope with panicky situations and panicky people.

'Titus, this is what we'll do. I'll arrange a locksmith and see to it that you get a modern and secure lock, or a completely new door if it's needed. And you need have no worries at all about the computer. Lenny – if it was indeed him – hasn't managed to get into it. The breathalyser lock is restricted so that it will only react to your unique enzyme combination, it is only your breath that can start the computer. I didn't want to tell you this earlier, because you would only have blown your top and shouted even more about Winchester's undercover tricks. I took a saliva sample from a beer can when you were at my place after the festival and the technicians fixed the rest.'

'What are you saying? So that breathalyser thing was your idea from the very start? You said it was Evita's idea!' mutters Titus.

'Sorry.'

'Damn it, Astra. I thought you were on my side.'

'But I am! You must admit that it has worked rather well!'

'Yeah… I suppose.'

'Well then you can relax. I can guarantee that he hasn't seen any of your files. Sit down and try to work again. As soon as I'm back home we can meet and then I'll start reading.

'As soon as you're back home? What do you mean? Where are you?'

'In Antiparos, in Greece. Didn't I tell you? I'm on holiday.'

'Oh, right. Nice. Okay, ring me when you're back. Have a nice time!'

Titus feels calmer. Astra is good for him. She thinks about everything. A perfect woman. And if she was pretty before, then what is she going to look like after a few weeks of Greek sun? Oh my God, if only I had a bit of Zorba in me, thinks Titus.

He blows in the tube and looks at the message: fifty-eight minutes and thirty-five seconds left.

He is keen to see with his own eyes that the manuscript is still there. If anyone has stolen it, he might just as well top himself straight away. He would never be able to find the energy to re-write the whole thing.

No, he must think through his routines better: check that the windows are shut when he goes out and lock the door properly, check it is locked by pushing the handle down and keep a discreet eye on the entrance door a couple of minutes after he goes out. Urgh, he is all nerves. Just take it easy, Titus, everything will be all right, he thinks.

Another blow in the tube: fifty-six minutes and seventeen seconds.

Time crawls along.

Titus goes into the kitchen alcove and turns the coffee machine on. He makes a sandwich using a slice of Cheddar and slices up a green pepper to put in it. He fills a glass with orange juice. The fridge doesn't look like an ice desert in the Arctic anymore, now that he has his eating habits under control. A balanced diet. Regular mealtimes. Things will sort themselves out. Breathe slowly.

He looks out through the window. The white-haired lady is still sitting on her balcony. Now she is pressing the buttons on the radio on the balcony table.

Yeah, why not? Good idea, thinks Titus, and turns on his little kitchen radio.

The signature tune fills the room. It is *Summer*. Probably the most popular radio programme in Sweden of any category. Swedes known and unknown who have something exciting or interesting to talk about are given one and a half hours each at lunchtime during the summer to enthral the whole country. They intersperse their stories with their favourite music. The result is often extremely personal and occasionally rather provocative. Nobody is indifferent to what they hear. The evening tabloids usually get on the bandwagon and do a messy re-write or a sick distortion the next day to sell a few extra copies in the summer news drought.

The signature tune fades away. Titus wonders who it will be today.

Good afternoon, Sweden.
Hello, Swedes!
My name is Eddie X.
I am an author and poet.
I live on water, bread and love.
And music.
You can do that too.
Today I'm going to show you my life.
Because it is your life too.

You and me.
We are very similar, don't you think?
Just as fragile, just as strong.
Just as repulsive, just as beautiful.
Today I'm going to show you my memories.
And I shall play music that has gilded my memories to
something priceless.
You will be there with me when I made out the first time.
You will be there with me when I made love the first time.
Does that sound like fun?
It was.
But first you are going to come with me to my nursery school.
You.
You are going to paint my willy with finger paints.

Here we go. Titus sits down on a kitchen chair and listens attentively. He forgets the time and that the breathalyser lock is ticking away to imminent liberation. Eddie's cosy voice fills the room. He has a faint northern accent which increases the sincerity; no one else in the whole world could get away with such a bombastic balancing act like this one of Eddie's. But it never becomes ridiculous, not for a single second. Eddie X never degrades himself to become a silly court poet with a starched collar. He is rock'n'roll in poetry format, a stick of dynamite in a velvet casing.

Titus is hooked. Spellbound. He and the other little children play with Eddie's willy at nursery school, he follows Eddie to a children's party, starts school, looks at the lady schoolteacher's bouncing breasts, sneaks up on the girls in the gym showers, laughs at the dragon fancy dress, wets himself at school camp, feels the popcorn taste of the first tongue kiss, has an uncontrolled ejaculation in his pyjamas, makes out with the girls with new and firm breasts, acquires a taste for it and makes out even more, scrumps apples from local gardens, eats his way through every ice cream flavour on the list, goes mountain-biking in the forest, makes out in a frenzy, watches TV, drinks strong beer, writes poetry, drinks copious amounts of strong beer, writes exceptionally good poetry, performs at a Poetry Slam competition, wins the audience's hearts, makes love even more, writes even more poetry, paints a red heart on his chest for his medical for military service, is declared unfit for duty and sends the certificate in a pink envelope to the Secretary General of the UN, Interrails all over Europe, goes island-hopping in the Mediterranean, moves into a commune, makes love, becomes obsessed with love and conveying it, becomes a legend in Poetry Slam circles, travels the length and breadth of the country visiting festivals together with The Tourettes, preaches the gospel of love, publishes collections of poetry and makes recordings.

Eddie X plays only Swedish music to accompany his memories. He has no taboos about what is beautiful or ugly, permitted or forbidden. In Eddie's *Summer* programme, Ace of Base and E-Type have just as much cred as The Hives and The Soundtrack of Our Lives. Twenty-five years of the best of Sweden in a wonderful and amusing whistle-stop summary in one and a half hours.

Titus can almost hear through the walls how the Swedish nation is cheering joyfully. A new jewel in our national treasure chest has been found. First Bellman, Taube, Lundell and Hellström. And now – Eddie X.

When the programme ends, Titus texts Eddie:

Congratulations! Laughs + tears + laughs again. Thanks + cheers. Titus.

When he puts the phone down, it suddenly hits him like a fist right in his solar plexus. He feels the blood emptying out of his head. He has to sit down on the floor. He rubs his crew-cut head hard. Bloody fucking hell. How could he *not* have thought of it earlier? Fingernails scratching his scalp. A struggle to breathe. Hyperventilation.

Eddie didn't say a word about his paranoid dad! When they met at the City Library he was doing research for his *Summer* programme! Digging into the past and learning more. Confronting nasty memories and all that sort of thing to be able to bare himself to the Swedish nation. And then: a single long harangue about the fun and games of growing up in Sweden. Just memories, no analysis. Not a word about what it was like to grow up with a dad who had mental problems.

So Eddie had lied to his face. He would never have thought that possible. So much for the loving message. A wolf in silk clothing.

Before Titus faints, he sees it all clearly: Eddie X, the new national hero, is also busy writing *The Best Book in the World*.

Meltdown.

CHAPTER 22

Other Sides

The doorbell rings.

Titus doesn't know how long he has been lying there out cold. Could have been minutes, could have been twenty-four hours – it feels like an eternity. He gets up cautiously and staggers out into the hall, a bit dizzy but able to stand. His mouth feels dry and dusty. He must have been lying there in the kitchen quite a while. He looks at himself in the hall mirror, and sees he is as pale as a corpse despite the sunbed short-cut at the gym.

The doorbell rings again.

Who can it be? Is it Lenny coming back to steal the whole computer this time? Titus looks through the spy-hole. He sees a muscular guy in blue dungarees holding a gigantic toolbox, his mobile phone in a holster and blond streaks in his hair.

Then he remembers the conversation with Astra. It's the locksmith of course. He got here so quickly. Then again, how does Titus know that? He could have been unconscious for ages.

He opens the door.

'Hello, are you the locksmith?'

'That's me. I came as quickly as I could, mate. There seemed to be a bit of a panic here they said.'

A local guy. You could tell from his accent. Good, somebody he could rely on, Titus persuades himself.

'Come in.'

'Yeah, right you are. It was this door, I gather.'

'Yes, that's the only door to the flat. Was it Astra Larsson who phoned you?'

'Yeah, that's the one. Nice lady. Phoned from Greece. Said it was urgent. So I came at once.'

'The same day? Did she phone today, I mean?'

'Yeah, right. I was busy with something on Hornsgatan before this. Took a bit of time. But got it done quickly anyway.'

Titus breathes out. In that case he hasn't been unconscious for long.

'I'm glad you're here. Do what you have to do. Just go ahead with it.'

'Yeah, you know, you can't have this sort of door nowadays.'

'No, I've noticed.'

'I mean, just look at this. Come out here.'

The locksmith takes Titus out into the stairwell outside the flat and closes the door from outside. Then he pulls out a credit card from his wallet and slides it into the chink between the door and the doorpost just above the bolt. He pulls it downwards in the chink more or less like on an ordinary card reader in a shop. The card catches the bevelled bolt and pushes it easy as pie into its hole in the door, which opens without resistance.

'Get it? You can't have it like this, you realise that don't you? Even a kid could get in through this door.'

'Oh dear. Can you fix that?'

'Sure. That's why I'm here, isn't it? She, the Greek lady, said that I should do a real state-of-the-art solution. I'll make it like a bank vault, you know.'

'That's great. Thanks.'

'Yeah, you know, first there'll be an eight-millimetre titanium plate along the whole edge. Then there'll be triple locks: an ordinary lock, a seven-lever and a nine-lever. Or do

143

you want a code lock too? You can get them with combinations of up to ten digits.'

'No, I think it's enough having to keep track of three keys.'

'Okay, that's settled then. It's your door, you know? I'll have to re-bevel the hinges too. Fix a plate all the way down. Then nobody can get at it, you know. Idiot-proof. The lady is forking out for this, don't worry.'

'Okay. Can you manage on your own now for a while?'

Now that Titus is awake, he wants to get into the computer as soon as possible to check that everything is still there. He leaves the locksmith, who immediately starts measuring up and pulling things out of his toolbox.

Titus blow-starts the computer.

```
Hello, Titus! Welcome back. After six hours I will
shut down and save your work. Then you will have
at least a two-hour break as usual. If you don't use
me for three days then you will have to start from
scratch. Have a nice day!
```

Titus is amazed at how the message varies every time he turns on the computer. It must be a very complicated program that Astra has installed. No wonder the poor authors only get a quarter of the sales proceeds from their books, the software developers in Silicon Valley have to have their share, he thinks. It must cost a fortune to construct breathalyser locks that check enzymes.

Click, click, click. At last he gets to the folders on the hard disk. Everything is still there! The manuscript is where it should be. He opens the file and breathes out. All the characters are still there, every single one.

Now he must think. His worst fears have proved right. Eddie has conned him. It is extremely likely that he is fully occupied with writing *The Best Book in the World*. The *Summer* programme was just standard Eddie stuff, he had probably used most of the material earlier in his shows. He only had to gather it together, go into the studio and dazzle the public. Eddie X can do that – arousing emotions is his speciality. And perhaps Eddie is sitting somewhere working on a matchless book manuscript this very second! He is going to entrance people with that too.

Titus has got big problems. Eddie is the worst competitor imaginable.

And on top of it all, Lenny is trying to break into the flat. It must be Lenny, after all. Who else could it be? But what is he after? What could it benefit him to steal a manuscript? He could never publish Titus' book under his own name, there would be an outcry on the arts pages and a much publicised trial about copyright infringement. No, this is more a question of intellectual espionage: Lenny is trying to steal his ideas. There is no copyright protection for ideas. Anybody can steal an idea, at any time, even Lenny. That means there are two possibilities. It's possible that somebody is trying to pinch ideas for their own use, but how likely is that? Lenny doesn't feel like an entrepreneur who develops ideas. Lenny is a rocker. If it was about pinching a sketch for a tattoo, well perhaps. But ideas for *The Best Book in the World*? Hardly. Which leaves us with the other possibility: Lenny is stealing on somebody else's behalf.

Eddie.

It is Eddie X who lies behind this. That's how it is. It can't be anything else. The sweet poetry evidently has other sides. Hidden, dark, dangerous sides. Titus can hardly believe his own thoughts – is it possible? Who would have thought that Sweden's new darling is a liar and a burglar?

Titus looks at his watch. Half-past four. He decides to try to phone Christer Hermansson at the City Library and ask if Eddie has perhaps come back to his reading room after the radio programme. On the other hand, Eddie would never miss an opportunity to receive the adoration of the public. Titus knows that. He is probably sitting at the Association Bar and drinking wine, mingling with beautiful and happy people. Laughing and smiling, making hormones race. The personification of friendliness.

But it's worth a try. In any case, he has no better strategy. He feels empty. He must find out what Eddie is doing. Titus hopes that Christer Hermansson isn't on holiday, but he doesn't seem to be the type who likes summer holidays.

'Welcome to the Stockholm City Library. You are speaking to Christer Hermansson, acting Library Director.'

'Hi Christer, Titus here.'

'Well, well, Titus Jensen,' Christer Hermansson answers with his most reserved voice. 'Nice of you to call. May I recommend an excellent book: *Emperors and Generals: The Men behind Rome's Successes*?'

'Always amusing. No, Christer, I want to ask you a favour.'

'Of course. *Ich bin ein bibliothekar*. Your book request is my command.'

'I don't want to borrow anything. I wonder if you would be really kind and go down to Eddie's reading room and see if he is in it, or if somebody else is there. Please, Christer, can you do that?'

Christer doesn't answer immediately. He must delve into his conscience and see whether Titus' request conflicts with some library regulation. No, it doesn't: a librarian evidently has every right to supply the names of people who have visited the library. Christer Hermansson has never been asked before, but is sure that he is right. He always is.

'Yes, that's okay. I can arrange that.'

'That's nice of you. Super.'

'Hold on. I'll switch this call to the portable phone.'

Some clicking sounds follow. There is silence for a moment, then the buzzing returns. Titus hears Christer's footsteps in the library. Half a minute passes. The footsteps fade. Christer opens a door. Footsteps again, a bit slower now. At last he is inside Eddie's reading room.

'Hello, Christer! Are you there? Hello?' Titus shouts loudly.

The locksmith looks into the room and stares at him, all eyes.

'No, I'm called Tommy. Not Christer.'

'Oops, I didn't mean you. I'm talking on the phone,' says Titus and makes a hushing gesture with his hand.

'Christer, are you there?'

'I'm here. The room is empty. There is no Eddie X here. No books either. Nothing.'

'Are you sure it's the right room?'

'Yes, of course. But hang on. There is a note attached to the desk lamp.'

'What? A note? Read what it says! What does it say?'

'It says: "Eddie X wishes everybody the best summer in the world", in capital letters.'

CHAPTER 23

Now We'll Get the Bastard!

Offender profile: Serial Salvador

Profiler: Detective Chief Inspector Håkan Rink.
The most likely character features/functions/ dysfunctions of the 'art murderer'.

General description: pleasant appearance. Perhaps handsome, possibly even very handsome. Very likely to be young or youthful. Popular among both women and men. Primary driving force: does everything in his power to gain people's confidence/ admiration/appreciation/love.

Inside: chaotic. Hard to live up to his own tenderness. Troubled with evil thoughts. Regards these as hard to control and immoral. Secondary driving force: fighting his evil side. Primary and secondary driving forces contradictory. Explosive effect on personality.

Interests: art/culture/literature/eccentric impulses/ bizarre ideas/crazy inventions.

Physical evidence from scene of crime investigation: long black hairs, possibly dyed/ discoloured, cloth traces from clothing items in soft material: silk/raw silk/velour.

Database searches and comparisons with other serial killers: the offender has a very creative personality/eccentric appearance/obsessed with his appearance/sucks his thumb/sleeps in foetal position/continually looking for mirrors.

Analysis: the evil side of the offender is growing all the larger. **Look out for cracks in behaviour among the group of suspects we are interested in:** exaggerated friendliness/unforeseen laughter/unexpected outbreaks of anger/missed meetings/sudden contact difficulties/apathy without any obvious explanation.

Now it's war. Titus is not going to give in without a fight. If Eddie X has stolen Titus' book idea, he has no choice. He shall render him harmless for all time. For an eternity of eternities. That is an author's only real privilege: to be able to crucify the objects of his hatred as long as the paper and the printer's ink in the book lasts.

Serial Salvador is going to borrow some features from Eddie. Or rather: Serial Salvador *is* Eddie X. When Håkan Rink really gets to know his adversary, towards the end of the book, he will pull his trousers down once and for all. He shall hunt him down, lock him up, humiliate him. Peel off his personality and put his rotting insides on display for general despair and amazement. The readers shall come to hate this beloved person. The handsome boy in the house next door shall be transformed into a bestial serial killer. Then the mob shall whip him to death. Shut him up in a torture chamber. A cold dug-out, a damp godforsaken abandoned earth cellar. Bury him alive. Stamp on his grave. Knock over his gravestone. Piss on him. Strip him of every last vestige of human dignity for all time.

These inspiring images drive Titus forward.

He sees himself as a victim of crime. Somebody has broken into his home. Somebody has tried to rob him of his brain, ideas and vital energy. The wrongs are unforgivable.

It would be easy to expect that these misfortunes would floor him and send him back to the haze of drugs, spirits and nicotine. But, strange though it may seem, he gains strength from adversity. Better to be obsessed than dependent, that's his mantra. Titus delights in the force of the writers' battle. Eddie can sit there and thumb through bestsellers as much as he wants. Try to copy styles and themes. An idiotic idea. Eddie hasn't got a chance against Titus' fury.

Titus is in the midst of his best period ever as an author. He writes in six-hour sessions without leaving his chair, for at least two sessions a day. During his breaks, he eats, exercises, goes on the sunbed, and sleeps. He flosses his teeth regularly, and is rapidly losing weight although his muscles are getting bigger. He likes himself more and more.

He searches the Internet and returns to the library to find information that supports his story. Not once does he sneak a look at how other bestselling authors have done it. It's great to let yourself be inspired, he thinks. But to inspire, that is even greater. He is on the right track.

Titus and his manuscript are slowly but surely developing into magnificent specimens.

The weeks go by.

The oppressive heat of July turns into the more relaxed summer feeling of August. The old lady on the balcony next door sorts the mushrooms she has picked, or weeds her flower boxes.

The evenings start to get darker.

Titus works away.

The innumerable press conferences and all the easy-to-understand metaphors made Håkan Rink popular with the media and the nation. He had their full confidence even though Serial Salvador hasn't been apprehended yet. But they knew that he was near. Håkan Rink was a man they could rely on. A father, a father of the nation even. Even the prime minister expressed his admiration. He was invited to talk shows and attended celebrity opening nights. And when, in his bass voice, he said that 'they saw light at the end of the tunnel', his eyes glistened in the camera flashes. He too knew they were getting close now.

Better to be obsessed than dependent. This is my job. Trees grow up towards the sky, birds fly through the air, waves lap against the shore. And me? I write masterpieces, Titus thinks.

Sometimes Titus wonders what Eddie is doing. How far has he got? Will it be good? Or is it only about love? Despite Titus' growing self-esteem, there is every reason to worry about the situation. He must think realistically. Eddie is a skilled craftsman. He can perform tricks with the alphabet. At the same time, Titus wonders if Eddie has the ability to concentrate; a writer of novels must be able to shut himself in for long periods, with only himself for company. Can Eddie really manage that?

He wishes he could tell Astra that he is racing against Eddie when he writes, but of course he can't tell her. When he sold her the idea, he hadn't mentioned Eddie at all, he had simply said that he had thought up a brilliant idea for a book, not that it was something he had cooked up together with Sweden's hottest contemporary poet during a very drunken night. And that the poet was published by Babelfish, one of Winchester's fiercest rivals! If Astra had known that, she would never have got Evita to back him, and he would still be sitting at the Association Bar and smelling like an ashtray. Now it was too late, he must go through with it.

Besides, he can hardly prove that Lenny did the break-in at Eddie's bidding. He can't even prove that it was Lenny who was inside his flat, and now it was probably far too late to secure fingerprints. Plus the police were not nearly as alert in reality as Chief Inspector Rink and his colleagues – they would just yawn and laugh at his accusations. What crime had been committed, did you say? Some unauthorised person has blown into the breathalyser lock on your computer? And as if that wasn't enough, he is forced to play a double game hereafter. Astra and her computer demand total sobriety. He has come to appreciate that, it's not a problem. But he did risk it all when he openly showed Lenny that he was sober and alert, talked about the writing he was busy with, mentioned how hard he worked. That sort of talk put everything at risk. No, he doesn't need any more gold-diggers wondering what it was that had revitalised him. From now on, he must play the old faded Titus Jensen if he is going to manage to keep the competition at bay: tipsy, seedy-looking, lean and cold under the surface. That can work. He has learnt so much about himself this summer; if anyone can portray the tired old Titus Jensen, then it is the new strong Titus Jensen!

That's how it must be. He has painted himself into a corner. Now he is standing there, surrounded, pushed up against the wall.

But he has a fucking great manuscript on his hard drive.

Almost finished!

A bit too good to be true?

CHAPTER 24

The Best Nautical Metaphors in the World

To reach people one should use language that is full of imagery. Several investigations by American presidential election campaigns show that the candidate who uses the most metaphors wins the election.

The following metaphors are recommended for tight situations at press conferences and can be easily adapted to different branches and situations. The selection is based on quotes from the legendary Detective Chief Inspector Håkan Rink.

Regrettably, we have only seen the tip of the iceberg.
Now we must look beyond the horizon.
We must weather the storm.
A bit of spray never hurt anybody.
There is something fishy about this.
Now we've got the wind in our sails.
He has sunk very deep.
Other serial killers are waiting on the lee side.
They are splashing about in a backwater.
Like ripples on the surface.
We are following a strong lodestar.
And we have an inner compass.
We pour oil on the waters.
It's a question of staying afloat.
Now he'll have the wind against him.

The mist is lifting.
Full steam ahead.
Time to sever the hawser.
Now we'll launch her.
We'll reach shore yet.
The coast is clear.
We'll soon be in harbour.

CHAPTER 25

Teambuilding

Astra is back from her holiday and has arranged a little meeting. Since only three people know about the project, they are gathering at Astra's flat. Titus usually only visits Winchester's either when he's got a new book coming out, or if there is a party there. There is no reason to turn up now and start speculation as to what is in the offing.

Publishing people are experts on speculation and conspiracy theories. One might well think that book publishing is their core activity: to refine the work of their authors with the best interests of the readers in mind, to do everything in their power to market and sell books in the best way possible. And, indeed, they do all of that. But what really absorbs most of their time and energy is speculation and conspiracies: buttering up agents to try to steal profitable authors from other houses, getting authors with falling sales figures to write less often or even to switch to another publisher, watching every step that their competitors take. If, for example, another company publishes a book by an author they have turned down, they must be on their guard – the wrong rhetoric at that stage can lead to devastating articles on the arts pages, and their brand name could be undermined. If the sales figures are bad, then they must get their message out quickly: 'We said no to that manuscript straight away. No commercial potential at all – a child could have seen that.' If it's a success, then the opposite applies: 'Yes, we were sent the manuscript. We got it first, as usual. Unfortunately we were in the midst of a rather complicated re-organisation at the time because things are going so exceptionally well for us. The selection process fell between two stools. But we would like to be the first to congratulate the author.'

Astra Larsson plays the publishing game brilliantly, but on two important counts she differs from many others: she is more interested in succeeding than she is afraid of failing, and she spreads positive vibes which soon extend in good circles. She loves her publishing house. Her publishing house loves her.

Of course, she gives Titus a warm hug at the door.

'Hello, Titus, you're looking really well!'

'Thanks, same to you. Wow, I don't think I've ever seen you with such a tan before. Have you had a good time?'

'Fantastic. A real holiday. Snorkelling, eating good food, renting a moped. I didn't even have any sticky manuscripts with me, I read completely ordinary books. It was great. Come in!'

They enter the living room. There sits Evita in an enormous egg armchair in reddish-brown leather. When she sees Titus, she gets up and approaches him with open arms.

'Hello Titus. Been a long time!'

'Indeed. Lovely to see you.'

Titus hugs Evita and sits down on the sofa. Astra asks if he wants a latte or double espresso. He chooses espresso and Astra goes into the kitchen area. Soon there is a hissing and buzzing from the coffee machine. They chat about the summer. Evita says a new baker has come to the island where she has her summer house. He bakes unbeatable Karlsbader buns. Astra wonders what they are. Evita explains how wonderful they taste instead of answering the question. Astra describes her island-hopping in Greece. Evita wonders aloud if there are still a lot of guys on the beaches trying to pick you up. Astra describes the Greek food instead of answering the question.

Titus doesn't say much. He realises that he has hardly done anything special at all during the summer, but it has been one of the most exciting periods in all his life. He has penetrated deep inside the brain of a serial murderer, he has done research on how human relations work in the police force, he has learnt lots about surrealism, art history, cooking, the behaviour of drug addicts, losing weight, the mass media and a whole lot of other useful stuff. He has produced great experiences without having to experience the slightest bit of them himself. Not since his visit to Dr Rolf, at any rate.

'So, what's your summer been like?' Evita wonders, looking at Titus.

He's looking really young, she thinks. She remembers him as bigger and more heavily built. Not exactly bloated, but lacking sculptural form. Now he looks really fit, with decent proportions. Hasn't he got a bit of a tan too? Mm, what a smasher, she thinks, and tries to catch Astra's eye to exchange a meaningful look.

Astra sees it and responds with a smile, neutral but not too encouraging. She knows that Evita devours men like builders devour burgers and she doesn't think Titus is particularly interested in that type of attention. But sure, he does look like a new man. She is glad for Titus' sake. It is a good omen.

'It's been a good summer. A bit rough at the beginning, but it got better and better,' says Titus, who realises that they are curious as to how things have gone.

Now it's a matter of delivering the goods. He doesn't beat around the bush.

'The structure works well. It is short and concise, just as we discussed. Now I'm incorporating a really juicy crisis. This is going to be something quite extraordinary.'

'Gosh, how exciting. Tell us!' says Astra enthusiastically.

Titus gives them a serious look and, after a theatrical pause, lowers his voice to a minimum volume.

'After a long chase, Håkan Rink and his team know who the murderer is. They have even ascertained his whereabouts. When the police go in to grab him, it transpires that the whole thing is a gigantic set-up. The murderer has his own agenda and has steered the investigation exactly where he wants it. He is aware that Håkan Rink has become a national hero through his press conferences, which are broadcast live at prime time. Rink has solemnly vowed to bring an end to the surrealist terror. The murderer is fed up with all of that, and he is going to show that it is he who is in control. To the very end.'

Titus is silent.

'Then what happens?' Evita asks eagerly.

He looks at her thoughtfully.

'I'm not going to say any more now. I think it's bad karma for the project to talk about things that haven't been written yet. But this I can say: it will be very degrading for all parties. Very, very unpleasant.'

'You can't do this,' Evita shouts and laughs. 'It sounds terribly exciting!'

Titus smiles at her. He believes her. He knows it is good.

She stops laughing and looks at him. There is something about his eyes that touches her. He looks so resolute. There is something incredibly attractive about resolute men, she thinks, especially when they work for her.

Evita is pleased with her investment. Astra and she have evidently got this right. The early reports had of course pointed in that direction, but now that impression has been confirmed. Titus Jensen is back in business. Stronger and better than ever. And more handsome.

She turns towards Titus and puts her hand on his arm.

'Can we read it soon?'

'Yes, indeed. I've got the manuscript with me. Like I said, there are a few chapters still to do, and I'm going to go through the whole manuscript again, several times. But on the whole this is what the book will look like.'

Titus fishes up a little memory card from his jacket pocket and puts it on the coffee table.

'Here's the flash card. You'll be careful with this, won't you?'

'Naturally, Titus, you know that. We'll do the same as the first time: we shall only read it on our e-book readers – no emailing, and we won't save anything on the company servers for a while yet. This is still our little secret, isn't it Evita?' says Astra, looking at Evita.

'Absolutely. I loved the first bit I read and I can't imagine it is any less good now. Yes, this is our little secret. But – I have actually started to leak a little,' she says with a knowing look.

Titus stiffens. What does she mean? Hadn't they agreed that it would be super secret?

'I have spoken to the people at Winchester Agency. They are the ones who take care of our international rights, as you know.'

Titus knows very well what they do, even if he himself hasn't been a success on the international market. The agents are the people who negotiate the rights for foreign books for translation to the Swedish market, and it is they too who sell Swedish authors to other countries. The deals are made at the big international book fairs. In Sweden the annual book fair in Gothenburg is the most important meeting place. There, the agents present their new titles and compete with the other agents to buy and sell the latest fad book.

Fad books might be ones that have been an unexpected success in one market, or they could be the result of a deliberate PR campaign around a long-awaited author comeback. But a genuine fad book is a book that sticks out on its own merits, one of those exceptional books that appears once in ten years and which the whole world wants to read just because it is so wonderfully unique. People who devour books love a fad more than anything else, and the best fad books are picked up fast as lightning by the professional commentators on the arts pages: journalists dig up exciting background stories and the myth grows all the larger. Booksellers love fad books, too; when somebody has read a fad book, sales of other books get a big boost as people rediscover the joy of reading, tell others what a great read the book is and buy more by the same author or books with a similar theme. A really good fad book can even get people who have never before read a book to go into a bookshop, and once they have acquired the taste for book adrenaline they immediately want even more experiences. Suddenly people are talking about literature during lunch breaks and starting to watch culture programmes on TV. They buy even more books, and spread their new-found delight to children and friends.

Yes, fad books are the very blood cells of the circulatory system of the book industry. Without a fad book now and then, the business would wilt. Evita loves fad books and wants to be involved with them.

'I have told the agents that we are bringing something really exciting to Gothenburg at the end of September. I haven't said what it's about, I've just told them to book in the largest international publishers for personal presentations with me, Astra and a secret author who has written a book with a considerable international potential.'

'Gosh, now you're making me a bundle of nerves,' says Titus, looking very worried.

'It's all right Titus. I know what I'm doing.'

'Are you sure? I don't like celebrating victories in advance. I suppose I'm a bit superstitious. Not just a bit – I am terrified by this stuff. You know that I've always been drunk when I did that sort of thing before.'

Evita puts her hand on Titus' arm again. She looks deeply into his eyes.

'Everything's going to be okay. We'll take care of this, Astra and me, we'll fix it. All you have to do is come along with us to Gothenburg. We are staying at Park Avenue. You'll go upstairs to bed when the others go to the bar, eat a VIP breakfast in peace and quiet on the top floor, go to a few, important meetings at the International Rights Centre down in the fair hall. What do you think?'

Titus is silent. He looks at the flash card in the middle of the table. A well-developed embryo, a foetus which will soon be born as a baby and have a long and rich life. Should it just lie there? Can't Astra take care of it straight away? He thinks it looks abandoned, but he doesn't say anything because he has no wish to give an unnecessarily nervous impression.

From the other side, Astra stretches across and lays her tanned hand on Titus' arm.

'It'll be fine, Titus. This way everything will roll along much faster. We'll release the book in Sweden just after the February book sale and then it can be published in other countries in the autumn. Nowadays books have about six months in the limelight – we must turn as many spotlights on as we can during that time.'

'Okay…'

'Fine,' says Evita. 'It'll be okay, won't it? Will you finish in time? In that case, we shall prepare a really thorough presentation. Synopsis and author portrait, some decent reader's reports, we might even translate a few chapters. We shall print a fancy folder a few days before the fair – glossy, the exclusive touch. That will work for Frankfurt, too. Astra and I will be going there a week or so after Gothenburg. And you, Titus, we must take some photos of you too. You look so… good at the moment.'

'Thanks. Yes, I'll certainly finish in time. As long as nothing unexpected happens…'

'Haha, and what might that be?' laughs Astra, and flashes a big smile at him. 'Everything's going perfectly.'

Now Titus smiles too. It does undoubtedly feel tip-top. He has been working like a maniac all summer. Despite this, he feels strong and rested. He knows that the manuscript is good and that it is going to get even better before he is finished with it.

This is the first time for ages that he has felt the frisson of female company. Evita's hand on his arm has stirred him; every time she touches him, he gets a tickling sensation on his neck and down his back, in a pleasant way. He regards it as yet further proof that he is on the way back to a real life. She isn't by any means the she-monster that people say, he thinks. She is lovely. Pretty, too, with a sexy appetite for life and not just conventional feminine allure. That said, her feminine attributes tick all the boxes, too: skin and legs and décolletage and red lips wherever you look! She is sort of steaming a little. Simply fabulous. Wonder if she's got a man at the minute?

The three of them continue chatting a while and discuss the details of the schedule. Titus describes how he is going to create several crises in the story before he ignites the final crescendo. Astra talks of the importance of building up the characters slowly so that the tension is retained throughout the book. Titus agrees with her, that is precisely what he has done. Evita has some anecdotes from the media world, asks whether Titus remembers when they launched *Baroque in Their Blood* and she fell asleep in the middle of the reading at the release party. He doesn't remember, but Astra does, and she jokingly puts her hands over her ears and shouts out that she doesn't want to remember or hear a single word about it. Evita laughs and touches Titus' arm. Titus shivers with pleasure. Evita eats him with her eyes. Astra smiles with the whole of her face and loves her job.

There is a delightful atmosphere. All three feel that they are important parts of something exciting and great.

Then the doorbell rings.

CHAPTER 26

Come Aboard Amour

The bright yellow silk shirt is unbuttoned almost down to his navel. His taut chest is tanned and freshly shaven. Even his nipples look tanned. Eddie X is leaning against the doorpost, twirling a strand of orange hair around his fingers, when Astra opens the door. His brown eyes smile. His white teeth glow.

'Astra, beautiful Astra. May I offer you my simple company?'

When Astra sees Eddie standing there she lights up like a sun.

'Hi, Eddie! Oh dear, we are in the middle of a little meeting.'

That doesn't stop Eddie. He steps into the hall and looks into the living room.

He smiles at Evita, who radiates happiness. She instinctively pushes her bosom out a little and turns her head to one side without losing eye contact. You look your slimmest like that.

Eddie even smiles at Titus Jensen, who looks as if he has lost his winning lottery ticket… Titus' chin drops a little, and if you had looked really closely would have noticed that his tongue was resting like a small piece of steak on his lower lip and the bottom row of teeth. It is obvious that Eddie's entrance affects different people in different ways.

A poet who sells well is unusual, and Evita Winchester is of course not slow to turn on the charm for the new national poet. You always have to keep the door open for new sales possibilities. She is proud to see that Astra has the same attitude and has got to know Eddie so well that he even comes to visit her at home.

'Come in, Eddie. What a fantastically amusing *Summer* programme you did! I listened to it when I was out on the island. It seems as if everybody in the country heard it.'

'Thank you, do you really think so? It cheers me to hear you say that. May I take a seat?'

Eddie doesn't wait for an answer, but sits down beside Titus. Titus is speechless, and just stares. What is he doing here? What is this all about? What's happening? A moment ago, he was happy and full of energy. Now he is deflating like a leaking balloon.

At the same time, the room is filled with Eddie's self-confidence. He puts up both arms on the back of the sofa.

'Has Astra told you that we've started dating?'

Astra blushes behind her tan, and lets out a little giggle.

'Dating? Now take it easy, Eddie. We have had dinner together on one occasion.'

'Yes, and it was the best dinner I have eaten in all my life. I don't remember what we ate, but I do remember every single word we said and every single look you gave me. A magical evening with twinkling stars and a twinkling Astra.'

Evita laughs at Eddie's romantic torrent of words. As usual with Eddie, it never feels ridiculous, just feels heartfelt and delicate. Evita really thinks he means what he says. She looks at Astra.

Astra is seized by the giggles. In the course of a minute she has been transformed from a businesslike publisher to a crooning maiden.

Titus wonders what on earth is happening. If this isn't a question of intellectual espionage then I'll eat my hat, he thinks. Is he really so terribly cunning that he is going to seduce Astra and try to pump her for information about the project? How much has he found out already?

He must warn Astra in some way, and demand an oath of confidentiality. At the same time, he is convinced that he would risk everything if he revealed that Eddie knows about the book idea. Both Astra and Evita could feel cheated. Who knows, they might be furious and cancel the whole thing.

Besides, there is no reason to show Eddie how smart and alert he is now. Rather the opposite, he ought to act like the old Titus. In Eddie's world, Titus is a pathetic specimen. Let sleeping dogs lie!

He slides down a little lower on the sofa and tries to look tired and a bit the worse for wear.

'You seem to be having a good time,' says Eddie jovially.

'Yes, indeed,' says Evita, 'We're sitting here discussing the future. The idea is to publish a paperback trilogy with *Storm Clouds*, *Treacherous Charades* and *Baroque in Their Blood*. Completely black covers with dark grey typography in relief on the front, perhaps with Titus' eyes looking straight through the reader. It feels rather exciting to do all three together, don't you think?'

Wow, that woman knows what she is doing, thinks Titus, and feels a little less concerned. He can evidently rely on her. But what about Astra?

'An excellent idea,' says Eddie the full-blooded diplomat. 'I love everything Titus has done, and everything he's going to do. Titus is a piece of Swedish literary history.'

Titus pretends to hiccup. At least that is easier than trying to say something. Eddie looks at him.

'How are you doing, Titus?'

'*Comme ci, comme ça.* I am fairly tired,' he says, trying to rasp.

166

'What a coincidence that you are here! I've been thinking of asking if you can come and do a reading at Södra Teatern on 6 September. They're arranging the Spoken Word Festival there and it would be a wonderful bonus if you could come, people love it when you read. I shall be the MC and will be doing some of my own things between the acts.'

Titus starts to perspire. How can be wriggle out of this? No way is he going to humiliate himself and read nonsense in front of a guffawing crowd. Not now that he has sorted his head out.

'Err, well, I don't know…'

'Come on, it'd be really great, Titus. And the fee is four thousand kronor, too.'

Four thousand! Titus hasn't got much in his bank account. A reading would actually mean a considerable improvement in his situation. Four thousand? How does that work? He gets four thousand to read nonsense, about one month's worth of his annual royalties, and that for books that have taken several years to write. It is just daft.

'Yeah… well… I suppose I could do it.'

'I'm glad to hear it. Great!'

The small talk goes on for a little while and Eddie continues to dominate the room. He lists the names of the international guests who will be coming to the Poetry Slam Festival, he speaks of all the emails he has received since the *Summer* programme, and he reveals that the entire programme will be issued as a double CD with extra material ready for the Christmas shopping season. Evita wonders how clever it is to release a summer CD in the winter. Astra says that it might work because it's a sort of 'opposite approach'. 'Exactly!' Eddie shouts. Evita hums and haws. Titus sits and nods, trying to look tired and a bit tipsy. No way is he going to reveal that he is a viable human being in front of Eddie X.

Astra and Evita don't notice how weirdly Titus is behaving since all their attention is focused on Eddie and what he says.

'But I haven't come to talk about myself,' says Eddie suddenly, and looks solemnly at Astra. 'It's such a lovely day that I thought I'd ask you if you want to come for an evening sail in my boat. I have a little Neptun cruising yacht called *Come Aboard Amour*. It's moored by the Blockhus promontory out on Djurgården. I thought we could go round the islands in the sunset and then I'd serve you dinner in the cockpit. What do you say, Astra?'

Astra looks in open-eyed wonder at Eddie X. What sort of guy rushes into somebody else's business meeting and invites them to a romantic dinner? You can't help but admire his self-confidence. And you can't help but love him.

'That sounds super, Eddie. Of course I'll come!'

'Great, then I'll pick you up at six. Is that okay?'

'Absolutely. Aye, aye, captain!' Astra giggles.

Eddie gets up to leave. When he passes Astra he lets his hand caress her shoulders. He says he can find his own way out. Both Evita and Titus stare openly at Eddie when he goes out through the room. If a resurrected Jesus had gone through the room at the same time, nobody would have seen anyone but Eddie.

Astra, Evita and Titus sit in silence for a few moments after the romantic wind has blown the outer door shut.

Titus can't restrain himself any longer. He must give expression to his worry.

'Do you think that he… I mean, why did he come just now? Was it just a coincidence or…'

Astra looks surprised. She has no idea what he is getting at.

'What? No, but, well of course he knows where I live. I told him that when we were out eating.'

Evita is equally unable to grasp what Titus is worried about.

'He's just delightful! Entirely governed by impulse. He must have been nearby, the sun was shining, and he felt that he wanted to sail this evening. No sooner said than arranged. And now he has a date.'

There is a vacant look on Titus' face. He is absolutely convinced that Eddie X is more interested in getting hold of book ideas than in getting hold of sailors. Besides, he knows how men function. The hunt comes before romance.

'Please Astra, you must promise me not to mention *The Best Book in the World*. Not to a soul, and especially not to Eddie.'

'But of course, Titus! Why ever would I do that? You can trust me. *The Best Book in the World* stays between the three of us.'

Titus gives a wry smile. He is by no means convinced.

CHAPTER 27

The Evening Breeze Blows up

Titus totters out onto the street outside Astra's flat. Astra's coffee was not at all satisfying. The coffee is good of course, and the milk hot and frothy. But where are the cakes and biscuits? Not a bun to be seen! No cakes, no sandwiches, no Danish pastries, no croissants, nothing. The only thing on the table was an enormous fruit bowl: organic fairtrade bananas, apples and plums. Sure, fruit can be tasty, but it isn't what you expect when you go for a coffee. If you have fruit with coffee it ends up as something quite different to a coffee break – a damned fruit break, like in a children's nursery. A jolly little fruit break. Kumbaya, my lord. Titus gets the shivers when he thinks about himself as a little boy at nursery school. It was on the whole quite unusual for kids to go to nursery when he was little, most stayed at home with their mothers, playing in the yard with nice new toys from the new Co-op department store. Miniature mechanical diggers. Footballs made of real leather. But not Titus. His mum cleaned offices instead of looking after him, and since he was delicate and a bit different, he always got to sit next to teacher when they assembled for a sing-song in the afternoon after the outdoor break. They all sat in a circle on the grey-beige linoleum floor and held each other's hands. Miss Leaf (Titus had never heard her first name) had cold sweaty hands and fluttering but kind eyes with little lumps of that black stuff on her eyelashes. A shrill voice: Kumbaya my lord, Kumbayaaaah! Morgan sat on the other side of Titus. Meany Morgan. He had tough paws and he used to mangle Titus' hand so that his fingers sort of rolled up inside Morgan's dirty fist, back and forth until his little hand was round as a cigar. Morgan's victory cigar. Scornful milk-teeth pegs. And then – fruit break. Brown-spotted bananas. Soft apples. Morgan's teeth-marks. Swedish nursery schools in the shadow of the expanding welfare state in the early 1970s.

Titus is hungry and dissatisfied. He is not only in a bad mood because fruit acids and coffee are extremely unsuited to each other. Most of all he is angry with himself. He doesn't function properly in company any longer, he just sits and is grumpy as soon as he meets anybody. He doesn't participate, just juggles with a whole load of unfounded suspicions inside his own brain that slowly but surely is being transformed into a centrifuge that is out of balance. And the idea of pretending to be more or less tipsy, what nonsense! Damn it, he is an adult, he tries to convince himself.

Titus must cure himself. First something to eat that is rich in proteins and carbohydrates. Then he needs the company of an old friend or colleague to get a bit of perspective on life. Perhaps he has quite simply imagined that Eddie X is out to get him? What proof does he actually have? A weird meeting at the City Library, a *Summer* programme that wasn't about what Eddie said it would be, a forgotten note with a cryptic message, an imagined break-in without any witnesses and with nothing missing – just the lid of the laptop that had been lifted up. Hardly something to turn out Interpol over. A police investigation wouldn't even call that circumstantial evidence; Håkan Rink would just have snorted and muttered something about his NPNC-doctrine: No Proof, No Crime. No, Eddie was probably fully occupied with charming the world. He couldn't give a damn about me, Titus thinks. Or could he?

Titus walks past a sign announcing: *Dish of the day, fifty kronor.* Irresistible, without a doubt. There is a solitary but nice table outside the Chinese restaurant. He takes a seat and waits for someone to take his order.

Eddie's Neptun yacht is well looked after down to the tiniest detail. The cover on the deck is painted in a dark lilac colour, the hull in a lighter lilac tone, with large ornamental letters from midships in black: *Come aboard amour.* One might well assume that Eddie had christened the boat; the name matches his poetry perfectly. But it was the first owner, the legendary entertainer Sven-Bertil Taube, who named his shining new yacht at the boatyard together with his wife at the time, Inger. The name is said to have come about by chance when the elegant gentleman held out his hand to help her aboard. To rename a boat means bad luck, and Eddie X would never deliberately court ill fortune. Besides, he is certain that he garners considerable benefit from the amorous Taube inheritance, and he never misses the opportunity to tell the story.

The mast is of rigid and sturdy Oregon pine. All the ropes run across the roof of the cabin back to the cockpit so that the boat can be sailed by a solitary person without them needing to leave the helm. Eddie likes to be in control. He also has a considerable weakness for the old-fashioned romantic world of sailing. For example, all plastic is forbidden on board; you must eat on proper china and drink from proper glasses. When dishes are to be washed, or decks be scrubbed, you haul up the water with a bucket made of waxed sailcloth. That's what Sven-Bertil used to do too, according to Eddie. The bunks in the cabin have chalk-white cotton sheets and old eiderdown bedding, which can get a little damp if it rains, but no worse than can be steamed away with a few old oil lamps.

Eddie has timed his sailing tour with Astra perfectly. When the hot afternoon air finally leaves Stockholm's roofs and slowly rises, the vacuum is filled with cooler air from the archipelago which in turn is chased inland by the almost cold air in the open Baltic. As soon as they have left the jetty, the lukewarm onshore wind catches the foresail and the mainsail. The Neptun cruiser sets off like a spear through the water. Adrenalin and a sense of well-being spread through Eddie as the water ripples all the faster around the bows. He looks up at the sail, now perfectly taut in the light wind. He trims the mainsail further and the boat heels a little more. Astra is sitting on the lee side in an orange Helly Hansen life-jacket from the 1960s. When the water splashes up beside the railing, she starts to laugh.

'Eddie, this is like a big dipper!'

'Is it the first time for you?'

'Yes, you must promise to be careful.'

Both become silent when they realise the ambiguity of the conversation. They look at each other. Then they burst out laughing. The ice is broken. This is going to be a wonderful evening.

Titus looks at a large heap of sticky rice and the three small pieces of deep-fried chicken. He sighs deeply and heaps soy sauce over it all in an attempt to save the meal from impoverishment. He tries to get a good grip with the chopsticks. Pah, it won't work. He takes the fork and scoops up a first mouthful.

I need a plan of action, he thinks. If only I could do something completely different for a few hours, then perhaps I will see everything in a new light early tomorrow morning, probably realise that this is just some crazy paranoia and that I can forget the whole thing. Or, I'll become even more convinced that Eddie really is trying to steal my ideas. And that would be okay too, because then I can start collecting evidence.

That seems sensible. Have a rest and take it easy. Do something else.

Titus eats slowly and reflects. Do something else. Nothing comes to him. What does it mean, do something else? What could that be? All summer long he has been crazily obsessed with the book. He hasn't got any friends any longer. The few he had are presumably sitting at the Association Bar, 'celebrating' as they call it, as if they had an official excuse to be there every day like a job, an important task. They pretend to be intellectuals but all they manage to read nowadays are the evening tabloids' sports pages. Evening after evening, the same story: today we're celebrating that Djurgården had a home victory, today we are celebrating that they managed a draw in an away match, today we are celebrating that the Champions' League is starting, today we are celebrating the Champions' League final.

No, he can survive without that. He is forced to start afresh, find new friends, create a new life. Perhaps there might even be a woman in that new life, a woman who wouldn't slam the door behind him after only a couple of days. But for the time being, that feels extremely distant. This new sober life is bloody boring, he thinks. But at least it is a real life. Better late than never. I'm never going to touch a drop again, he thinks solemnly. It is wonderful to be boring.

He thumbs through an evening paper that an earlier guest has left behind. Is there a good cinema to go to? Stand-up comedy?

'Now we're going to feast on prawns!' Eddie shouts.

Come aboard amour has berthed beside some flat rocks in a little bay on the western side of the Fjäderholm islands,

174

a mini archipelago between Lidingö and Nacka. The sun still warms you, and the August darkness won't overtake the evening for a couple more hours.

Believe it or not, Eddie even has a cooler from the 1940s in varnished mahogany. It is full of ice and contains two bottles of wine. Astra laughs at Eddie's weird equipment.

'Lovely, Eddie. Yes, I'm ravenous. And thirsty.'

Eddie has rigged up an old picnic table in the cockpit. On the thwarts he has laid out piles of blue sailing cushions with short white bobbles in the middle. There are linen serviettes and he has even managed to make some toast in the storm kitchen's frying pan. He lifts the lid on an old ceramic jar and smells the contents.

'Ah! This is delightful chili mayonnaise. I made it myself from my mother's recipe.'

They eat the prawns, throwing the shells overboard as they go. Lots of small and medium-sized fish snap up the bits and swim to the nearest tuft of seaweed to continue the feast in peace and quiet. The little bay bubbles with sensual pleasure.

'Here's to the month of August. Cheers!' says Eddie, and raises his old crystal glass. The locks of his hair are matted from the wind.

'Cheers for letting me come along!' Astra responds, and her hair is just as matted. Her camisole is all askew, slipping down one shoulder.

'Cheers for your *wanting* to come along!'

'Cheers for all of this.'

'Cheers.'

The newspaper has four spreads with tips for activities, but Titus can't find anything to do. He is simply unable to shake off his paranoia. How can he possibly relax now, knowing that Eddie and Astra are out sailing together? Of course Eddie is pumping Astra for all she knows about Titus, and how easy can it be to resist Eddie's charms when he turns on the charm? He'll certainly be trying to wheedle out of her details about *The Best Book in the World*. She is probably quite capable of slipping out of his clutches, but still… How long can she resist him? Titus is absolutely convinced that the only thing going on inside Eddie's brain is the creation of an immortal masterpiece – at Titus' expense.

He is facing a situation that most people never find themselves in during their whole life. This very evening, his entire future will be decided. He can let Eddie X reign, or he can take charge of the situation and make sure he can realise his plans without Eddie putting obstacles in his way just as he approaches the finishing line. Attack is the best defence, and if he must fight this battle without allies then so be it.

He puts a fifty-kronor note on the table and gets up. He stands erect, with a determined look. It is wonderfully boring to be sober. Damned unpleasant, but refreshing at the same time, like taking an ice-cold shower. Better to be obsessed than dependent.

And better to break into somebody's house than let your masterpiece be appropriated by a handsome romantic poet.

The wine bottles are empty. The last rays of the sun are slowly being tucked away in the cumulus clouds over the rooftops of northern Djurgården. The evening breeze has blown away and there is not a ripple on the water. The oil lamps are lit and ready to struggle against the darkness of night.

Now Eddie serves freshly brewed coffee and ice-cold Carlshamn Flaggpunsch. The charged atmosphere has been further filled with laughter and talk. Eddie tells about when he and some friends sailed into Sandhamn stark naked during the big Gotland sailing race week. The old guys in the luxury yachts did not appreciate the naked teenagers at all, but the few luxury wives and mistresses that had been allowed to accompany them appreciated the boys all the more.

The mood by the jetty became somewhat agitated, to put it mildly, and in the end a fat harbour master wearing a yacht-club blazer came and informed them that they were not following the 'regatta dress code'. They could either get dressed that very minute or he would arrange a forced transfer to the Stavsnäs winter port. Eddie imitates the harbour master. He stands up, salutes and clicks his heels together.

Astra almost chokes with laughter.

They are having a good time together.

And it's going to get even better.

Titus has guessed right. Since Eddie too lives in an old listed building, the locks are just as old and useless as they were at his own place. It is not difficult to find Eddie's door: a big heart cut out from an old red blanket decorates it. The pointed end of the heart ends with an arrow indicating the letter box. 'Put love letters here!' announces a little hand-written note.

It is easy to force the lock bolt back with some pressure from two credit cards pushed together into the door chink. Titus silently thanks the locksmith.

He sneaks into Eddie's flat. It looks as if somebody has thrown a feng-shui bomb into the place: two rooms and a kitchen and not a single superfluous object to be seen. White ceiling, white walls, white lye-treated floor planks, white curtains, white-stained old kitchen chairs and wooden

177

furniture. Almost everything is white except for an enormous bed-cum-sofa which takes up a large part of the gigantic room. The place is full of colourful cushions of different sizes, and one of the shorter walls is covered with a floor-to-ceiling poster of a naked couple walking on a beach with a setting sun in the background. The contrast of the light room and the kitschy poster is fascinating; Titus remains standing there for a few moments before he enters the other room. As expected, there is a desk and a computer. The little study has more of the character of a traditional writer's den – the walls are covered with bulging bookshelves, and books, brochures, newspapers, clippings and print-outs cover the greater part of the floor.

Titus starts by going through the bookshelves. A bookshelf tells you everything about a person, partly by showing you which books are in it but above all by how they are arranged. The books in the collection don't actually tell you what the book-owner has really read – the selection is more about the picture the person wants to present of himself. But the way they are ordered, you can't hide that, it reveals everything. The people who have read the most start by arranging their books according to genre, with biographies and fiction in separate sections, likewise cookery books and photo books, and so on. The more genres, the greater the interest in literature, and after that of course there is strict alphabetical order according to the author's surname in each category. The least literary person arranges his books according to size. It is dreadfully ugly and almost impossible to find anything. On the other hand, nobody ever takes a book out of that type of bookshelf. Some maniacs even try to arrange their books in colour groupings, but they are few. Eddie belongs to the first category, excluding the many books stacked in heaps due to shortage of space. But within every letter of the alphabet there is complete chaos:

Dostoevsky comes before Dahlström. Kosinski before Kafka. He is a combination of a structure fascist, someone who goes by size, and a common-or-garden nutter. Strange indeed, thinks Titus. He looks in J, where his own books ought to be, but there is just a big gap.

Titus finds the Jensen-books in a heap on the floor next to the desk. Oh my God! Some sort of espionage is clearly going on. He thumbs through the books but can't find any notes or comments inside them. In fact the paper feels stiff, almost as if they haven't been opened before. What sort of spy can't be bothered to do proper research? Titus feels angry that Eddie hasn't even read his books, despite having buttered him up and flattered him so many times.

Titus looks out of the window to check if anybody is watching him. There doesn't seem to be. He turns the computer on and sits down on the desk chair waiting for the program to start up.

Ha! You don't need a password to get in! He starts frantically to search among folders and files. The hard disk is mainly music, pictures and films. Titus bypasses these and soon finds a folder called 'MANUSCRIPTS'. He opens it, and one of the sub-folders immediately catches his eye.

The hair on Titus' arms stands up when he reads the name: *The Best Book in the World*.

Out on the Fjäderholm islands, calm has descended. The day-trippers who come with the ferry have long since gone home. The guests at the inn on the other side of the island are either in the restaurant or out on the jetty drinking whisky in peace and quiet. The taxi boats won't be coming for another hour or two.

In the little bay where *Come aboard amour* is moored, it is calm too. The cockpit is empty and both the crew and the oil lamps have moved into the cabin. Eddie X and Astra are lying among the warm eiderdowns, flirting. A bit of kissing, and switching between nonsense and serious subjects of conversation. Eddie wants to know what it is like at Winchester's. How do they look after their authors? What sort of contracts do they have? How much do the editors interfere with the texts? When it comes to Winchester's, Astra is super-professional. She is a like a catalogue and only reveals carefully balanced information. She is more interested in how things are at Eddie's publishing house, Babelfish. Does he think they market him properly? What would make him change to another publisher? What does he think of Winchester's? Does he want her to arrange a meeting with Evita Winchester, completely informally?

Titus starts reverentially poking around in the folder called *The Best Book in the World*. There is a Word file called 'synopsis'. He opens it and reads a short list of bullet points:

- **The funniest T-shirt print in the world:**

THE WOOD GROUSE IS THE BIGGEST
HEN BIRD IN SWEDEN

- **The best aphorism in the world:**

IT IS JUST AS LIKELY THAT THE WORLD
WAS MADE BY GOD AS THAT THE MOON
IS MADE OF CHEESE

Is that it? Titus thinks about his own way of making a synopsis. He can easily fill an entire pad with handwritten notes before he even starts on the book. But this? What on earth is it? Either Eddie is trying to make a fool of him, or he has got writer's block. Creative paralysis.

Slowly but surely a lofty calm spreads through Titus' body. Perhaps Eddie quite simply isn't capable of doing battle with him. He has obviously tried, but without success. Eddie has sat down and started to note the contents of the book and the only things he has been able to think up are a weird T-shirt print and an aphorism, albeit a fairly clever one. But that is hardly a sustainable start for a bestselling non-fictional novel of decisive importance that is going to change the world. Such an idiot! Titus shakes his head.

The next file is called *Comeaboardamour_bestpoemintheworld*. An expectant smile spreads across Titus' face. Of course, he clicks that file to open it too.

Beloved Astra, come to my yacht
Work Eddie's pump, give it a shot
Come aboard and share my berth
There's lots of room; plenty of girth
Dearie me, did the wave splash you?
Take off your shirt before you're wet through
We have man-rope, tackle and leather
The right equipment for all sorts of weather
The keel is long with anti-corrosive iron bolts
The varnish shines all shiny, the tiller bucks like a colt
Come hither and I'll kiss your curvy railing
Serve you a full suit of sails and learn you some sailing
And when you finally ask me to fill your sails
I'll gust from the south with all that entails
Let go the topsail, clew up, hold fast!
Sheet home my foresail and blow on my mast

We'll sing a sea shanty, drink grog, make mirth
Make for the headland and tack up the firth!
Ship ahoy! Come into my berth!

Titus's eyes are like saucers. What is this? Never in all his life has he seen such rubbish. Surely this couldn't have been written by the brilliant romantic poet Eddie X? Titus reads it again and gets stuck on 'The varnish shines all shiny, the tiller bucks like a colt...' Shines all shiny? this must be the worst ever combination of a verb and an adverb, Titus says quietly to himself, and lets out a laugh.

He starts thinking. Either the poem is meant as a joke, or Eddie has lost his marbles. Or his ability to express himself with words, at any rate.

Suddenly, the meaning of the poem becomes clear to Titus.

Eddie is going to seduce Astra! Evidently, there are no limits to how far that man is prepared to go. His creativity has become completely blocked somehow. He has lost the ability to write and is becoming a desperado. Frustrated artists can become furious, as Titus is well aware. Who knows what mad plans Eddie has to regain control?

I must stop him, Titus thinks.

I must warn Astra!

Out by the Fjäderholm islands, Eddie is starting to become slightly drunk. He has drunk so much punch that his lips and mouth are sticky from all the sugar, and he has to tense his jaw muscles when he speaks so as not to slur his words. And like all tipsy boys he can't manage to kiss and do the small talk for more than a short while. Suddenly he frees himself from the eiderdowns and opens his arms wide.

'Come on, now, Astra. We're going swimming!'

He opens the cabin hatch and jumps up into the cockpit. There, he hastily tears off all his clothes with sweeping gestures and sets off round the deck in a wild Indian dance. He stops on the foredeck in front of the mast, thrusts a little with his hips and swings his dick a few rounds in the air before diving down into the black and glistening water.

Astra is not quite as drunk as Eddie, but is just as exhilarated. When she comes up on deck and sees Eddie already in the water, she too undresses quick as a flash. She holds her nose and her bosom when she jumps into the water.

'Lovely, isn't it?' Eddie shouts, and with a toss of his head clears his long fringe from his eyes. He swims a few metres in the bay and waves to Astra to follow. She swims after him. They stop and tread water a while without talking, just looking at each other.

'This is heavenly! How can it still be so warm in the water?'

'I love August! Look over there towards Lidingö, Astra. Can you see?'

'What?'

'Look at the water! Look how it's shining all shiny! I love it when it shines all shiny!'

'Yes, it is beautiful when it shines all shiny. I like it.'

'Hello, you have reached Astra Larsson at Winchester Publishing. Leave your name and your telephone number, and I shall phone you as soon as I can. Thanks for the call.'

Damn, damn, damn! Titus shakes his mobile phone in the air as if it were to blame for Astra not answering. What the hell should I do now? Phone her again and leave a message? Text her?

And in that case, what would he say? In the long run it is usually best to tell the truth. At the same time, he knows that Astra has fallen for Eddie. It would be hard to convince her over the phone that Eddie is a maniac. It would only rebound on Titus himself. He would look like a jealous nutter with a conspiracy theory. So what should he do? He must act, otherwise Astra might be tricked into something unpleasant. And, most important of all, Eddie might ferret out lots of secrets about *The Best Book in the World*.

Titus comes to the conclusion that a white lie is the only proper solution at this stage. Whitish, at least. Off-white, he thinks, and sends off a text message.

Then he simply turns off his phone.

Time will tell, he thinks.

The night bathers are back in the cabin. The swim and the charged atmosphere have already done for a large part of the alcohol. Astra and Eddie sit wrapped up in each other's towels and eiderdowns, kissing for all they are worth. They caress each other's hair. Their emotions are on fire. The oil lamps flicker sensually in time with their wide-open mouths. The dampness has started to leave their bodies and now settle as a mist on the small windows. They aaaah and ummmm as they kiss each other, sometimes with closed eyes that allow their hands to discover new wonders, sometimes with wide-open eyes that ladle in even larger portions of pleasure. Their legs are entwined. The towels and covers fall off. There is a great deal that is shining all shiny on the boat just now.

Suddenly, the text alert on Astra's telephone cuts like a machete right through the cabin. Robot-like, she stretches out for the telephone and opens the message before she has time to think – a message from the outer world can destroy a sexy moment easy as pie. But Astra isn't thinking clearly, it is her muscles and nerves that decide. Her eyes and hands leave Eddie's body and concentrate on the telephone display. Answering the phone is evidently a reflex that has a higher position in Astra's needs-pyramid than the impulse to mate with the best man in the flock.

RELAPSE. HELP ME. NOW. TITUS.

'Oh no, what the hell…' whispers Astra.

Not many seconds pass before the erotic atmosphere leaves the cabin. Astra's pupils whirl around in her eyes, as if trying to help her brain find something to cling on to.

Eddie sits up a little and pulls the covers over his navel.

'What's happening?'

'I don't know. Something has happened to Titus. He seems to have gone on a binge again. He wants help.'

'Oh dear. Has he tried to become sober? I thought he personified the everlasting party,' says Eddie quietly, caressing Astra's arm.

Astra mutters some curses to herself and tries to phone Titus. But he has turned his phone off, and he hasn't got an answerphone function turned on either. All she can hear is the telephone company's automatic message which speaks in staccato.

'I must go home,' says Astra and looks desperate.

'Really? Are you sure?'

'I must. Anything at all could have happened. Can we do that, can we go home now?'

'Yes, of course. I'll start the engine and we'll be back in the harbour in fifteen, twenty minutes.'

'Great,' says Astra with a slightly sad smile. 'Eddie, this is just crazy. I really don't want to break off this evening. You have been absolutely fantastic. You *are* absolutely fantastic. You make me horny as hell, and I think that I am actually a little in love with you. Really, really magical, all of it. I'm terribly sorry.'

'It's all right, Astra. Nobody can destroy what we two have here. Now let's be on our way. We must save Titus Jensen for posterity.'

Eddie gets dressed quickly and starts doing things with the boat so that they can sail home. He connects the petrol hose to the outboard motor, squeezes the petrol pump a few times, pulls out the choke and starts the engine at the first pull. It chugs quietly while he loosens the mooring ropes and pulls the boat out with the anchor rope. Astra untangles the mess of sheets and towels, and tidies the bunk which fills half the cabin. She curses Titus for being so hopelessly immature. Who knows when she'll get to see this lovely bunk again?

Eddie hangs up an oil lamp in the mast as a lantern. The old Neptun cruiser chugs slowly back to its home harbour through the calm waters. A few other boats can be seen here and there. The evening is not over yet. The summer is not over yet. The sky above Stockholm is lit up by street lights, flats and lots of lively pubs and restaurants.

Eddie holds the tiller with his right hand, putting his other arm around Astra's shoulders when she comes and sits beside him.

'Has he tried to be sober for a long time?' he wonders.

'Yes, indeed. He has been totally dry since the beginning of summer. He has even stopped smoking.'

'Oh, goodness…'

'The thing is, he is working on a new book. Or rather, it is almost finished. I think it is going to be really, really good, but not if he starts boozing again. That would be the end of it. Evita's going to be absolutely livid.'

'Wow, have you been able to read any of it then? What's it about?' Eddie wonders.

Astra looks at Eddie, somewhat surprised. What does the plot of the book matter at this point? Eddie looks away.

'I mean, I wonder how he's feeling? I wonder what's happened.'

'I just don't get it. I thought he was in good balance. He looked young and fit didn't he? You saw him at my place earlier today.'

Eddie's eyebrows rise a centimetre or two. Now he looks genuinely curious.

'Young and fit? Well, actually I don't think he did. I thought he looked a bit tipsy. I think he had probably already had a shot or two.'

'I don't know about that. No, something must have happened this evening.'

As they approach the harbour, Astra phones and orders a taxi. Eddie asks if she wants him to accompany her. She doesn't. Or rather, she does, but she knows that Eddie makes Titus nervous. He has nagged her so much not to talk about what he is busy with, and especially not to Eddie X. No, regrettably she must track down Titus on her own.

Something is happening to Eddie. His mouth looks like a line. His eyes are smarting. He grips the tiller so hard that his knuckles turn white.

Titus looks at his watch. It's well after midnight. He realises that the sailors could be back in the city any time but that he has no idea if his text has actually been received or if Astra has even seen it. It was a bit of a shot in the dark, and now he really has no idea which strategy he should follow.

He sneaks out of Eddie's house and starts walking home quickly. He must air his brain, think and try to sort out his alternatives.

Option one. He hits the bottle quick as hell and hopes that Astra forgives him for this one and only escapade. He'll grovel at her feet, petition for mercy and hope she will still have faith in him. At the same time he will warn Astra about Eddie. But why should she believe him? And what should he claim to be the danger from Eddie? No, he can't hit the bottle to save himself. That would risk everything. Better to be obsessed than dependent. Forget it. Not a good alternative.

Option two. He tells it like it is. That his paranoia drove him to break into Eddie's house and that he had searched his computer and now considered he could prove that a historic theft of ideas is under way, and that Eddie is intending to carry out a pretentious seduction of Astra with the help of horrible sailing metaphors. No, that isn't going to work; he cannot reveal to a single living soul that he, Titus Jensen, has deliberately broken into the home of one of the most popular figures in the country. Christ, no. He drops that idea too.

Option three. He can resort to yet another white lie and concoct a half-truth. He can say that he sent his 'relapse' text purely to arouse Astra's attention. That much is true. And then he can say that he happened to meet Eddie's mate Lenny in town, and that according to him Eddie has boasted about how easy it would be to get Astra into bed, that she has completely fallen for him and now all Eddie has to do is to bait the hook. Titus can say that he does of course know that Astra is fully capable of looking after herself, but that she nevertheless must be informed as to the rules of Eddie's dirty game. If Eddie only sees Astra as a trophy, then she must be appraised of the fact. It is his obligation as a friend to tell the bitter truth. He apologises for his abrupt text message but felt that something special was required to gain her attention. Titus realises deep inside that a teenage-like seduction boast doesn't fit in very well with Eddie's character, but he also feels that he doesn't have the time or the ability to find other ways out of his dilemma. He has to give it a try, and it is at any rate not a completely rotten strategy. With a bit of luck it might just hit home. Or rather, it simply must work.

He is soon home again. He turns his phone on and waits for Astra to ring. Because she is going to, isn't she? Surely?

When Astra climbs into the taxi, she is rather bewildered by all the emotions rushing around inside her. She has had a wonderful evening with Eddie: wild sailing, romantic dinner, intimate conversation, night swimming and kissing in the nude – all within the course of a few hours. What a pace! They are probably beginning to fall in love with each other, she thinks, and smiles to herself. She would never have thought that she would fall for a guy with extra-large coloured silk shirts. She is usually waylaid by blokes with expensive suits and smart hairstyles. Astra has no idea which women Eddie has had, but she doesn't think they usually have an electronic calendar and ten-thousand-kronor shoes in their hall. But evidently opposites attract each other; the greater the charge at the ends, the greater the magnetism.

She tries to phone Titus again. Perhaps he has turned his phone on now.

Titus is sitting at the kitchen table staring at his mobile phone, and answers immediately when it rings:

'Hi Astra. Where are you?'

'I'm sitting in a taxi. But where are *you*? What's happened?'

'I'm at home. Can you come over?' he says in a serious but short tone.

'Sure. Are you all right?'

'We can talk more when you're here.'

Titus doesn't even notice that Astra has no make-up and that her hair has that after-sex look. As soon as she comes in, he takes her hand and leads her to the computer. He bends

189

down and puts the tube into his mouth. The breathalyser-lock approves his breath and the computer welcomes him to a new work session. He spreads his hands.

'There, you see? I'm sober.'

'Yes, I see that. I'm very pleased, I must say. What the hell are you playing at, really?'

Titus looks seriously at Astra and says that he'll tell her everything.

And he does.

He tells her why he was forced to send her a false text message. How and why he came across Lenny. That Lenny was sloshed and blurted out everything Eddie had said about how he was going to mount Astra. How Lenny laughed and was twitching and jerking at the same time as he was obviously deeply impressed by Eddie's ability to seduce women. How he imitated Eddie's obscene gestures with which described that the final conquest would take place on all fours. That Titus hadn't really believed Lenny, but that Lenny could even quote from a poem Eddie had written about Astra. Some rubbish about something that 'shines all shiny' and how he would shag her on his boat *Come aboard amour*. And that Eddie had said to Lenny that as soon as he had Astra on the hook then he would start pumping her for information about Titus' new book.

That last bit wasn't really planned. It just sort of slipped out.

Titus becomes silent and realises he can't just keep on gabbling non-stop. He must give Astra a chance to digest it all.

The strategy has worked. He can see that from her long face. He isn't proud of himself, but he does feel that what he has saved is of considerable value.

'I didn't know what to do! All I knew was that you were

on a sailing date with Eddie. And I know Eddie, he can twist anybody round his little finger. I just had to do something. Do you understand?'

Astra stares at Titus. The words from Titus' outburst whirl around inside her head, but don't form any proper meaning. Shines all shiny… shines all shiny… shines all shiny… the words create a little whirlpool in her brain like water draining from a bathtub. At first you hardly notice anything, there is just a little trace of movement on the surface. But soon the laws of gravity and the forces of nature get the upper hand. The whirlpool makes demands, and it takes with it everything it can see on its increasingly wild clockwise journey. It can even suck a big toe into the drain.

In Astra's head, the shines-all-shiny whirlpool whizzes around faster and faster. It soon sucks down common sense, which until now has managed to swim calmly and sensibly on the surface. Perspective and discernment join the roundabout too. 'Shines all shiny' grows into a maelstrom. She recognises that expression all too well: they are Eddie's words, no doubt about it. She feels disgusted, partly by the idea that Eddie had planned his romantic attack upon her. Can it really be true? She is also disgusted to have been a subject of discussion between two cultural misfits at a pub as if she were just some damned plaything. She has no wish whatsoever to be the focus of their conversation. Why is she sitting here in the middle of the night in the flat of a nutty has-been who not only interferes in her life but also thinks he is capable of writing a book that can top the bestseller lists in several different categories? How did she get sucked into this swamp? This is crazy, why couldn't she have an ordinary job instead? Lawyer, accountant, bank director, any bloody job at all?

But no way is she ever going to descend to Titus' Neanderthal level and start crying or talking it out with him.

Never ever. Coolness and professionalism, these are the only things that work with these decrepit old men.

'I don't know what to say, Titus. This is just too much. You make me so tired.'

'I know, Astra. I'm sorry that it turned out like this. At first I didn't know what I should do. But I was forced to tell you the truth.'

Astra inhales a slow breath through her nose and exhales it the same way. Then she gets up and leaves Titus.

She feels like she has gone down the plughole herself.

CHAPTER 28

Working Period

A few days pass. August comes to an end and September takes over.

After his visit to study Eddie's home, Titus feels a great sense of calm. Eddie has obviously had the idea of starting on *The Best Book in the World* since he has a folder in his computer with that name. But everything he touches is lacking in substance. It is useless. He is never going to succeed by himself. That is most satisfactory, in Titus' opinion.

Titus, however, is churning out chapter after chapter for his concise manuscript. It is brief, powerful and without a load of boring digressions into detail and recourse to cliché. He is going to keep his readers on tenterhooks and treat them to one cracker after the other.

He finds several wonderful recipes that will allow Håkan Rink to stick to his ABC Method. Soon he'll have a fully fledged cookery book. The parallel track around fulfilling yourself and finding your self-respect is also becoming much clearer as Håkan Rink and his team achieve major break-throughs in their personal lives and in their police work. Titus writes checklists and provides examples of concrete plans of action so that the readers can build up speed with their own successful lives as soon as they have finished reading. No end of doctrines, tips and good advice. Meanwhile, the thriller itself is most captivating; the run-through of Serial Salvador's driving forces is not only an exposé of the dark side of mankind, but also an excellent guide to the history of the twentieth century seen from the perspective of the most important 'isms' of the whole period. Titus writes several short essay-like sections which he indicates with an indentation of the text so that the readers will understand that they can just skim through if they are feeling impatient. It is vital keep the readers on-side.

Surrealism lay to a large degree behind the rapid development of business imagination, the entertainment branch and communications industry during the twentieth century. But there was a dark downside when the subconscious creativity took up such a lot of space. Many of the worst genocides carried out during the last century would presumably never have taken place if there hadn't been that green light to live out your innermost dreams in reality. The relationship with Nazism is very clear:

Surrealism celebrates the inner superman; Nazism the outer.

Both these 'isms' gathered strength at about the same time, in the depressive shadow of the First World War. Mental strength was celebrated, and at the same time there was a trend for narcissistic examination of not only one's own neuroses but also of one's own power, which risked breaking out into black psychoses and war. That one's own personal strength could be used to protect those who were vulnerable or to learn to understand dissidents was not something that was embraced by these 'isms'. Everything was geared towards trying to win personal independence, an imagined increase in freedom that would benefit the ever-advancing collective. The freedom gave a spiritual experience which, as opposed to a purely religious and emotionally based experience, was built upon theoretical – albeit fragile – foundations. To become a free person, you must first come to grips with your own reason, your morals and your aesthetics.

But, as always, art and politics led to essentially different consequences. Guillaume Apollinaire, Tristan Tzara, André Breton, Franz Kafka, Salvador Dali and all the others who worked with a free flow of the senses can hardly be blamed for the horrible deeds of which Adolf Hitler was later guilty, much as Albert Einstein was not responsible for the atom bomb being dropped on Hiroshima, nor Marilyn Manson for the lethal shootings at Columbine High School.

These days, with summer nearing its end, have turned into yet another intensive working period for Titus. He follows his routines of gym training and regular meals. He skips the sunbed because he risks at any moment ending up looking like a cultural drunk who has gone to seed, not least when he does that reading at the Poetry Slam Festival that Eddie persuaded him to agree to. Muscles and senses on full alert, that is the order of the day until the book is finished. Better to be obsessed than dependent.

He doesn't have any more contact with Astra. She doesn't answer when he phones, and he doesn't leave any messages on her answering service. He knows very well that everybody at the publishing house has lots to do in the run-up to the annual book fair in Gothenburg at the end of September, and as regards the advance presentation of the project *The Best Book in the World* he is fully confident that Astra and Evita will produce a smart brochure which will have a knock-out effect on the buyers from foreign publishers. Evita thinks with her wallet and normally succeeds in everything she touches. Titus Jensen is not going to be an exception, he thinks, hopefully.

Astra is also slaving away. After the evening sail she has turned off everything which isn't connected to work. She has allowed a bomb to explode in her calendar which is now full of meetings with authors, book-cover designers, marketing people and literary agents.

Eddie tries to phone her many times. He sends flowers and poems. On one occasion, he even sends her an old cuddly hamster soft toy that plays David Bowie's *The Prettiest Star* when you squeeze its tummy. Astra can't help smiling a little when she thinks how many vintage shops he must have trawled through to find that.

She refuses to see herself as a victim. What does it matter if Eddie has talked with Lenny about how he is going to seduce her? Isn't it rather charming for a guy to know what he wants? And how many times hasn't she herself objectified Eddie and appraised his bottom instead of his poetry? No, this isn't about Eddie's intentions – it's the double-dealing in his behaviour that she can't accept. You can't act as if you are an androgynous poet and the next second trans-mogrify into a babbling male chauvinist pig. Is he a man or a teenage boy? She wants a decent mix of oestrogen and testosterone, not to feel like she has been picked up after a boozy evening at a bar by somebody who tastes of caveman. Her feelings for Eddie are mixed, and she decides to take a break from everything to do with emotions. Leave it for a few weeks and see which feelings survive and which go up in smoke. The next time she meets Eddie, she wants to be certain that her brain and her loins will cooperate.

And as for Titus, at the moment she is simply hopelessly fed up with him. She knows that he has tried to get in touch but as long as he doesn't have anything important to deal with, they can just as well each work on their own. He has a one-track mind and probably isn't thinking about anything besides himself and his book project. And she has done so much to make it easy for him: arranged his computer to force him to take breaks, got him a gym pass and fixed all sorts of things so that he can get a life again. But does he show the slightest bit of gratitude? No, he doesn't. Everything, simply everything, revolves around *The Best Book in the World*, and even if he doesn't say it straight out, she can feel that Titus' world is becoming increasingly full of weird threatening situations and shady conspiracy theories. He seems to be high on speed, and the whole thing is extremely irritating. But she isn't surprised in the slightest. It must be harmful to throw yourself from one extreme to the other like Titus has done. One moment he is a hard-drinking cultural has-been, the next he is a hard-working artist who delivers superb texts. She is a little worried that it will soon be like pouring ice-cold water onto a rock that has been many hours in the full sun – when he cracks open, the explosion will be powerful.

'He has been inside my home. He has stopped my love. He has stolen it!'

Eddie X slams his hand down on the desk so that the computer jumps up. He can't concentrate on work. He can't write, not a single word. Something is churning away inside him, an unpleasant sensation which is increasing all the time. Sometimes it feels as if he had swapped something valuable. Sometimes it feels as if he had lost it forever. And he can't get hold of Astra either.

He is tired and feels apathetic. The blood is draining out of his veins. Words disappear from his mouth. Ideas evaporate from his brain. What is left is a vacuum, an empty space. He will soon implode.

It doesn't help to go into vintage shops and buy colourful clothes. It doesn't make it better to smile at people he meets in town and who expect a friendly reception.

He wants to be able to kick an empty beer can without people wrinkling their nose at him.

He wants to be able to disappear like a chameleon against a wall.

He wants to sleep.

But he can't.

He has been reading. And, sure, it is an obvious theft. They are going to discover that. Now he must work, regain the initiative. That is the right path.

He knows what must be done, and he is concocting his plans.

CHAPTER 29

The Return of Nadersson

A call from an ex-directory number. I hate people who don't dare show where they are ringing from, Astra thinks irritably when she answers:

'Yes, hello?'

'Yes, hi. I wonder if you are the person responsible for your company's security issues?'

'No, I'm not.'

'Well, my name is Fabian Nadersson and I'm phoning on behalf of Maximal Security. Can you spare a minute?'

'But I said that I am *not* responsible for security issues. Are you deaf?'

'No, not at all. On the contrary. The thing is that at the moment we have a good campaign for automatic back-up copying via the net. All of your company's computers can upload a complete back-up file every day without the users having to do anything. You don't need any extra bandwidth, and everything is stored on double servers in Maximal Security's vaults.'

'But I don't care. I AM NOT RESPONSIBLE FOR SECURITY ISSUES.'

'I see. But you might be interested in signing up for a trial period? The first week is free…'

'No! You must phone the person responsible for security issues!'

'Okay, who is that?

'I haven't the faintest idea…'

'But it is just a trial period. You don't commit yourself to anything. The first week is completely free and after a week you can contact us if you don't want to…'

'Stop, stop, stop! I don't want to talk to you any more. Thank you and goodbye!'

'Okay, we're agreed then?'

'Wait. WAIT. What do you mean "we're agreed"?'

'That you're signing up for a trial period. Aren't you?'

'No! We are *not* signing up for any damned trial period! Is that understood?'

'Absolutely. Thank you for your time. Goodbye.'

'Goodbye.'

Astra throws the phone down onto her desk and leans backwards. She is angry. Just now, everyone is an idiot, especially people trying to sell you things over the phone. Only sadists become telemarketers. They sit there and delight in retaining their icy cold attitude while the person they are talking to gets all the more irritated. In eight out of ten cases it ends with the person who has answered shouting down the phone and cutting off the call. And the pleasure-loving telephone sellers, what do they do? They record the whole thing and listen to the worst conversations time and time again. They praise their own calmness and laugh scornfully at the victim on the other end.

Automatic back-ups. Yawn. Who gives a damn?

She continues the dreary task of answering the day's emails and shakes her head at that telephone seller Fabian Nadersson and his hopeless attempt to get her to buy something. And anyway, Nadersson? What sort of name is that?

She thinks about Titus and his computer. There, the security is already tip-top. Her company already has an excellent security department and she hasn't the slightest inclination to let any horrid telephone seller plague their lives. It was quite right to cut off that Nadersson fellow and his ex-directory number.

Then it struck her. The back-up copy...

Hadn't Titus left a memory card at her flat when they had that working meeting with Evita? Where did that get to? Bloody hell, it's time she gave Titus some feedback. She really ought to read the manuscript and phone him. It really isn't his fault that Eddie is a blockhead. Did she take the card with her to work? No, she can't remember that she ever picked it up. Yet she is absolutely certain that Titus put it on the coffee table. Is it still there?

When Astra gets home she can't find the memory card anywhere. She looks behind all the cushions and under the rug. Nowhere.

She recapitulates the meeting she had with Titus and Evita. They talked about the book launch and that they would translate some chapters for the book fair so that they had something to show the international agents. And when they had almost finished, Eddie rang the doorbell. Did Titus put the card on the table before or after Eddie had come? He must have put it on the table long before Eddie turned up. And since she didn't pick it up, that means the card lay there when Eddie came in...

Surely, it isn't possible...

Could Eddie have...?

No, why should he...?

She dismisses the ridiculous idea. Now she is starting to become as paranoid as Titus. Let's look at this sensibly. No, the card must have been mislaid when she cleaned, or something like that. She must have had her mind on other things. And by now the card has either ended up in the rubbish, or she has put it somewhere and forgotten where.

She must phone Titus and ask him for a new memory card. That's probably just as well. Then she'll have an opportunity to check progress and she'll get a more up-to-date manuscript. But she can't tell Titus that she has gone and lost the first one. Then he would just fall to bits.

She phones him, but he doesn't answer. Where can he be? She looks at her watch to check the date. The sixth. Wasn't it today that Titus was going to read at that Spoken Word Festival at Södra Teatern? Yes, of course it was.

She decides to grab a bite before she goes. She finds some Parma ham and marinated zucchini in the fridge and she grates a little pepper and parmesan over it. I'll have to eat quickly, she thinks, I must get some make-up on too. And find something really attractive to wear.

Eddie X will be there of course, and she is not going to treat him to the sight of her looking tired or miserable. That idiot.

Really she doesn't want to go to that spectacle at all. However, she is Titus' publisher. Her conscience gnaws and tells her she ought to give him all the support she can, despite his having behaved in such an annoying manner.

These readings are usually out-and-out freak shows. Clownery and sick humour of the worst type, albeit nicely hidden in a cultural cloak.

But now that Titus is sober, perhaps he at least can retain a fragment of his honour?

CHAPTER 30

Theatre at the Theatre

In Stockholm in the beginning of September you can't be sure of anything. Is it summer or autumn? Are people happy after their holidays and life-sustaining activities? Or are they already beginning to become depressed, faced as they are with eight months of darkness? If they have let themselves go over the top with summer delights, they can lose their minds in the winter when the dreary contrast casts its shadow on their senses. And if they have completely shut out the summer, their bodies might have been exposed to too little sunlight and the consequent vitamin D shortage will knock them straight into an autumn and winter depression instead.

In Sweden it is a question of balancing your feelings and spreading them out over the year: not too much and not too little. The Swedes have a special word for this – *lagom*. They pride themselves on this word being totally Swedish, and claim that it doesn't exist in any other language. In Sweden you need to be *lagom*. A Swede rations his or her experiences. Only somebody who is *lagom* can keep their cool.

But in recent years Sweden has started to lose its footing. *Lagom* is getting a bit wobbly. *Lagom* has sprung a leak. Swedes are beginning to lose their minds.

It began back in the 1950s and 1960s with American cultural hegemony: a magnificent flood of sitcoms with canned laughter. Historians will come to see that it was Lucille Ball and her *The Lucy Show* that disturbed the equilibrium for all time. A red-haired dame in black-and-white TV, with conical breasts and a crazy laugh – it was simply hilarious, yet still attractive and human in some way. In and out through doors, up and down stairs. What was this? And why was it funny? How could the meek Swedes ever be the same again after this experience?

Then came the immigrants with their weird spicy food and hot feelings, which they liked to serve with joyful voices and wild gestures. They started to call each other and the Swedes 'pal', ignoring the fact that it actually takes a lifetime to acquire a friend in Sweden. And as if to really bowl these *lagom*-Swedes over, they started to mix all cultures any old how, their own as well as that of the Swedes: kebab on pizza, cinnamon in coffee, sprinkles on strawberries!

Other cultural imports that have created sensory distortion are Poetry Slam and Spoken Word. They are stage actors, poets, authors and stand-up comedians who in various ways perform on stage so that their texts will reach the public. There are no rules. The one who reaches them best, wins the public's hearts. You can be funny, sincere, political, ironic, in fact anything at all that arouses emotions and makes the public feel they are an important part of a large, loud and weird world.

Summer meets autumn. Euphoria meets depression. The calendar has reached 6 September. This evening is the Spoken Word Festival, a party evening for brilliant texts. Not quite so geared to hysterical laughter as stand-up comedy, but just as memorable and entertaining. The best talents in the country are gathered here, and even the odd legend from abroad has been invited to join them.

When Titus Jensen gets to Södra Teatern, Stockholm's alternative crowd has already started to meet up in the square outside the theatre. They hug one another and laugh. Hair in all colours of the rainbow, tattoos and piercings, funny clothes, new clothes, ragged clothes. Emotions and life. Nothing *lagom* as far as the eye can see.

Titus, however, is not especially colourful when he stumbles on the steps to the entrance. The black-clad figure with his shaved head is obliged to make use of the railing to ascend, a sight that is all too familiar. The pathetic Author with a capital A has come to provide entertainment for the people. And he looks just as sloshed as usual.

Not everybody thinks Titus Jensen is pathetic. Halfway up the steps he is stopped by an enthusiastic young couple. Both of them just as black-clad as Titus. They are bobbing up and down as they stand and both talking at the same time.

'Oh, Titus, can we have your autograph? We love you. We got together when you read *Manual for Housewives* at the Peace & Love Festival last year. Like, without you we'd never have become a couple. You gave us love. Do you get it? You are the greatest!'

Titus stares at them. This has never happened before. Nobody has ever, in all of his career, expressed their love or admiration in such an unrestrained and direct manner. He takes the felt-tip pen and writes his name on their arms. The blood rushes to his cheeks and he feels the blush spread. A weird sensation. Somebody likes him. Indeed, two people like him. The couple bounce along further up the steps and Titus follows them with his gaze for a moment before moving on.

Inside the foyer, the marble floor makes the background buzz especially loudly. The intense theatre atmosphere is so strong you almost think you can hear a chamber orchestra tuning its instruments despite the fact that many a year has passed since there was an orchestra pit at Södra Teatern.

On the left, some young wardrobe attendants are leaning over the counter with nothing to do. It is still too warm for overcoats. Besides, wardrobe fees are not included in the budget for today's young public. Instead, they slowly pour in through the doors to the right, up the staircase and towards the bar. No active cultural experience without stimulants. Titus follows along with the flow and wonders if he too will have time for something before his entrance. For the last few days, the very thought of performing has made him feel uncomfortable, even though his performance doesn't necessitate a single minute's preparation. He only has to be himself, to treat them to himself, he has tried to convince himself. As Eddie X sometimes shouts out when he introduces him on the stage: 'Everybody has a bit of him in themselves. Yet there is only one Titus Jensen – and that is TITUS JENSEN!'

But nevertheless, today it doesn't feel as simple as it usually does. Something important is absent.

When Titus gets to the top of the stairs and is about to enter the bar, somebody puts a hand on his shoulder. A strict voice:

'Ticket please!'

Titus whirls round.

A big smile. Brilliant white teeth, velvet-brown eyes that can melt glaciers.

'Nice to see you, Eddie,' says Titus with a slight nod of his head.

'You are late,' says Eddie and puts his whole arm round Titus' shoulders, giving him a half-hug. 'It doesn't matter. Come on in, we've time for a beer in the green room before we get started. Great to see you!'

Today Eddie X is wearing a knee-long batik tunic in various shades of purple. Down below, a pair of creased grey-black and rolled-up linen trousers stick out. On his feet, some shabby ox-blood coloured Dr Marten boots without laces. His dead straight Indian hair with orange and blue streaks is twisted into an erect ponytail. At the very top, his hair bushes out like a fountain above his head. There is something elevated about Eddie when he glides through the premises. He greets the public and shakes hands with a lot of them. Now and then he puts his left hand over the handshake as if to seal a lifelong contract of mutual love and fidelity.

It could be a magical evening.

Being drunk can be exhausting. But *pretending* to be drunk is even more of a drain on one's resources.

Nervousness, abstinence and anxiety are riding Titus Jensen. At the moment he has the main role in the stage play of his life. Every single nerve is at maximum tension and at the same time that he is sweating profusely he must smother yawn after yawn. It is as if his body is screaming at him to fill up with oxygen. Everything to retain control of the situation.

He hasn't got much more work left on his masterpiece and no way is he going to allow Eddie X to destroy anything. Eddie can go on thinking that Titus is a boozy has-been, but when the book is published, that love evangelist will be crushed once and for all. He will be crumbled into bits. The future belongs to Titus Jensen and *The Best Book in the World*.

In the green room Lenny is sitting and swigging a beer. He has thrown up one leg over the arm of his armchair and his foot bobs up and down in time with his shoulders which twitch now and then. He is all charged today; he is going to accompany Eddie's text-reading with an amplified contrabass. Just him, Eddie X and a large stage. Today there won't be any of the big band twitches from The Tourettes.

When Titus comes into the room he immediately falls onto the sofa inside the door. His panic increases. Now there are two people to act drunk in front of.

'C-c-cock in your ear!' Lenny yells when he catches sight of Titus.

'Hi Lenny. Hell, great to see you,' says Titus, slurring his words in an attempt to sound like his usual half-sloshed worse self.

Lenny gets a bottle out a little fridge and stretches across to Titus.

'You seem to be fairly sozzled already. H-h-here. Drink this fucker too. Amaze the world!'

Titus takes the little bottle and holds it to his nose. Vodka. Of all the spirits in the world, vodka is the easiest to drink. He feels the craving grow inside him, and he knows that he could drink the whole bottle in less than thirty seconds. He knows exactly what it feels like when the first calm spreads through his body purely from the knowledge of having access to alcohol, long before it reaches his bloodstream.

But it is better to be obsessed than dependent. When the human driving forces do battle, it is not always the strongest one that wins. You can use your brain too, and let cleverness win on points. Despite the proximity of the vodka, Titus feels totally relaxed when he conjures forth his reward image. The young boy with his life before him, lying on a woman's bosom, breathing in time with her. Out and in. Out and in. Moustache wet with fat milk. Lick it off. Become calm. Cognitive self-help. Vodka came, vodka went away. Hello and goodbye. He is going to get through this. Again. He can do it. He is good.

'Are you all geared up, Titus?' Lenny wonders. 'Has Eddie told you what you're going to read?'

'No, I never do that in advance,' says Eddie, and flashes a smile via the mirror at Lenny and Titus. 'It would spoil the magic. Wouldn't it, Titus?'

'Mmmm,' mumbles Titus, who realises that he must lie low with the talk so as not to out himself as a newly fledged teetotaller.

He presses his thumb hard against the mouth of the bottle, leans back on the sofa into a recumbent position and puts the bottle to his lips. Then he turns his head in towards the sofa, holding the bottle between the cushion and the back of the sofa. He releases his thumb. The vodka runs out, gurgling, down into the innards of the sofa.

Then he adopts a half-sitting position with a 'pah!' and wipes his mouth on the arm of his jacket and puts the empty bottle down with a bang on the coffee table. He pushes a sofa cushion over the damp patch and says:

'F-fanks, Renny… can I have a little snooze before it's time?'

Titus doesn't wait for an answer, but leans back with his eyes shut. He isn't following any special plan, just acting on the spur of the moment. Parry. Act. Live life like it's a pinball machine. He emits a short snore.

'Hey, Titus! Have you fallen asleep? You can't sleep now. Hey!' says Lenny.

Titus doesn't respond. Must play for time, reload. Soon they will expose him.

'Titus? Are you there?' Now it is Eddie who wants to know.

No answer. Heavy breathing.

'He is beyond salvation,' Eddie sighs. 'It's rather sad, isn't it?'

'It is fucking crazy. He just zonked out. Must be totally sloshed.'

Eddis tears himself away from his mirror image and goes up to Titus. He gives him a gentle shake.

'Titus…?'

No response.

'TITUS!'

Eddie gets hold of Titus' jacket lapel and pulls him up. Titus' head hangs backwards. A little string of saliva runs out of his open mouth. His body is totally limp. All his strength goes into being out of reach.

The stakes are high, Titus knows that. But it is a case of make or break. Snore.

Eddie lets go of him. Leans over Titus' ear and says in a calm and friendly tone:

'Titus, I'll come and wake you five minutes before it's time for your entrance. In about half an hour. It's going to be fine. You'll manage it.'

'What the fuck! Are we just going to let him lie here?' is Lenny's loud contribution as he pokes Titus in his side.

'What choice do we have?'

'Yeah, well we can phone a hospital and ask them to send an ambulance. The guy is unconscious, you can see that!'

'Get a hold of yourself, damn you! So that they would send him to some fucking rehab clinic, or what?'

What was that? Titus reacts in his pretend torpor. A new tone. Titus has never before heard Eddie raise his voice against anybody. What's going on?

Titus hears that they leave him and move towards the door. It sounds as if they are pushing and shoving each other.

Titus decides to sneak a look and opens a minimal slit between his eyelids. He peeps out. What is happening?

Lenny stands by the door with his hand on the door knob. He is on his way out. Eddie is standing next to him. Legs apart, his arms crossed. Keeping the door closed with his foot. A tense situation.

'I just thought…' Lenny attempts.

'Don't fucking think anything,' Eddie hisses and pushes Lenny up against the door. 'If you let me down then I'll reveal the whole bloody mess. Then you are – *in deep shit.*'

'Yeees... or no. I mean, of course I'll do it for you. I'll pump him. I promised I would.'

Eddie X has the underside of the lower part of his arm up against Lenny's throat. He applies some pressure, hard and for a long time. His arm is trembling with rage. The knuckles on his clenched fist have gone all white. His jaw is tense. His upper lip twitches. A vein throbs on his forehead. Eddie is no longer handsome, just angry, extremely angry. With his teeth together, he hisses:

'You're going to help me see this project through. I have read more than half and it could just as well be my own words. It was fucking well my idea from the very first. That bastard has nicked it all. We must do whatever is necessary, do you get that? Whatever the cost.'

Lenny looks frightened. His eyes wide open, he stares at Eddie and nods.

Titus stares too, with his millimetre eye, from the sofa.

The fury.

Romantic poets can evidently have many sides to them.

When Astra gets out of the taxi outside the theatre, the square is almost deserted. It is a few minutes past eight and the festival has already begun. She hurries up the stairs and goes to the box office. She's lucky, there are still a few tickets left. The upper gallery, next to the spotlight ramp. Might be a bit hot there, but she can see and hear well. Only 190 kronor.

'I'll take it,' says Astra, and pays.

The opening act is something of a highlight: Legendary jazz and groove poet Gil Scott-Heron is on stage. The man behind classics like *Home Is Where The Hatred Is* and *Whitey On The Moon* gets the adrenalin going in the magnificent theatre auditorium. He is the opening act and will also

211

close the evening as the final act. In the 1960s and 1970s, he made a name for himself for his militant stance in the Afro-American liberation struggle. During his entire artistic career he has fought against injustice and discrimination by reading and singing revolutionary texts to funky background music. Lots of people regard Gil Scott-Heron as the father of hip hop, although he personally hates the way a large part of black music over the last twenty years has treated women in such a degrading manner. It is both sad and degrading that a people who have been the victims of apartheid can't raise themselves above the standard of their oppressors.

When Astra takes her seat, the whole auditorium is already on the verge of meltdown. Gil Scott-Heron's time machine has thrown the public back to 1970, a time when the revolution was raging. The old legend stands alone on the dark stage with only one spotlight right above him. He looks like a scarecrow: grey beard, grey jacket, black shirt, black leather cap. Everything is too large, too sack-like. Funky background music with bongo drums, lazy bass and indecent transverse flute. His head bent slightly forward towards the mike. You can't see his eyes. A hoarse, feverish voice. One hand gripping the mike stand. His other clenched fist up in the air, out towards the auditorium. Black power.

Astra just manages to hear the final words. Gil-Scott Heron's warm-up.

Whistling, cheers and foot stamping on the floor. The ovation seems to go on forever. Everybody loves what they have just experienced. Imagine, actually hearing *The Revolution Will Not Be Televised* live! Admittedly, more than thirty years after the event, but even so. This is the best revolutionary song in the world!

Tomorrow the audience will be back at their jobs earning the money to pay the interest on their mortgages for their expensive homes. But this evening they are all of them activists who can and want to change the world, and those who now and then hope there will be a revolution do at least have more fun than those who never hope for anything. Particularly when they do it together.

It is an enchanted evening.

After Gil Scott-Heron's magical opening, a stable and decent programme follows. The themes spread wildly and the performances are about everything from freedom of expression to sex. Eddie X does a great job as MC and manages to get the wild programme to hang together in a neat and warming way. He also reads some of his own poems in the intervals. Love spreads. The audience are delighted in their seats.

Astra thinks about Titus and wonders how he will manage the evening. It ought to be time for his appearance soon. She knows how confused and irritable he has been the last few weeks. Can he really manage to be teetotal and to stand up in front of a whole theatre auditorium filled with people who demand to be entertained? As long as they don't do that gimmick with the luggage trolley. Please, please, no trolley!

Now Eddie X returns yet again to the stage, his arms opened wide towards the public. He walks slowly up to the microphone and smiles.

'Dear audience! With us this evening we have a Swedish classic, as angry as Strindberg and as black as Norén. Yes, now, of course, you understand to whom I am referring. Perhaps you have already seen him read something from our unknown literary treasure trove earlier. Perhaps you have only heard about these celebrated literary occasions. Whatever, here he is – the full-blood writer, half pain, half blackness! My friends, please give a warm welcome to – Titus Jensen!'

Then a flashing stroboscope light starts up. The bass beat from White Stripes' *Seven Nation Army* booms out of the loud-speakers. Eddie looks as if he is jerking in the flashing white light although he is standing completely still.

From off-stage Lenny comes in wheeling a black-clad Titus standing on a yellow baggage trolley. He does a few laps of the stage to audience applause and laughter. A lot of people know what to expect. As Titus is brought up to the front of the stage and the microphone the music goes quiet and the usual spotlights replace the flashing lights. When Lenny stands the trolley up and tips off his load, Titus takes a couple of unsteady steps out on to the stage floor. He screws up his eyes against the light, holding his hand like a peaked cap to shade them. He sways slightly, his mouth open and slack, drunk as a lord and high as a pylon. He is embarrassing and hair-raising at same time. Is he going to pull this off? Giggles and laughter in the audience.

Astra puts a hand on her brow and squirms in an effort to shake off the repugnance she feels. This is just crazy, she thinks. How can people find this funny? Bloody parasites.

And what should she do now? If Titus has broken his promise of temperance then the book project is a write-off, that much is obvious. The manuscript will never be ready in time and Evita will cut off the funding the second she hears what has happened. Damn and blast, and after she had invested so much time in that blithering idiot.

Eddie rests his arm on Titus' shoulders. He looks at the audience but speaks to Titus.

'Hello, Titus.'

'Hello.'

'Nice to see you here!'

'Mmmm.'

'And now you are going to read for us?'

'Thank you.'

'What are you going to read?'

'Don't know.'

'Is it in Swedish, do you think?'

'Don't know.'

'Is it something good, do you think?'

'Don't know.'

'Do you want to know what we have chosen for you?'

'Okay.'

'We have chosen a fantastic book from the literary treasure trove, a rarity we found earlier today at an antiquarian bookseller's just near here. The book is called *What a Young Husband Ought to Know*. It was written by the American moral preacher and doctor of theology Sylvanus Stall about one hundred years ago and was translated into Swedish in 1930. Take it away, Titus!'

Eddie X puts a fancy little volume with a half-calf binding into Titus' hand, and backs off the stage. Titus remains standing alone together with the motionless microphone stand. There is an expectant silence in the auditorium.

Titus opens the book and looks at some random pages.

'Oh goodness, what tiiiiny print! Were people smaller in the old days?'

Laughter immediately. The audience has decided: this is going to be fun.

Titus digs out a pair of reading spectacles from his pocket and places them on the tip of his nose. He clears his throat and starts to read like an old Sunday school teacher in a 1930s film.

'Chapter Nine: about your future bride! "It is necessary now to call the attention of young husbands to the fact that in women there exists less sexual desire and satisfaction than in man. Perhaps of the great majority of women it would be

215

true to say that they are largely devoid of sexual pleasure."'

Titus exaggerates the 'e' in all words containing the syllable 'sex', making the words even more ridiculous than they already are. Seeeexual desire and seeeexual pleasure. This attracts howls of laughter from the audience.

Astra doesn't laugh. She sits there with her arms tightly would around her chest, as if in a straitjacket. She thinks that what she is seeing is quite simply the worst sort of humour, based on people's disabilities.

"'In regard to the seeeexual intensity of the seeeexual instinct, women might with some accuracy be divided into three classes. The first class, which includes the larger number, is generally supposed to be quite devoid of seeeexual inclination and feeling. The second class is composed of women who find in the marital relation a moderate and nooormal pleasure when they are in health, and if indulged in at times which are agreeable to them, and at suitable intervals."'

Titus is now up and running, Astra can see that. And the audience is with him. They laugh every time Titus pronounces something in a particularly funny or emphatic way. He stands erect and does actually manage to express a little human pride, despite everything. That's something at least, Astra thinks.

After a short pause for effect, he holds the book theatrically at an arm's distance and continues to read in a clear and distinct voice:

'And, my friends: "The third class represents the few in whom seeeexuality presides as a ruling passion. This class is by no means as numerous as some might imagine and such women should never be married except to men of good health, strong physique, large powers of endurance, and with a *pronounced* seeeexual inclination."'

Titus gives an exaggerated bow and gains applause. He turns the pages to a new passage in the book. Now he has really got up steam. He stands, legs apart, and glows with self-confidence. Astra relaxes a little. This is actually slightly amusing. Bloody stupid, but amusing.

"'Chapter Four: Essentials in husband and home. If your wife is to have a fair chance for a pleasant home and a happy and useful life, she will need a husband who can sacrifice his personal luxuries and self-indulgences in order that he may share with her and the family the comforts and blessings of their home – a man who will scorn the saloon, avoid the club, remain away from the lodge, *give up his cigar*, and spend his time and his money for the comfort and happiness of his family.'"

Even Titus laughs while reading. He never usually does that. Astra starts to think that Titus' eyes are shining in an extremely alert manner. Is he really sloshed? He doesn't look particularly intoxicated any more.

Titus turns the pages again and sticks his finger in at random.

"'Do not stimulate impure thinking by theatre-going , the reading of *salacious* books, participation in the round dance, the presence of *nude statuary and suggestive pictures*; avoid such bodily exposure and postures as mar the modesty of both man and woman. Marital moderation is most easily secured and maintained where married persons occupy separate beds; and, indeed, in many instances such conditions exist as render separate rooms not only desirable, but essential. Mr E.B.Duffey says: 'If the husband cannot properly *control his amorous propensities* they had better by all means occupy separate beds and different apartments, with a lock on the communicating door, the key in the wife's possession.'"

Yet again, time for a brief rhetorical pause. Titus looks out over the auditorium with a broad smile. Astra thinks that he seems to be enjoying himself. The audience is also in good form; they belong to a laid-back generation that can laugh at historic stupidities instead of being shocked.

A young black-clad couple on the front row have stood up holding hands and are reaching out their hands towards Titus. Some sort of message is written along their arms. They are jumping, dancing and look as if they love Titus more than anyone else on the planet. To think that Titus can arouse such emotions! That is something new.

His gaze searches up over the balconies, right up to the gallery where Astra is sitting. She gets the impression that he is looking for her, and they make eye contact, Astra is almost certain of that. What was that, did he see her, did he give a wink? Titus' gaze wanders further over the audience as if he is searching for somebody. But surely that was a wink? At least it was some sort of signal.

Titus reads some more short passages from the past ages of the moral preacher, before suddenly shouting:

'Now listen, here comes the last verse from our very own doctor of theology, Sylvanus Stall. Are you with me?'

The audience stands up, their hands in the air with fingers pointing towards the ceiling, stamping the floor. Titus Jensen is king.

'"Seeeexual excess is one of the most destructive forms of intemperance, degrading alike the body, mind and morals." So think about that, girls and boys – go home and fuck each other this evening! Have a nice time! Thank you for listening to me, my name is Titus Jensen. Today and for ever and ever!'

Shouts of laughter and applause. This was one of the high-lights of the evening, most of the audience agrees about that. Even Astra thinks that Titus made a good job of it. Perhaps these spontaneous readings are not quite as degrading when you get down to it; the public is laughing just as much at the ridiculous texts as they are at Titus. But of course it is pathetic that nobody cares about his own texts. Why can't they pass muster for a festival like this? They are just as good as most of what she has heard this evening, that's for sure. She decides to seek out Titus when the programme is finished. It is time to normalise their relationship again and besides, she must find out whether he really has broken his temperance vows.

After the festival, several of the performers and a large part of the audience hang around in the upper foyer and in the vicinity of the bar in the middle of the room. Since the weather is so nice and the evening warm, the enormous terrace outside is open, too.

Eddie X is holding court around a table in one corner of the terrace. He has had a good evening even though the energy drained away somewhat after Titus' climax. Eddie's interval act simply didn't strike home like it usually did.

Various refreshments are available on a large tray in the middle of the table. Titus has managed to fill his glass with something that looks like a large gin and tonic with lemon – without adding a single drop of gin. He bellows in time with his fellow revellers. His nervousness has gone and now it is as easy as pie to act drunk. He is sitting next to Lenny who is comparatively relaxed and doesn't have to shout out expletives all the time. Lenny is fairly drunk too, but for real. He twitches and stutters much less than usual, almost as though alcohol alleviates Tourette's, Titus thinks.

'F...fucking hell, you were really great,' Lenny yells. 'I don't think I've ever seen you read so bloody well.'

'Fanks, it was blooody fun,' says Titus, slurring his words.

'Fuck, Titus. You are almost a popular hero now, after all your readings. Aren't you going to write a new book now, so you can cash in on your popularity?'

'Yeah, purrhaps, purrhaps…'

'What, are you working on something new?'

'You never know…' says Titus, and tries to avoid going into the subject.

'What is it? What are you writing now? Tell me!'

'Well it isn't anything. I'm not working on anything special.'

'Ah, come off it, pull the other one!' Lenny counters. 'We have hardly seen you all summer. You must have something in the works. What is your book about?'

'One thing and another. Nothing special. Let's talk about something else.'

'Oh no, that's interesting. What are you writing about? I want to know.'

Titus wonders why Lenny is suddenly so overly interested in his writing. What plans are he and Eddie cooking up? Are they going to try to steal his ideas? The conspiracy theories wash over him again. But who would believe him? He needs concrete evidence before he goes to Astra and Evita and tells them that Eddie X and the Babelfish publishing house are going to produce their own genre-transcending book. Or should he go directly to the police? He is not sure if they care about immaterial theft. Just think how the MP3 pirates knocked out the entire record industry without the police so much as lifting a finger to help them. He looks quickly across the table to see what Eddie is busy with.

Eddie is sitting with his legs wide apart on his chair and with his arms behind his head. He's talking to Astra, who is standing next to him on high heels with her expensive handbag in a firm grip. Cautious, not to say suspicious. She looks extremely attractive this evening, a summery tan and with heavy black eyeshadow. Dressed for business, but with rather too many undone buttons on her blouse to suit a dusty meeting at the office.

Astra! Is she here? Then she must be convinced I'm drunk and have broken the contract, Titus thinks. In a slurring voice, he mutters something to Lenny about coming back and then rushes up to Astra.

'Astra! Astra, I must talk to you!'

'Nice to see you too,' says Astra and gives Titus the most tired of looks. She really wants to keep a certain distance from him, otherwise he will completely devour her with his manic behaviour. But she follows along when Titus pulls her over to an empty part of the terrace.

'Astra, listen to me now. I am one hundred per cent sober. I'm just pretending to be drunk so that they won't know I'm alert and writing again.'

Astra gives a laugh.

'Pretending to be drunk!? Come off it, are you twelve years old or what? Get a grip, Titus.'

'I promise. Have a sniff.'

He leans over her face and breathes out for all he is worth over her nose. She gives a start. It doesn't smell particularly nice. But sloshed? No, it doesn't actually smell like that.

'Why are you behaving like this?' Astra pushes Titus' face away from her.

'I must. They can't be allowed to find out anything.'

'Who can't? What are you talking about?'

'Eddie. And Lenny too, I think. I'm not sure. Something is going on there. They keep on pumping me about the book. They know something. And Eddie is not at all who you think he is. He is dangerous. Beware of him.'

'But...'

She doesn't have time to find out what Titus is babbling about. The velvet-eyed Eddie X has suddenly sneaked up behind her and put his arm around her waist. A feeling like a minor electric shock goes through her body and she remembers the moments among the eiderdowns on board the yacht. Life is complicated, nobody can say otherwise.

'Having a conference?' says Eddie and gives her a warm smile.

'Mmmm,' mutters Titus, who returns to his strategy of rationing his words.

'I didn't have a chance to ask you what you thought about the evening, Astra?'

'A success, Eddie. Really. Well done,' says Astra in a cautious tone.

'Thanks. Come and sit with us. There's some food coming in soon. Or, rather, "out". There's some food coming *out* soon,' says Eddie, and indicates the open night sky above them. 'I have longed to see you, Astra. I'd like to talk to you.'

He puts his hand on her arm, stroking it softly.

Astra thaws a little more and agrees. A lot of things need to be sorted out. Even though she has buried herself in work the last few weeks, she hasn't been able to forget what actually happened. Who has said what and to whom? Has Eddie really boasted to Lenny about how he would seduce her? Or was it Titus' abstinence that created such figments of the imagination? She doesn't doubt one second that Titus is unreliable. The very idea of calling Eddie "dangerous", for example. Ridiculous…

Once back at the table, Eddie devours Astra with his attention. They eat tapas, drink wine and chat together. Eddie is very interested in every detail of Astra's life. She feels as if she is really being seen for who she is. Slowly but surely, Eddie builds up his credibility again. Eventually, Astra also gets the answer to her question.

'Yes, it's true that I told Lenny how much I love you. And you know how he is, as soon as you say something serious he gets all nervous and starts swearing and twitching. Makes dirty gestures. Exaggerates. He can't do serious. If something becomes genuine and for real, he just wants to run away and talk drivel. I don't know how he has dealt with what I shared with him. I can imagine that he has said that to Titus. Yeah, told him I had said that. But of course I haven't.'

'Why does he behave like that?'

'I think it is from his childhood. His dad is a famous psychologist or psychiatrist or whatever it's called. He could never really accept that his own child could have Tourette's syndrome. I suppose he thought that he gave his son all the love and security he could. Yeah, he probably thought that Lenny shouldn't have Tourette's syndrome quite simply. But he does, whatever you say. Lenny's dad didn't even manage to alleviate the problem; I think that was what caused the problem.'

'No, you could say that again. The problem is far from being alleviated,' Astra cuts in. She has never really discovered what made Lenny tick. She thinks on the whole that he is weird and she has always found it hard to understand the greatness in the noisy music made by The Tourettes.

'Lenny always felt that his dad didn't take his situation seriously,' Eddie goes on. 'It was nearly always his patients that got all the attention. In the end, Lenny himself gave up trying to combat his Tourette's and started to accept his situation instead. Tourette's came to be his best friend, you might say. He let it go into full bloom. He opened all the taps, just let it run freely. Tourette's has made him what he is today. Today he is respected for the man he is. He wouldn't be anything without his syndrome.'

'And his dad? What happened to him?'

'I don't know. They don't have any contact today, haven't spoken to each other for many years. Perhaps the guy is even dead. Yeah, I think he probably is. I am convinced that Lenny doesn't actually care.'

'Sad.'

'Perhaps, perhaps not. The important thing is that Lenny can be who he really is, don't you think?'

They look across the table towards Lenny where he's sitting with his tics and talking to Titus and some others. He gesticulates and yells, laughs and swears. He looks as if he is having a whale of a time.

Titus, however, looks tired and keeps sneaking looks at Astra and Eddie X. He tries to attract her attention with his gaze. He has been doing it for quite some time.

'Pah, I can't cope with his puppy dog eyes any more!' Astra says to Eddie. 'He is always under my skin, it's driving me crazy.'

Eddie looks at her, surprised.

'I thought you loved Titus?'

Astra laughs.

'Love? Haha, no I am just his publisher, not his mother. No thanks, I don't want a whole load of emotions when I'm working.'

They sit in silence for a few moments. Astra doesn't know which thread she should unravel to find a more amusing subject of conversation. Eddie puts his hand on hers, a gesture of joint understanding.

'So you also think he has changed?' he says in a low hiss, and sneaks a dark look at Titus.

Astra reacts to his sudden hissing. She doesn't recognise that. She pulls her hand away.

'Changed?'

'Yeah, don't you notice how everybody looks at him,' Eddie goes on with growing anger in his voice. 'He is a superhero this evening. Before, he was a clown when he did his readings. Now people love him. Did you see how the audience cheered him?'

'But that's good, isn't it?'

Eddie snorts.

'Good? They hardly paid any attention to me this evening. It was just Titus, Titus, Titus, right across the board. And did you hear that he almost started talking about love? It isn't Titus who should talk about love, it's me!'

Eddie doesn't look Astra in the eye. Instead he is blinking feverishly and staring at Titus, clenching his fists so that his knuckles go all white.

'Can't you see how he's draining me? He stole me, he's emptying me! He's crawling into me, he's filling all my senses with his stinking blackness, and he just stands over there and smiles with his rosy cheeks. I fucking hate it!'

Astra looks at Eddie with growing amazement. Something seems to have cracked inside him. Nasty marsh gases are hissing out of Eddie X the love poet. How the hell could she ever have felt attracted to him?

These bloody artistes. She must get away. Quickly.

Titus sees Astra suddenly leave the party. She looks tired and irritated. A pity, he had hoped to talk a little more with her. Now there is nothing else to keep him here at the party. He decides to set off for home. He is dead tired and looking forward to having a moment to himself. He hasn't had so many social contacts for months. How did he manage it before, when he was nearly always at parties?

Titus says 'See you, then' to Lenny, who insists on following along a bit of the way, even though he is a bit unsteady on his legs on account of all the gin.

'Okay, let's go,' says Lenny.

Might be a good thing, thinks Titus. Now I can try to pump him about that break-in and what sort of mischief he and Eddie are up to.

They set off together down the narrow alleys. Near Hornstull they meet a bunch of Hammarby supporters with their green and white scarves. They joyfully greet Lenny and Titus as if it was obvious that the only thing people are thinking just now is that Hammarby has won a home match at the Söder stadium. Yes, this is a good day for Stockholm. Warm weather, a football victory and a legendary Spoken Word evening – could it be better?

Titus is most satisfied with his evening. He has delivered a top-notch reading and got paid 4,000 kronor cash. He'll be able to live on that for a while. The only fly in the ointment was that Astra and Eddie spent so much time together; he really hopes that Astra has listened to his warnings. In his heart he wants to believe that she is on his side.

Somebody calls his name from across the street. Titus turns around. He sees the young couple from the steps, the two who sat right at the front and who were so enthusiastic when he read. They each blow him a kiss, and give him a smile. He waves back, slightly embarrassed, puts his hand over his heart and gives a little bow. Just think: they became a couple thanks to him!

Titus couldn't be bothered to pretend to be drunk any longer. Anyway, Lenny is so sloshed that he won't notice. He decides to be direct, sink or swim.

'Lenny, I was wondering…'

'Yeah?'

'What exactly are you and Eddie up to?'

Lenny stops in his tracks and looks stupidly at Titus.

'What, how do you know?'

'I just know. But why?'

'I don't know. Eddie wanted to. It wasn't me.'

'Come off it. I saw you running away!'

'Yeah, well, I mean, it was me who was there. But it was Eddie's idea.'

'But why? What does he want?'

'I can't tell you, Titus. It's impossible, I've promised Eddie. But I was only inside your place a few minutes. I didn't take a single thing, I promise. I just looked.'

'For what? Tell me what you are up to! Admit that you are spying on me!'

'I can't say any more. Stop it now. Stop it! You are the one who must talk. Now you must talk. I have promised. Please. Talk now!'

And Lenny continues the same pestering that he has been busy with all evening. What is Titus writing? How far has he got? Will it be good? What is it about? How many people know what he is writing?

Lenny goes on and on about it, but doesn't hear that Titus never answers any of his questions. There is just Lenny's monotonous one-way nagging, completely without interactivity. This is a sort of admittance of guilt too, Titus thinks, otherwise why would he keep on with these stubborn efforts to try to discover what Titus is writing? Yes, there is absolutely no doubt about it: Eddie and Lenny are in the midst of a gigantic coup. They seem to think that they can steal the copyright to a literary work. Idiots. Nutters. Small fry. Don't they realise that they're too late? He has virtually finished. It is just a matter of days and then it will start: the long success story of *The Best Book in the World*, with Titus Jensen on the cover.

He looks at Lenny. Suddenly it strikes him.

Lenny is not stuttering.

Lenny is not twitching.

He is not even swearing.

He has… recovered?

CHAPTER 31

The Law of Happy Endings

There is a cup of steaming-hot herbal tea beside Titus' computer. He has slept a long time and now feels rested and strong. He isn't afraid of Eddie X any longer. Eddie and Lenny are just a couple of clowns, they can't get at him now. It's too late. When this summer started, he was a pathetic wretch. Now he is strong. And he is going to retain that strength.

The autumn sun sits lower and lower in the sky each day. A few rays find their way across the rooftops and into Titus' dark flat. He blows into the breathalyser lock and the computer welcomes him in just as friendly a tone as usual:

Hello Titus! According to my calculations you only have three pages left to complete your manuscript. Contact your publisher as soon as you have finished. Congratulations!

Titus feels as if he has been reincarnated. He is going to complete the project of his life. A crazy project in which he has had 250 pages to pack in lots of handy facts and practical lists, and a knockout blow to the jaw of hair-raising tension. A straight right from the left side of his brain and a left hook from the right.

Before he writes the final chapter, he must make a list of the ten best revolutionary songs in the world, which he will let Chief Inspector Håkan Rink have as his 'Revolt' playlist on his iPod:

The Revolution Will Not Be Televised	Clampdown
Imagine	Eve of Destruction
Get Up, Stand Up	Blowin' in the Wind
We Shall Overcome	Minority
Last Night I Had the Strangest Dream	Diamonds From Sierra Leone

Titus takes a deep breath. Now he is getting close.

There is really only one thing that publishers, manuscript experts and reviewers all agree upon: a book must have an end that gives rise to hope. Even if the story is dark and dismal, there must be a grain of a happy ending that gives nourishment to life's optimists. If a book doesn't have a happy ending, it will die a natural death. Un-reviewed, un-read and un-sold. The Law of Happy Endings is an ancient truth that can't be challenged.

But Titus refuses to deviate from his perfect sense of pitch. He has decided to turn his back on all the experts who think they can judge his work of art better than he can himself. He will leave it to the readers to decide what is consolation or despair. Over-explicitness kills and he is certainly no murderer: quite the contrary. Hope is strong and distinct in all the lists, recipes, tips and facts that run through the book. He hands out lots of matchboxes, but never pokes his finger in the reader's tummy. It is up to each and every reader to decide which candles they will light in their lives. But if you follow all the advice there is every possibility of becoming a complete human being, of that he is certain. It is, after all, *The Best Book in the World* that he has written. The actual plot around Chief Inspector Håkan Rink and Serial Salvador, however, has an uncompromising brutality to it. Because that is what life looks like too.

He who has seen the darkness, will be the first to see the light, he thinks.

Oh, how he delights in his own ability to express himself. Today, he is really good.

He has long since abandoned the idea of letting his personal vendetta against Eddie X blemish the end of the book. He has come further in his personal development. For a long time, revenge provided good motivation to write, but now he chooses to stand above the instinctive desire to defend himself. He is hardly aware any more that Serial Salvador has borrowed characteristics from Eddie X.

The Best Book in the World is not a meta project, disguising itself as a story about another story with complicated and obscure sub-texts. *The Best Book in the World* is a simply narrated and well put-together reference work about life. It is exciting, useful and helps to develop the reader's personality. And yet the whole work rises above the level of everyday life and reality. Together, the disparate texts form a pattern. They become – literature.

I have bared my soul, thinks Titus. I have turned the other cheek. Now I am empty.

The tears splash onto the keyboard while he slowly and solemnly types the very last chapter.

The big Entrepreneurs' Gala is to be broadcast live as usual on TV4.

Cool as ice, Håkan Rink counted on the information being correct. The source seemed highly credible even though the tip-off came late.

Serial Salvador would come to the Entrepreneurs' Gala. He had purchased an unnumbered ticket the day before the gala. Unfortunately that meant that he couldn't be checked against a list. The only thing the police knew at the moment was that he would most likely sit somewhere on the ten rearmost rows which were not reserved. Also, the old description was no longer valid. He had altered his appearance again. But the source was absolutely certain that his information was correct. You couldn't mistake those eyes. Brown velvet.

There had been little time but the Stockholm police force had managed to arrange it all. The effort was planned down to the tiniest detail. Rink's men were posted on every second row in a zigzag pattern. When they had identified him, they could nab him easily. As soon as the prizes had been awarded and the cameras turned off, that would be the end.

Håkan Rink himself was invited to present the prize in the most prestigious category – Entrepreneur of the Year. He had considered whether it was suitable to mix his roles. On the one hand, a hard-working detective chief inspector who needed peace and quiet to be able to focus on his task; on the other, a public security alibi from a pressured police force which was forced to deliver very soon. The sand in the hour-glass of patience was running out. But the triumph of being able to stand on the stage and perhaps even establish eye-contact with Serial Salvador moments before he would be rendered harmless had got the better of him. It would go well. It usually did.

When the spotlights were pointed towards him, he could immediately feel the heat. The audience cheered.

From the loudspeakers: 'A warm applause for Håkan Rink, Sweden's toughest detective chief inspector!'

He took some quick and light steps up to the podium at the front of the stage. His leather jacket glowed in the light. He screwed up his eyes against the spotlights and waited for the applause to die down, raised his hand and leaned over the microphone. Bass voice.

'This is the most important prize in Sweden. I am extremely proud to have been entrusted with this presentation. It is you entrepreneurs who shall make the future more secure for our children. It is you who shall save the planet from pollution. One can summarise what you do in five letters: G-R-E-A-T. As in a great job!'

The audience was familiar with Håkan Rink's predilection for combinations of letters, and they had a good laugh at his hearty self-irony. The mood was the very best.

Håkan Rink smiled at the spotlights.

He took hold of the rope which controlled the curtain in front of the big screen where the nominations in the very best class would be presented.

'And the nominated are...'

All cameras and spotlights were pointed at the stage. The lighting was excellent.

Håkan Rink gave the rope a firm tug.

With a crash, something large and heavy fell from the ceiling above the stage. The chief inspector ducked quick as a flash and shielded his face. A short murmur came from the audience before the terrified screams broke out.

A man hung from an enormous upside-down crutch suspended from the ceiling. He had a thin rope around his neck which was tied across the arms of the crutch. The body jerked in severe spasms. The large brown eyes stared hard at Håkan Rink. A long

232

mane of black hair hung like a curtain from his face, weirdly dyed strands of hair. His wrists were tightly handcuffed and the man beat his arms wildly against his own stomach. Perhaps he wanted to free himself. Perhaps he was trying to get his body to swing even more.

The volume of the screams lessened a little when the spectators realised that there were no explosions or shots in a second shock wave. This wasn't a terror attack. This was something else.

The man swayed slowly above the stage in the glow of the spotlights. His feet jerked violently for a further few seconds. The most clearheaded members of the audience tried to get their breath back and leave the rows of seats to reach the exits. Others held their hands in front on their eyes in a naive attempt to avoid being there. Panic vibrated in the air. The police had to struggle with the fleeing audience to approach the stage.

His eyes stared. His mouth smiled. There were no more jerks.

A beautiful corpse in a well-lit setting.

Serial Salvador's final work of art was a fact. Death had finally made him immortal.

Håkan Rink too became historic. The national hangman. The man who re-introduced the death penalty on one occasion.

Live on TV. During peak viewing hours.

CHAPTER 32

Autumn Leaves

Titus Jensen looks out of the window.

The lady on the balcony is busy tidying her flower tubs. The first night frost will come soon. She must save the plants and put them in her chipped winter pots. She does that every autumn. She puts the pots on the marble windowsill slabs, together with all the framed photos from bygone days. The plants will winter there and remind the old lady of the past life that might come back and visit if only she takes care of her memories. Her wrinkled face breaks into a cautious smile. Every time she remembers, she becomes beautiful in her curly and grey-white frame. She pulls off some dry leaves, lets the wind catch them, and follows them with her gaze as they fly away.

In the up-winds along the house facades, the plant leaves join the first autumn leaves, the yellow leaves from the outermost branches of the trees which have suffered so much in the summer sun and are now forced to capitulate even though it is still early September. Their safe and green sister leaves closer to the tree trunk, which still have a month or so to live, have not experienced half as much. They have only stared at one another all spring and summer, safe and dependent on the never-ending supply of nutrients from their thick mother branch. Inside, there amidst the cool greenery, they rustled in dignity now and then when the wind tore at their wild brothers and sisters on the tips of the branches. They have remained nice and green all the

234

time, but oh how boring it has been! Now the leaves that have lived a life are sailing away in the wind, down to the lawns and borders where they will compost themselves while waiting for reincarnation. They are going to come back, younger and wilder than ever. Next time they will find themselves even further out on the branch, experience even more.

The old lady looks sad, although she is smiling. A lot of leaves have left her. Perhaps she too will want to become soil. Perhaps she too will want to become young again.

Titus looks at the lady. In some ways he can understand her situation. But at the same time it is sad to just look back. All that we have is now and the future. Everything else is history. I am where I want to be, he thinks. Money? Yes, certainly. Appreciation? Guaranteed. Women? Absolutely. The memory card with *The Best Book in the World* on it contains everything he needs to be happy.

For the time being he can't write another word. He has run out of energy. He knows that he must eventually return to the manuscript and alter it when Astra and the editor have read though it carefully and made their comments. He wants to walk through Stockholm before the autumn makes the city grey and cold.

Astra's telephone answering machine:

'Hello. You have reached Astra Larsson at Winchester Publishing. Please leave a message after the beep and have a nice day.'

Beeep

'Hi Astra, Titus here. I'm on my way in now, hope you are there. I have finished. I'll bring the memory card with the manuscript. I'll keep the computer as I assume there will be a few rounds of editing later in the autumn. But I think the book is actually pretty good quality already, so I'm on my way in now. See you soon. Very soon. Kiss.'

Kiss? Where did he get that from? Jesus! So unprofessional! As if he was talking to his old mum. He blames it on the fact that his emotions are so vulnerable after a long and intensive working period. Astra will surely excuse him; she ought to understand what he has gone through. He has worked virtually every day all summer with his manuscript. Work – six hours, break – two hours. Work – six hours, break – two hours. Day after day. He did it.

He goes into his little bathroom and gets undressed. He stands naked in front of the tiny bathroom mirror and shaves his head with great precision. He trims his beard down to one millimetre and notes that his beard growth is acquiring an increasingly grey hue, not that it matters. He takes a quick shower in cool water and uses a file on his feet, something he has started to do this summer. Before, he hadn't even noticed that his heels had cracks. He dries himself thoroughly, even between his toes, and rubs in a rich moisturiser all over his body, this too a new ritual. He puts on a newly ironed black shirt and black suit from the wardrobe. He looks strong, handsome even. He walks up to the computer, puts the lid down and says 'Sleep tight'.

Locks the door. Chooses the stairs rather than the lift. Is aware of every step he takes. Feels the energy returning. This is one of the most important days in his life. Now he understands what it feels like to be on the way to a maternity unit. He faces a tense situation with a forced calm. If you are going to retain control, then you must go easy on expressing your emotions. Should he allow himself the luxury of a taxi in honour of the day? Say to the driver: 'Take me to Winchester Publishers. Make it quick, a novel is about to be published!' He smiles a little at himself when he gets down in the entrance hall.

But what is that smell?

Something isn't quite right.

A damp wetness settles on his face. The entrance hall goes black. Tiredness strikes quickly like the blow from an axe. He can't walk to Winchester Publishing. He can't even take a taxi. He must sleep instead. He tries to fight it. He *wants* to go to see Astra! Tries to shout out to her but gets cloth in his mouth. Takes a deep breath with his nose which is almost free. A pungent aroma. More dampness. No more air. Cloth in his nostrils too, like a wet hot towel in his face. Or a rag. His eyes smart. They are bleeding. He is forced to close his eyes under the dampness. Even more tired. Must rest. Falling. Tries to wave his arms to retain his balance. They are stuck to his body. Rough cloth around his body. First it was his shoulders. Now his legs. Everything is just stuck. Tight fit. Belts everywhere. Or ropes. Tighter and tighter. Round all of him. That's nice. Relaxes. He's going to sleep now. His legs leave the ground. He is an autumn leaf. He flies off. Or is carried. Sleep tight.

CHAPTER 33

Country Life

Astra is in a meeting at the office. They are talking about the programme for the imminent book fair and going through all the signings and programmes that their authors will be attending. The Gothenburg Book Fair is unique because both professionals and the public are welcome. That creates a special atmosphere and gives the book industry a unique gauge of what readers actually value. But for the publishing houses the fair is a comprehensive apparatus that costs a frightful amount of money. Nothing can be left to chance. For example, all the authors must eat well and stay at the most expensive hotel – they can't have different hotels for different authors, since officially they are all worth the same. Obviously, the bestsellers must have decent accommodation and that means all the 'cultural' authors automatically get the same treatment. So they must slim down the production and maximise every hour that an author is at the fair. Once there, every author will have a permanent companion from their publishing house to guide them around the fair floor between various signings, seminars and interviews. So they need lots of people from Winchester Publishing at the fair, but when it comes to their 'staff' accommodation a strict hierarchy applies: the bosses stay on the top floor of the fair hotel in the city centre while the plebs are spread out in rings around the city, according to their rank.

Winchester Publishing has a strong list this autumn, and the highlights will be presented at the book fair. Their competitors have lots of exciting things to present too. In addition, the fair will be hosting several interesting authors from abroad. There will be a delightful mix of high and low, from the lightest entertainment to unknown poets who write in dying languages – just what your average cultural consumer wants to read and hear the latest about. It is extremely likely that there will be (again) a record number of accredited journalists. Those who claim that literature is a dying medium have never been to the Gothenburg Book Fair.

Astra has got so far in her career that she has a fairly free programme at the fair. She is going to chair a couple of mini-seminars, host some dinners and help the agents at the international rights centre to present some really heavyweight titles.

She has put her phone next to the big planning calendar and sees when it starts to vibrate. Looks who is phoning. Titus, oh well. He can wait. The phone signals that the answering machine has recorded a message.

After a while, Evita looks in through the door.

'Astra, can I borrow you a moment…? There's something I need to ask you.'

'Sure.'

Astra gets up and takes her phone with her. She is going to check what Titus wants before she goes back into the meeting again. They go into the corridor.

Evita looks around to make sure nobody can hear them.

'Yes, well… this is the situation. The Bitch in Barcelona has just phoned. She wondered if we had booked the same suite as last year for Pablo Blando.'

Astra looks surprised.

'She phoned *you* about that?'

Are there no limits for that control freak, Astra wonders. Must she double-check with my boss too?

239

Evita seems to almost understand what Astra is thinking.

'Well, they have slightly different ways of going about things in the Latin countries. We'll have to put up with it. But I promised her I'd check with you. Can you email her about it?'

'I already have done… but okay, I can do it again,' says Astra brightly.

'And there's one other thing. A bit sensitive, perhaps that's why she phoned me. Pablo is beginning to get a bit old and evidently gets an awful lot of palpitations when he takes Viagra nowadays. So she has started to ration his dosage.'

'Oh, I'm glad about that, because it isn't so easy for me to get hold of…'

'Yeah, but the catch is that…' Evita interrupts her without completing her sentence. She looks down.

'What is it?'

'She wants us to get him some crushed reindeer horn instead.'

'What?'

'She says that it would be the best for his heart.'

'You're joking!'

'He has evidently seen a documentary about the effects of reindeer horn. When he was on a book-signing tour in Japan.'

'No, I can't believe it!'

'I agree, it is totally sick. But true. We'll laugh at it someday.'

'I really hope so,' says Astra and looks slightly worried. She knows what is coming now.

'So can you arrange it, do you think?'

'I suppose I'll have to.'

'Yes, I'm afraid so,' says Evita and tilts her head to one side. 'You're so incredibly competent.'

When Titus wakes up, he still can't move. He tries to remember what has happened. Yeah, right, he was on his way to Winchester Publishing with the manuscript. And then he fell asleep.

It is dark, completely pitch dark. He opens his eyes wide to try to see anything at all. Nothing. He tries to open his mouth. He can't. His lips are stuck together. It feels as if he has an iron band across his face on the level of his mouth.

He can tell that he is sitting and that he is stuck there. An iron band around his wrists and ankles too. Or is it tape? It is probably tape because he can't feel any sharp edges when he tries to wriggle his way loose. Tape round his stomach too. Two hard poles against his back. A kitchen chair?

His nose is free. He takes a deep breath. Cold, damp air. Is he down in a cellar? Or up in an attic?

He snorts. Umpf. Ummppff!

Not the slightest sign of resonance or echo.

Total silence.

It is as silent as in a grave.

Uuuuuummmmmmmpppppfffff!

Astra looks at her watch. Where has he got to? He said that he was on his way to Winchester's. The message was recorded at 11.32 and now it is a quarter to five. He ought to have been here ages ago. She phones him once more, but his phone is still turned off. Weird. Perhaps she ought to call in at his place on her way home? Check if anything has happened. Perhaps he's fallen ill? The thought of the manuscript makes her terribly curious. And just think – he stuck to the schedule! She would never have thought that possible when all this started. But it is thanks to her. She took an iron grip from the very first, just as Evita had said.

241

The breathalyser lock was a stroke of genius, nothing less. But where the hell is he? Why doesn't he answer his phone?

Many an hour seems to pass. Perhaps days. Titus can't be sure. No, it can't be a matter of days, he thinks. He hasn't pissed his pants yet. But of course he hasn't drunk anything since he ended up this darkness either.

How does it work? Do you only get the urge to piss if you drink? Or must you always piss? What do you piss out if you haven't drunk anything? He only has a slight urge to go, so presumably it has been only a matter of hours. Yes, that must be the case.

Astra rings the doorbell for a long time. Titus doesn't answer. She peeps in through the letterbox. Empty. No movement at all. She rings the neighbour's doorbell to find out if he or she knows anything about Titus. Nobody answers there either. She peeps in through the neighbour's letterbox too. There is a pile of advertising leaflets on the floor, the sort that comes with the post. Everyone gets it nowadays, it makes no difference if you have stuck up a sign: No advertising, please! The neighbour must be still at work, Astra thinks. If Titus got a similar pile of leaflets too, then it must mean that he left after the postman had been round. They usually come at about eleven, surely? So he must have left his flat just before lunch, which is round about the time he had phoned her on his mobile.

But where had he gone off to? Why doesn't he answer?

Titus is worn out. None of his ideas lead him anywhere. Everything just goes round and round in his head. It is absolutely loathsome to sit tightly taped to a kitchen chair in the pitch dark. Now and then he falls asleep for a while, and it is almost a nice feeling when that happens. Body and brain must rest a while.

Titus dreams that Lenny tips his chair on to a trolley. He is wheeled out through a little door. It is dark, it is night. The place is surrounded by dark trees, an awful lot of trees. Forest. There is a dull rustling. He is in the countryside, what a nightmare.

Then Eddie comes up to him. He smiles at Titus. Puts his hands on Titus' shoulders. Gives them a little pat.

And then he slaps Titus violently on his cheek.

Titus wakes with a start.

But he can still see Eddie before him wearing that friendly smile. What? Isn't he dreaming? What is this? Uuuuummmmpf!

His cheek is stinging from the slap, and it doesn't feel any better when Eddie rips off the silver tape from his mouth so that his beard stubble goes with it. Titus opens his mouth and takes some deep breaths.

They stare at each other.

Eddie looks almost as if tears are coming to his eyes when he starts to speak.

'Hello, Titus.'

Titus stares at Eddie, and at Lenny, who is standing next to him. He lifts his head a little, as if to show that he still has a certain human dignity.

'Titus, you have forced me into a difficult position,' says Eddie with a strained voice.

'What…?'

'Yes, you have indeed. You can't deny it.'

'What do you mean?'

'I have read nearly the whole book.'

'What? What is this?'

Titus gradually starts to realise his predicament. He has been kidnapped. He looks around him. He is in some sort of farmyard out in the country. There is some light coming from a window on a little cottage close to them. A typical old tithed cottage it looks like. Perhaps it's red, you can't really tell in the dark. It could be grey, too. It is surrounded by a solid mass of trees except for the yard in front of the house where they are now. He can see an earth cellar with the door open. His prison. He smells damp.

Eddie continues hoarsely.

'You left the memory card on the coffee table at Astra's to provoke me. That was how it started. You wanted to make me unbalanced. Show that I couldn't produce anything any longer.'

'I've no idea what you're talking about,' Titus mumbles, in despair.

Eddie paces back and forth in front of Titus.

'I did what you wanted. I read the book. As much as you had written, that is. I read the manuscript the night after me and Astra had been out sailing. Fucking hell, Titus. I would never have believed this of you.'

'What?'

Titus follows Eddie with his gaze as he paces back and forth in front of him. Lenny stands next to them to one side, completely still. He looks almost relaxed, not at all his usual self. He too follows Eddie with his gaze.

'It's such a dirty low trick, what you've done,' Eddie goes on in a low voice. 'To think of all those times I've given you a helping hand by arranging readings! Haven't I given you love? Haven't I? Answer me!'

'Love? Do you call this love? Shutting me in a damned earth cellar?' Titus protests.

'I was forced to. There are limits to what even I can put up with!'

'Oh really, so we should feel sorry for you now?' Titus shouts in resignation.

Eddie comes to a halt in front of Titus and crosses his arms.

'What you have done is a deadly sin. You have stolen my ideas and drained me of energy. I don't know how it has happened but you have written almost word-for-word what I was going to write in my manuscript.'

'You what…?'

Titus can't believe his ears. This is simply too much, he can hardly take it in. Eddie is claiming that he has stolen *his* ideas! While in actual fact it is the opposite – that Eddie and Lenny all summer long have tried to spy on him. Just a few seconds ago, Eddie even admitted that he had nicked the memory card at Astra's. And besides, they have kidnapped him and tied him to a fucking kitchen chair in a pitch black earth cellar in the country!

'I have read nearly all of it now, even the ending which you had with you today. Sentence for sentence, word for word, letter for letter, you have stolen my text. You have done it skilfully, I'll give you that. It is an extremely good book, Titus. Incredibly good. You must be clear about one thing: I am the one who has written it. Not you. You have simply stolen everything. Like I said, don't ask me how you've gone about it. But that is what you've done. We have to agree on that.'

'Like hell we do! I'd rather die than go along with something like that! You're crazy. You have completely lost your grip!'

Eddie puts his hands on Titus' shoulders and smiles sadly.

'We're going to come to an agreement, Titus. We certainly are. That's what we're going to do. All in good time, all in good time.'

He strokes Titus' shoulders.

Then he pushes lightly with his thumbs into the hollow between Titus' shoulders and collar bone. Applies pressure. Harder and harder. As hard as he can, for a long time.

'Owwww! Stop!'

As soon as Astra wakes up, she tries to phone Titus. No answer.

She phones the locksmith that she arranged when he had a break-in during the summer and had to get a new lock. Even though 'things are pretty busy right now, you know' she manages to get him to agree to a special turn-out charge and they arrange to meet at Titus' flat in half an hour.

She only has to wait there ten minutes before he turns up. Although the guy is just a mountain of muscles, she can't help wondering how he can carry such a big toolbox in just one hand.

'Hi there, lady! Yeah, this is it. And this, this is a really good door. I installed this lock myself, I remember that distinctly, you know.'

'Yeah, right,' says Astra. 'It was me who phoned from Greece if you remember. Then you sent a rather padded bill to Winchester Publishing. Perhaps you remember that?'

'No, it's not me who sends the bills, you know. Ellen does that, she's married to the boss.'

Astra realises that she shouldn't get involved in a discussion about prices at this juncture. That was stupid. He mustn't start making difficulties now.

'Okay. But I need to get in here.'

The locksmith puts his toolbox down. Crosses his arms.

'Oh really? But it was a bloke what lived here, you know? It said Titus Jensen on the door then. And it still does. Can you see?'

'Yes sure, the thing is he works for Winchester Publishing. And now he has disappeared. I've got to check whether there are any clues inside here.'

'Yeah but… if I let you in here, you know, it'd be like a break-in. Can't do that. Very risky, that sort of thing, you know. That's not what we locksmiths get paid to do, you see. Crime and punishment, you know. Then you need a risk surcharge.'

Astra gets her wallet out of her bag and pulls out a thousand-kronor note.

'Would this work?'

The locksmith grabs the banknote and then produces the largest keyring that Astra has ever seen. He rattles the keys in a demonstratively loud manner before finding the right one. Jangle and click. One, two, three and the door is open.

Astra goes through the flat with the guy shadowing her, his muscular arms crossed.

'For goodness' sake, leave me alone!' Astra exclaims, irritated.

He slouches out and stands in the stairwell. Mutters something grumpy about how he perhaps ought to phone his trade union. You know.

The flat looks like your average bachelor pad. Not exactly chaos, but nothing pedantic either. She looks inside the fridge. It doesn't look as if Titus had planned a long absence. There are opened cartons of milk and some leftovers rather carelessly packed. The little airing window in the kitchen is open. Astra gets the feeling that Titus has left the place all of a sudden.

She goes up to the computer in the living room and blow-starts it, keeping an eye on the door while waiting for the pop-up. She hopes the enzyme program works as promised.

> Hello, Astra! If you want a back-up, then you must stick the memory card in the socket on the right-hand side of the computer.

A good job she is one of those people who thinks of everything.

When Titus wakes up he is back in the dark. He isn't tied up any longer. The last thing he remembers is Lenny putting a rag over his face and becoming incredibly tired. Now he is lying on a mattress, at least that's what it feels like. With his hands he feels outside the mattress. A cold stone floor. He is back in the earth cellar.

He crawls along the floor to what he intuitively knows is the way out. He comes to a solid door and searches with his fingers for a doorknob which isn't there. But a keyhole? Is there a keyhole? He touches a bit of metal which feels rough and rusty. He twists it aside. Light! Yes, the bit of metal hung over the keyhole. He bends down and puts his eye against the hole.

Out there it is daytime. He can see a lawn with a large oak tree in front of a little cottage painted red. A little gravel path in front of the cottage. A porch and a window. No sign of life.

He bangs on the door, which is so thick that his bangs make no impression. It feels like banging on a tree trunk out in the forest. Who is going to hear him?

He puts his mouth up against the keyhole and shouts:

'Hello! Help! Is anyone there?'

He looks out again. A squirrel scuttles across the yard and up into the oak.

Everything is still.

Titus continues to bang on the door for quite a while. In the end he realises nobody can hear him. The cottage doesn't even seem to have any neighbours. Are they going to let him die here?

Desperate and snuffling, he crawls back to the mattress.

He huddles up and puts his arms between his thighs and stomach and his forehead against his knees. All his energy and determination is lost. He cries and sobs.

Astra is becoming increasingly worried. After a couple of days with no sign of life from Titus, she has a very uncomfortable feeling about it. The book fair is rapidly approaching and she very much wants Titus there when *The Best Book in the World* is going to be marketed to the international agents and Sweden's booksellers. Since Lenny is the last person she knows talked to Titus before he disappeared, she looks for him too. But he has vanished as well, and Eddie doesn't answer the phone either. What's happening with everybody? Can't they answer the phone?

Eddie is sitting in the little kitchen in the cottage and staring at a half-full can of beer. An old cobbler's lamp with a broken shade hangs above the kitchen table. The naked light bulb is transparent and the red glowing thread matches the whites of Eddie's eyes, which are now pink. He has some beard stubble and the usually so shiny hair is un-brushed and matted. He inhales deeply on his cigarette. What has he done to deserve this? Hasn't he always been so nice to people?

In front of him on the table are three mobile phones. When one stops ringing, another starts. And all the time it is Astra who is calling: first to Titus, then Lenny and then Eddie. Over and over again. It never stops. But he is unable to talk to her or even listen to her messages. Because what would he say? That she can't be his publisher until Titus admits his theft? That all his love has come to an end?

Lenny comes into the kitchen.

'He's woken up now. He's banging on the door.'

'Mmmm.'

Eddie looks at Lenny with tired eyes. Is Lenny really on his side? Or does he just feel forced to help him? Does he even understand what Titus is guilty of? It really is a bit steep to have the whole world against you. There is just no gratitude!

'Can I phone Malin?' Lenny asks. 'She'll be wondering where I've got to.'

'No, not now. Not one call is going to be made from here. They are hunting us. She is trying to find us. You can do it later. When he has admitted his guilt.'

'But please. It won't take a second.'

'NO!'

Ought she to ring the police and report him missing? How credible is it to issue a description of a middle-aged single man who has only been gone a couple of days?

Perhaps she ought at least to discuss it with Evita? Evita is always interested to know everything about Titus. You'd almost think that he makes her feel a bit horny. Mind you, there'd be a hell of a fuss about jeopardising the success of the book fair and that she isn't focusing on the right issues. No, she can't talk to Evita, not yet.

But can it really be a coincidence that all three have disappeared? Could Titus have been right after all with his nutty ideas about Eddie and Lenny? Have those two cooked up some mischief?

She must get hold of them.

Who might know something?

Hang on a moment, isn't Lenny with that pretty girl who works at the Moderna Museet café? What's her name? Lena or Linda? Something like that. Lina… Malin…? Yep, Malin, that's it! Definitely.

Astra calls directory enquiries and asks to be connected to the restaurant at Moderna Museet. There is a murmur from the guests in the background when they answer.

'Hello, could I speak to Malin please?'

'One moment.'

Astra takes a deep breath. Why the hell hadn't she thought of Malin earlier?

'Hello, Malin here!'

'Hello, Malin. My name is Astra and I'm a friend of Eddie X and I know Lenny too a bit.'

'Yeah, hi.'

'I need to talk to them about something. Have you any idea where they could be?'

'Yeah, I think they were going to the country to rehearse something.'

'Ah, so that's it! The country... whereabouts?'

'Well, I haven't a clue where it is. It's sort of an abandoned cottage deep in the forest in Sörmland. It's sort of always empty. In the middle of fucking nowhere. Like for real. I haven't the faintest where the place is!'

Astra tries to press her a bit more about where this abandoned cottage might be, or if she knows anything more about what they were going to do there, if Malin had heard that the author Titus Jensen was going to go with them. No, she hadn't. She knows nothing about anything. Lenny had simply said they were going to take it easy and rehearse a few days. Then they went off. That's all she knows.

Titus wakes out of his torpor when something that sounds like an old radio starts crackling.

'Hello, are you awake Titus?'

It's Eddie's voice, on a speaker. Perhaps Eddie is sitting inside that cottage and talking to him from there? With a walkie-talkie or some such apparatus? Maybe its one of those baby monitors he's seen on the TV ads.

'Have you thought about my offer?'

Titus isn't sure whether there is a microphone in the earth cellar. Can Eddie hear him if he swears? He'll try speaking in a low voice:

'What? Which offer?'

'My offer to you. If you admit that it's my book, then you'll be free. You must sign the contract. I'm the one who wrote the book and you know that. You have stolen it. You have nicked every single idea from inside my head, and pretended to Astra and Winchester Publishing that you are the one who has written it. That's what you must sign. Then you'll be released.'

'No fucking way!' Titus shouts for all he is worth. 'It's my book. I have written every single word in it! I have put my soul into it. You don't know what you are talking about!'

'Oh yes I most certainly do!' Eddie yells back through the speaker. 'I know very well what I myself have thought up! They are my ideas, straight off. I said all of that already during that evening at the festival. But you were so drunk you've chosen to forget!'

'You didn't at all! You're lying!'

For a moment, silence reigns. Titus can hear Eddie breathing into the microphone. He seems upset.

'Titus?'

'Yes, what do you want?'

'Do you confess?'

'No, I've told you! Never!'

Silence again. A moment's heavy breathing.

'Then I'll have to turn the lights on.'

'What?'

'If you don't confess, then I'll turn the lights on!'

'Yeah, right.'

Is he joking? Is this candid camera? Will they come any moment and open the door and throw confetti and shout that it's all over and laugh at him for falling for everything? No, hardly.

The only alternative is that Eddie is in the midst of a severe psychosis. Titus has never come across such extreme obsessive-compulsive behaviour in anybody else before. It is decidedly unpleasant.

'Do you confess? Will you sign it?'

'No. You can let me out anyway. Let's forget all this. Perhaps you aren't feeling very well, Eddie?'

'Last chance: sign or I'll turn the lights on.'

What a bizarre threat, thinks Titus. He would much rather be imprisoned in a lit-up earth cellar than in one that is pitch dark.

'Eddie, I'd rather die than give up the copyright to that book!'

Eddie breathes into the microphone for quite a while. Then he says:

'Okay. I'm turning the lights on.'

Quite a few seconds pass. Still dark. Then there is a buzzing sound in an electric cable. A fluorescent lamp up on the ceiling starts to crackle and blink. Titus puts his hand over his eyes, not having seen any light for a couple of days. When his eyes have acclimatised he looks around him.

He sees a portable loo with a large container in green plastic in one corner. In the other there is a little camping table and a folding chair. The walls have shelves fixed all around the earth cellar. From floor to ceiling.

But there aren't any jam jars or sacks of potatoes on the shelves.

They are full of bottles and cartons.

Titus realises what he is looking at.

The shelves are packed with wine, spirits and beer. Several cartons of cigarettes. Lots of multi-packs of tobacco. Smoked sausage, crisps and cheese puffs.

The earth cellar is all kitted out for a party.

CHAPTER 34

Renewed Efforts

'Hello dear, everything under control?'

Evita is radiantly happy and drums with her long nails on Astra's doorpost when she looks into her room. Her hair is even more jet black than ever. She pouts her red lips at the little mirror just inside the door and gives herself an appreciative wink. There is always plenty of room for humour and self-mockery in Evita's life. Presumably that is why people feel so comfortable in her presence.

Astra twirls around on her office chair. She looks rather concerned.

'What? Oh, hi Evita. Under control… Yes, yeah. I suppose it is,' says Astra in a more tired voice than she usually has.

Evita goes in and sits on the chair opposite Astra's desk. She crosses her legs and supports one arm on the back-rest. She is one of those women who always look just as relaxed regardless of whether she is sitting in an armchair or hanging from a trapeze. Nothing can dent her self-confidence.

'The book fair will be starting soon. It is going to be really great.'

'Yes, well…'

'I've just been to Micha's and got my hair done. Did you know that it's his niece who does the shampooing? She can't be very old. Fourteen at the most. It can hardly be okay to work full-time when you're so young.'

'You look really lovely. Have you had some colour added? There's a nice glow.'

Evita stretches her head back and gently shakes her hair over her neck.

'Thanks. I've just done the usual. I don't really know what's in those dyes but I don't suppose they are particularly organic,' Evita laughs and goes on. 'Did you get Titus' manuscript? Did he get it finished on time? He must be very pleased with himself now, don't you think?'

Astra avoids looking Evita in the eye when she formulates her vague answer.

'I've got it. It looks really good. I've sent some selected chapters to be translated too. The printers at the book fair will arrange everything. All the sales materials will be waiting when we get down there on Thursday morning. So, yes, it should all be ready…'

Evita is a tough lady. But she hasn't reached her position because she is thick skinned. On the contrary, she is extremely receptive and considerate. She immediately cottons on that something isn't quite right and fastens her green eyes on Astra.

'But…? I can feel that there is a big "but" here…'

Astra takes a deep breath. She looks at Evita. Take the bull by the horns, she thinks. Sink or swim.

'Evita, I don't know where Titus is. He's disappeared.'

'Disappeared?'

'I don't know where he is…'

'What do you mean? A grown-up man can't just go up in smoke. Have you tried the Association Bar? Perhaps he's "had a relapse" now that he's finished the book,' says Evita, adding quotation marks with her fingers as she borrows the alcoholics' own terminology.

'No, it isn't like that. Titus has disappeared. For real…'

Astra's eyes shine all shiny when her tear ducts can't withstand the pressure any longer. But they never overflow.

'Astra, my friend. Tell me what's happened. I'll help you of course.'

Astra takes a deep breath and recapitulates the events and non-events of the last few days. She tells how Titus has all the time had an inexplicable worry that Eddie was going to steal his book idea. That she had come to the conclusion that it must be that Titus hasn't told her everything about how he got the idea for the book because every time Eddie's name is mentioned then Titus adopts an extremely defensive position. There is something fishy about Eddie and *The Best Book in the World*, that's all there is to it. Titus has not been completely candid. She also tells how Titus has accused Tourette's-Lenny of a break-in at his flat, instigated by Eddie, and how all three of them have disappeared. None of them answers the phone. Nobody has heard from them for days. Perhaps they are in an abandoned cottage somewhere, but nobody knows where it is situated.

When Astra tells her of the mess, Evita sits there quietly. She looks pensive and decisive at the same time. Astra observes her to try to ascertain what her reaction is going to be. Angry? Resigned? Will she scrap the project now? Say 'What was it I said?' about placing so much responsibility on an old alcoholic like Titus?

But setbacks have never stopped Evita Winchester before. They rather serve as spurs which make life worth living. A determined smile spreads across the Amazon's face.

'Now it's war! This is what we shall do. I'll put the legal department on it straight away. We'll protect the title all over the world. The day after tomorrow when the book fair opens we'll issue a press release in which we present the book, synopsis and the entire campaign for marketing it in Scandinavia. We'll do a worldwide press release; the press office will fix that. There will certainly be some notices and small articles here and there. That will help to protect us in future copyright actions. We were first, there's never going to be any doubt about that. The others haven't got a chance. I'll stamp Babelfish back into the same earthen floor that they have crept up out of.'

'Babelfish?' says Astra, surprised.

'Yeah, it's obvious there must be another publishing house behind this. I ought to have thought of it before. And they will be running Eddie X as a poster name.'

'Poster name…?'

'Yes. He's the author. The front man, so to speak. They will have got a whole team of editors to write the actual manuscript, I guess. Eddie X couldn't put together a book like this, but he'll look heavenly on the cover, I'm sure that's what they're thinking.'

'But do you really believe…?'

'That's how it is. No doubt. Now it's war. And we're going to win,' says Evita and breaks out into a big smile. 'There's just one thing you must do, Astra. You must find Titus. You must find out where that abandoned cottage is and go and fetch him. Titus Jensen – he is going to the book fair, dead or alive. Sure, there isn't much time. But you'll manage it. You know I rely on you one hundred per cent.'

Evita abruptly gets up from her chair and gives Astra a hug where she is sitting. She looks if anything even happier than when she turned up at the door a little while ago.

'God, what a fun job we have! Now to work! See you in Gothenburg!'

Astra is relieved by Evita's reaction. She ought to have told Evita several days earlier. It was incredibly stupid of her to wait so long, but what's done is done. Now she must look ahead. There was still time to fix this. She feels her energy return. Evita is the best boss one could imagine. Oh, how lovely it feels finally to have told her.

She gets up and paces back and forth in the room, strokes her hair with both hands and massages her scalp. Think, think!

The cottage, the cottage, the cottage. She must find out where that cottage is.

She decides to seek out Malin again. It was admittedly almost impossible to get any sense out of her last time, but she can't think of anything else at the moment.

She takes the lift down to the garage where she has her large SUV parked. The parking space is a company perk and more often than not the car remains unused for weeks on end. Astra prefers the underground or a taxi when she only has to transport herself short distances in the city, then she can avoid the wretched parking situation in Stockholm. But today she is going to travel a bit further. She really hopes so, anyway.

She drives the short stretch across the Old Town, past Nationalmuseum and across the bridge to the Skeppsholmen Island and Moderna Museet. There aren't many visitors today so it is easy enough to find a space below the museum.

In the restaurant there are just a few mothers with small children and the odd pensioner sitting beside the panorama windows, enjoying one of Stockholm's most beautiful views. Calm has once again settled in Stockholm. The cries from the attractions at the Gröna Lund amusement park have died away and the queues to the children's Junibacken have disappeared. Across the water at the Vasa Musuem some guys in colourful protective clothing are rigging up scaffolding. A couple of green-clad museum pedants are standing behind Nordiska Museet, busily raking even though only a few leaves have fallen so far. It is autumn, so one uses the rakes.

Malin is sitting with nothing to do in her black-and-white waitress-style uniform behind a cash register. Her long hair is deliberately matted and she has put it up into a loose bun round a fork. Bored, she barely manages to hide a yawn with her hand when Astra approaches her.

'Oops, excuse me.'

'Hello, do you recognise me?'

'Yes, you're Astra, aren't you?'

'Exactly, we've met a few times in the crush. And we talked on the phone the other day…'

'Yeah…'

Astra looks around to be sure nobody can hear her. She lowers her voice and whispers.

'Malin, I've been thinking about that cottage. I think that Eddie and Lenny have gone there together with Titus Jensen. And I must get hold of Titus. So now I must find out where the cottage is situated. Are you absolutely certain you don't know where it is?'

'Well, I *know* where it is,' says Malin gesticulating with her hands as if to defend herself.

Astra notices the tattoos on Malin's forearms. Strange entwining letters. Quite attractive, but Astra can't recognise the alphabet. She thinks Malin is a bit weird.

'What? You know where the cottage is? Why didn't you say so?'

'Listen. I don't know *where* it is. But I know what it *looks like* there, I mean. I don't know how to get there. I've been there for parties several times but I've always been in the back seat when we've driven there.'

'Would you be able to find it if I drove?'

'I don't know. I don't think so. Perhaps, perhaps not.'

Astra feels herself becoming irritated by Malin, but it would be daft to get angry at this juncture. Now she must

259

play her cards right. Malin can't know how serious the situation is. Astra decides instead to get Malin to cooperate by quickly confiding to her selected portions of the story.

Malin listens, all ears, and nods, as Astra tells how Lenny and Eddie might have some dirty business in the offing. At any rate Eddie, she thinks, and perhaps he has lured Lenny into trouble too.

'I knew it!' says Malin. 'Lenny hasn't been himself at all this summer. He has ground his teeth every single time we have slept together, and several times he's said that Eddie is so fucking weird and a pain. What on earth, I thought. Eddie isn't weird in the slightest, is he? He is always the nicest guy in the world. But Lenny says that he is different sometimes.'

'Different in what way?' Astra wonders.

'Yeah, well, he's become sort of jealous. He doesn't think that anybody likes him any more, that everybody thinks his poems are ridiculous, that when he says something funny then they laugh at him instead of with him, if you get what I mean. And that he's started drinking rather a lot. All the time.'

Malin goes on to say that Lenny doesn't want to talk about Eddie any longer. The week before they went off to the cottage, he didn't say much at all. As soon as she tried to ask him what was wrong, he just wanted to change the subject, became irritated and swore even more than usual. It was as if his tics got worse as soon as she entered the room.

Now she has tried to phone him loads of times the last few days, but he doesn't answer. And nor does Eddie X.

Astra and Malin talk for a while. They are agreed that everything is not as it should be and that they must do something. Now. The question is – what? Perhaps they can try to find the cottage by just driving around. It ought to be somewhere in Sörmland, because Malin is pretty certain they passed Södertälje when they drove there. And then they sort of went off to the right. What would that be? West? There was a lake somewhere near. Perhaps Malin could find the way if they just set off in that direction. But probably not. No, it wouldn't work.

'But Astra!' Malin suddenly exclaims.

'Yes…?'

'We'll talk to Lenny's dad. I know where he hangs out. We'll go there!'

'Why?' Astra wonders.

'Yeah, well listen. It's Lenny's dad who owns the cottage. He is there in the summer.'

'What? Does somebody own it? You said it was an abandoned cottage.'

'Well nobody lives there… it's, like, an abandoned cottage,' Malin says defensively.

'It might not be permanently inhabited, but that doesn't make it an abandoned cottage! An abandoned cottage is a house that has been forgotten, that just stands there. It isn't an abandoned cottage if somebody owns it and goes there in the summer. It isn't abandoned just because it's in the middle of nowhere. Oh, why didn't you say so from the start? Then I would have been able to find it immediately!'

'Well, I'm very fucking sorry then,' says Malin and rolls her eyes. 'Hello, how should I know…'

'But isn't Lenny's dad dead?' Astra breaks in when her brain has worked out what Malin has actually told her. 'Eddie said he was dead.'

'No, he isn't dead! Did Eddie say that? He and Lenny don't keep in touch any longer. He is alive and well from what I've heard, but I've never met him. Lenny knows where his dad hides the key to the cottage, above the outdoor lamp in the porch. It's the same place as when he was little. So he has, like, done a break-in at his dad's house. But then we have always cleaned up after us. His dad has no idea we've been there. It has always been at weird times, like in the middle of the week or a weekend when it's been pissing with rain all the time, when no normal person would ever think of going off to the country, like. Shall we go and find the old guy? I know where he is.'

Astra puts her hand on Malin's.

'Come along, let's go. Can you take time off?'

'Of course,' says Malin gravely. 'It is up to us now.'

CHAPTER 35

The Laws of Nature

Titus walks beside the shelves. Despite the cold dampness, he can feel his face starting to sweat. It is as if his body wants to become one with the cellar. The same dripping unpleasantness, the same controlling icy cold. He wipes his forehead with the shabby sleeve of his jacket. The black shirt and jacket have become rather dirty from the stay in the earth cellar. The perspiration is dripping from his scalp like melted margarine when you fry pancakes. There is a flow in his armpits too. His back, his crotch, all his sweat pores are wide open and pulsating with tiny thirty-seven-degree steam puffs. Off with his jacket. Unbutton his shirt. He is like a wet dishcloth. Losing liquid quickly now. Everything is flowing.

His fingers feel along the edges of the shelves. Nervous, exploring, trembling.

Titus remembers a question-and-answer game that he and his mates at the Association Bar used to liven up monotonous evenings. It was called 'the rest of your life' and could go on for hours. There was no particular order to who would ask the questions, you just chimed in and it got louder and shriller. 'Now here's one: if you had to listen to only one song for the rest of your life – which would you choose?' And that would be followed by an endless discussion about how this or that song was so good because it both made you happy and you could listen to it when making love, or that another song was better because it was such a complex production so it would be the least likely to tire of, or that yet another song was so extremely simple and it would harmonise with your heartbeats for years without disturbing you. Of course they never came to any agreement. Everything would have to be looked at from every angle and examined down to the tiniest detail. 'One single position for sexual intercourse – which would you choose?' And so on. The pros and cons of various sweets and goodies, governments, types of weather, sandwich fillings, diseases, novelists, newspapers and holiday destinations were analysed in extreme detail. The bickering turned into endless theorising with lots of laughter and bawling.

If Titus had been at the Association Bar right now and been forced to list the wines, spirits and types of tobacco to choose if he had to live with them for the rest of his life, then his choice would have been more or less identical with the selection on the shelves here in the earth cellar. Here are several red Bordeaux wines heavy as lead. He can really feel the zinc aftertaste on his tongue. Mmmm. Here too are some Chablis wines, light as a feather, their sweetness being perfect to wash down summer-warm strawberries. Ah, exquisite!

And look there! A Lagavulin! That superb Islay whisky which is like a parody of smoky Scotch single malt whisky. That's one I would certainly choose, Titus thinks. But there's a Laphroaig too! Perhaps I ought to choose that. It would surely be more balanced in the long term…

Then his gaze falls on a packet of red Marlboro. The cigarette that has led to an early death for hundreds of millions of people. Oh, so tasty! I'll take that, Titus thinks. He knows exactly what the first drag on the cigarette feels like, when the hot cloud of tar spreads inside you and the tastes in your mouth are replaced by the smell of the smoke. Absolutely, if I've got to choose one brand of cigarettes for the rest of my life, then it'll be Marlboro. Preferably the extra-long ones that make your cilia dry up as quick as a baby's hair under a dryer.

The attempts to think negative thoughts about cigarettes completely misfire. The craving creeps up on him like an influenza epidemic. It starts with a churning feeling deep inside him, and soon his entire body is on fire. He wants a smoke. Now.

Titus rips the cellophane wrapping off the cigarette pack and opens the flip-top. Presses his nose against the twenty wonderful cancer sticks sticking up. Takes a deep breath. Holds his breath with the tobacco smell in him for a couple of long seconds before breathing out with his mouth open and his eyes closed. It would be so good, he thinks. Just one measly ciggy, that's all he asks for. Have one ciggy, Titus, you deserve it. You are actually locked up inside a hole in the ground with neither bread nor water. Just one fag, that's the very least you can ask of life just now. Have one fag and then you can get out of this dammed prison. One fag will empower you. Just one.

'Idiot!' screams another part of his brain. Better to be obsessed than dependent: have you already forgotten your mantra? Without poisons in your body you can do whatever you want with your life. If you are clean, you can perform miracles. You've already written a classic manuscript, now you must see it through to the end. Better to be obsessed than dependent, never forget that!

Then he is a little boy again lying on a young woman's bosom, her breasts heavy with milk. He breathes calmly. He keeps time with her. She strokes his head. He has that downy soft baby hair. Her nipples are still and beautiful. He puts his lips around one of them and lets a wet tongue lick round it.

Titus can feel calm returning to his body. This cognitive self-help therapy with reward images saves him yet again. With a trembling hand, he puts the open cigarette packet back on the shelf.

A crackling comes from the colourful baby monitor on the table.

'Cheers, Titus!'

It's Eddie.

Who is he really, thinks Titus. He who just a couple of months ago was a good person has now been transformed into a repulsive monster. Why? What have I done to deserve this hell?

'Hello? Hahahaha! Woof, woof, you pathetic drunken dog. Did you find something tasty?'

'Eddie, why are you doing this?' Titus asks in a calm voice. He looks at the wall behind the walkie-talkie as if trying to establish eye contact with Eddie.

'Haha! And you wonder why? Haven't you understood anything? Ever since we thought up the idea of this book, you've been tormenting me. I could perhaps have lived with you writing a version of your own. But I can't allow you to steal all my ideas.'

'But I haven't done that!'

'Yes you have, every single word is stolen. Don't you think that I can see what you've done? Do you think I'm an idiot? But perhaps I could even have lived with that theft too. If you hadn't…'

The walkie-talkie goes silent.

'If I hadn't… what?' Titus wonders.

'If you hadn't infected me.'

'Infected you?'

'You have infected me, Titus Jensen.'

'With what?'

'Your confounded darkness. I can't shake it off! It's driving me crazy. I wake up every morning and the only thing I want to do is go to a bar and have a large, strong beer. I can't write a single sensible word. But you will bloody well confess that you've stolen my book! You have stolen my idea, my manuscript and you have infected me with all of your damned Titus depression. To hell with you! But I want my life back, do you understand? Cheers! Hahaha!'

There is a click from the walkie-talkie. Eddie has gone.

'Hello?' Titus attempts. 'Are you there?'

No answer.

Locking up a sober alcoholic in an earth cellar full of spirits is not a kind thing to do. It is torture.

Titus shakes his head. Eddie has gone completely nuts. What's with the 'infected' thing? He can't help it if Eddie has lost his touch. Just because he has got his energy and *joie de vivre* back this summer, surely that doesn't mean that it must disappear from somebody else? As if the energy had simply transferred from on to the other?

He sits there, on the camping chair by the table, and thinks over his situation.

Energy cannot be used up – he remembers somebody having said that. You can't destroy it and you can't create it. The energy that exists can only be transformed and redistributed. Energy goes round and round, a system complete in itself. For example, you pump up oil from under the sea, make it into petrol and use the petrol to create kinetic energy for a car. And around the car thermo-dynamics are created in the air, that is, energy which in turn affects animals, insects and sound waves, and the energy is knocked further into the atmosphere. Round and round, like a perpetual motion machine.

The thoughts inside Titus' head whirl round all the faster.

What if the same applies to human energy? The energy and love in the world just hops around between different individuals! Why shouldn't the laws of nature be the same for humans as for the sun, wind and water? You can't use up human energy and love. But you can transform it, move it.

In some perverse way perhaps Eddie is right. The mind boggles at the idea. But just imagine if it actually is true that Titus has functioned well all summer because he has got his energy from Eddie? All that time he has been under the impression that it is his actual work with *The Best Book in the World* that has kept him away from the hard stuff, but he can't deny that the idea cropped up when he was boozing with Eddie. What if he was really charging up with a load of energy from Eddie then? And at the same time emptying Eddie!

He stares in front of him, glares at the shelves filled with the best alcohol, tobacco and snacks in the world. Is he in his true element now? He feels empty inside.

He thinks about those young people who wanted his autograph at Södra Teatern. What did they say? That they had became a couple because of him? That he had given them love... Had he really been infected with Eddie's ability to give love? Could he, Titus Jensen, have given love to those young people...?

No, it's an impossible equation. He can never become Eddie X, and Eddie X can never become Titus Jensen.

The craving washes over him again. Just one glass of whisky – that would make him see clearly again. He must test who he really is. Is he the new energy-creating Titus or is he the same old drunk of a writer that he always has been? If he tastes the whisky, he'll have the answer. He will either pass the test and put the glass aside once and for all, or he will get totally sloshed as usual.

The cognitive behavioural pattern makes one more attempt to save Titus. The mantra chants repetitively in his head: better to be obsessed than dependent, better to be obsessed than dependent. But it sounds more feeble than obsessed. When he tries to find the reward image of himself on that soft woman's breast, he can only see a toothless tramp with a grey beard who laughs scornfully at him. The old wreck has lain down on top of a woman who sobs vainly and has turned her face away. Titus waves his hand in the air in front of his eyes but this figment of his imagination won't disappear. The man stretches up a bony and filthy hand in the air holding a mug of cloudy beer. The man says something. Have a glass, brother Titus! You have earned it. Cheers, damn it!

'He'll soon sign the paper, you wait and see,' says Eddie, and grins under the light bulb above the kitchen table.

'I really hope you're right,' answers Lenny.

'Yeah, for sure, he'll soon be himself again. And then everything will be business as usual.'

Lenny looks at Eddie with a sorrowful expression.

'Nothing can ever be the same after this.'

'Of course it can,' hisses Eddie. 'Who we are and how we are regarded is a zero-sum game. One man's loss is another man's gain. I'll soon be the usual Eddie X again, and you the same old Tourette's-Lenny. And Titus, he is Titus. A fucking booze-hound.'

'Stop, I'm not sure I want to be a part of this any longer…'

'You what? Stop pretending to be scrupulous, damn it, it doesn't suit you. Why are you here in that case, if I may ask?'

'You know why.'

'There you are then.'

'But I don't know if I care any more…'

'Hahaha! So you want to live the rest of your life as a bluff? "Do you remember Lenny, the guy who was the rock star in The Tourettes? But who was just a fake." What, is that how you want to go down in history?'

'No… but it's all this stuff with Titus. What if he never comes back? I think we're going too far.'

'I'll go just as far as I must to get that damned thief to admit his guilt,' says Eddie with clenched teeth.

'And then what?' wonders Lenny with a sad sigh. He is weighed down by the thought that his friendship with Eddie has been seriously dented. Carrying out crimes together creates a bond between people, but it wouldn't be right to call it friendship. They were friends before, close friends. They went on tour together, partied together, and spent boring weekdays together. They know all about each other's strengths and weaknesses, there was a mutual respect that made them strong and self-secure. It was a friendship that bordered on love. They felt happy deep inside from the presence of each other. But now that friendship had been transformed into a state of dependence. Lenny still hopes that there are values that haven't been smashed to bits, something upon which they perhaps can build up a completely new friendship when all this is over.

Now Eddie is a different person from the one Lenny has known for so many years. His hands tremble and little twitches can be seen in the corners of his eyes. He doesn't look kind. His voice is tired.

'Then… then you can do what the hell you want. I'll get back the rights to my manuscript and you can do what you want. I'm not going to say a word. I keep my promises if you keep yours. Everything will be as usual. Give me the fags.'

Perhaps he is right. Hope so, thinks Lenny, and slides the cigarette packet across the table top.

'O-okay.'

'Aaaaahhhh!

Titus has really worked himself up in his enforced lone-
liness. He must bring about a change. He must interrupt his
thoughts and push Eddie X out of his brain. Away with the
evil, away with the energy. Empty out, down to zero. He is
Titus Jensen and nobody else. He hasn't drained anybody.
He refuses to accept that his willpower has been stolen
from Eddie. If that power is not his own, then it isn't worth
anything. The thoughts whirl around at a crazy speed.

Titus screams as loudly as he can. His voice cracks.

But the whirling thoughts don't stop. They just get worse.

'Aaaahhh!'

He lies on the mattress and bangs his hands on the floor.
The despair has settled over his chest and whips him hard
on his face, drooling its cold sweat over his forehead. The
pressure is colossal, it is hard for him to breathe. His ribs
will break first, then his lungs will puncture, his heart will
explode. It is only a matter of seconds now, then he'll be
dead.

He uses the last of his adrenalin to break his way free.
He gets up and stands with his legs apart and his arms
stretched up towards the cellar ceiling. Scrapes with his nails
on the cold and loose mortar. He can break this off. He must
get away. Now there is only one way out left.

'Aaaahhh!' he roars as loud as he can and goes up to
the shelf. 'It is me who is Lagavulin! I am intense, smoky
and dry, full of richness and a salt flavour. But there have
been women who have said that I have sweet undertones.
I remember them all.'

He turns to the walkie-talkie and yells:

'My heart is coloured by amber! I have a slight aroma of
tar and seaweed. Stored best at an even temperature! Year
after year. Do you hear me – I am Titus Lagavulin Jensen!'

He stamps his feet on the stone floor, rapidly and heavily, like an anonymous execution patrol being rushed to their posts to fire their superiors' deadly shots.

'Can you see me? Do you hear me?'

He pulls the cork out of a bottle with a plop and throws it at the cellar door.

'AAAAaaaahhh!'

Puts the bottle to his mouth. The gulps run down his gullet. A lot of the whisky ends up outside his mouth and runs down his chin and neck. He drinks almost a fifth of the bottle before stopping.

'Aahh, Jesus that was good!'

Another large gulp and then he puts the bottle on the table with a crash.

'Now it's party time!'

He rips open a bag of cheese puffs and tips the contents onto the table. He takes a fistful and puts them in his mouth, chews wildly and laughs out loud. Yellow flakes of cheese fly around him. He wipes his forehead with the sleeve of his jacket. He isn't quite so sweaty any longer. His fluid balance is returning to a normal level.

'Hahaha! At last. The cognitive picture therapy can go take a running jump. It might suit everyday problems. But not earth-cellar torture! Farewell reward images! Goodbye threat images! When it comes down to it, no therapy in the world can prevent a person's true driving forces. Cheers, Titus Jensen! Welcome back to life! Where have you been? I've missed you. Hahaha!'

Before the whisky has even started its journey from his stomach and out into the bloodstream, he uncorks a dusty bottle of Cabernet Sauvignon from 1998. He gulps that down too, in a hurry as he is. Gulp, gulp, gulp. He wipes his mouth with his jacket sleeve.

'*Bienvenue*, Titus Jensen.'

He lights a cigarette and inhales greedily a few times before releasing it from his lips. He leans his head back and shuts his eyes, balances on the two rear legs of the chair and rocks slightly back and forth. Smoke blows out through his nose. He inhales deeply again and puffs out two perfect smoke rings.

'Oh, how delightful.'

He means what he says.

The intoxication is now charging through his body. The nicotine gives him a few minutes of inner softness and rest while the alcohol makes every cell in his body wake and tremble with expectation. There's a party going on. There's a good time on the way. Soon everything will be much better.

It is a liberating feeling. The anxiety about his relapse and failure lets go of him, and Titus smiles widely to himself. He picks up a large beer glass and some cans of beer.

'Silence. Take one. Listen to this.'

Titus opens can after can slowly and solemnly. He quivers with pleasure when he hears the wonderful tiny fizzing sounds. Pjui. Pfff. Pssff.

'Cheers.'

Titus pours out a cold beer, letting it run down the side of the glass to limit the froth. He doesn't want to have to wait unnecessary long seconds for the froth to settle before the drink can reach his thirsty throat. Jesus, an ice-cold beer tastes so good! After having gone through a hard and sober working period, you must surely be allowed to be human again? Yes, right on, that's the least you can ask for. He is going to get through this.

Titus' body has lived a comparatively long time without alcohol, which means that the first intoxication quickly turns into a severe drunken state. Had he been his old self, he might well have coped with such a tough start to the party. Now he gets sloshed in just a few minutes, lightning drunk in fifteen and unruly after thirty.

He cheers and yells and gulps and smokes like nobody's business. There is a very crazy one-man party taking place in the earth cellar.

Now and then he takes a few unsteady dance steps with an imagined party princess by his side. He bows, curtsies and gesticulates wildly. Now and then he shadow-boxes: a clumsy punch here and there, roughly like he thinks boxers do it, ducking and dancing around.

But then he gets a grand idea. There isn't enough singing in this cellar.

'But hello there! Isn't there going to be any schnapps at this party?'

He collapses like a heavy sack of potatoes onto the chair and starts singing the Swedish drinking song *Helan går* at the top of his voice while unscrewing the cork of a quarter-litre bottle of Norwegian Linjeakvavit.

'…And the one who doesn't take the whole / Doesn't get the half either / The whole gooooooooes / Sing hup fol-de-rol la la!'

Gulp, gulp, gulp.

Bang, crash, thud.

Bottoms up.

CHAPTER 36

On the Road

There are relationships between people where the bond has crystallised. Such 'cement' formations arise both in families and between friends. When these people get together, there is only room for predictable information and expected events. You are who you always have been. You think what you always have thought. And should perchance anything actually occur that transgresses the boundaries, then it is best for all concerned to pretend that nothing has happened, otherwise the roles and the friendship start vibrating dangerously and the foundations can crack. Cement people socialise regularly and serve each other nicely packaged, boasting and completely predictable successes and failure. When they later slowly crumble away, they do so in controlled harmony.

Then you have the relationships where people are suddenly gathered together by chance. It could, for example, be a major experience or a crisis. It can happen to anybody at all, even to cement people. When it occurs, they can suddenly become totally open and share their innermost thoughts while at the same time being really anxious to get to know their fellow human being. The sense of presence is total, and they are absolutely convinced that they have created an honest and open bond that will last forever. And that of course might happen. But at home in the cement factory of everyday life, the miraculous relationship can often stiffen into a strange and unfamiliar lump.

Astra sits behind the wheel and speeds southwards from Stockholm in her large car. Malin is sitting beside her on the passenger seat, and Lenny's tall dad is half-lying across the rear seat. It wasn't easy to find him, but they succeeded in the end.

The situation has got all three to open their hearts to each other. There are no cast-iron roles here. They realise that they must get to know each other in a hurry, so they are almost all speaking at the same time.

Astra tells the story of Titus Jensen and his important book project. Of a man who was going downhill but who now is on the verge of a new, perhaps final, possibility; that there is something fishy about the relationship with Eddie X and that it looks as if Lenny too is mixed up in it some way or another. Now she must get Titus to the book fair, whatever the cost. Eddie X would also be at the fair, he always is. As a rule he performs in the middle of the fair floor, in the crowd, and is usually a mega-success every year. She says that she has been close to falling in love with Eddie but that she can't really interpret her feelings. Is he a charming guy or just a charmer? The last time she saw him, he was obsessed with Titus. Mysterious and suspicious. Where Lenny fitted into all this, she couldn't really say.

Malin is very worried about Lenny. She tells of her relationship with him and about his strained relationship with Eddie. The two of them have been mates all their lives, and sometimes Lenny cares more about Eddie than he cares about her. It is not fair. She can't understand why Eddie has such a strong influence on Lenny. And actually 'influence' is the wrong word; 'power' is nearer the mark. Eddie lords it over Lenny. Lenny is Eddie's slave, almost. Yeah, Lenny has been super weird all summer and she doesn't know at all where she stands with him. She wants him to take some medicines but he just gets grumpy and says it's not necessary. Perhaps he has started with hard drugs instead. She has read that lots of people with Tourette's and similar problems medicate themselves with alcohol and drugs.

Lenny's dad for the most part sits there listening. He asks a lot of supplementary questions and wonders how this and that 'feels'. His face is sad. Sometimes he takes deep breaths and releases cavernous sighs. Now and then he directs Astra so that she takes the right road to the cottage. He says that he has known this day would come sooner or later. When Lenny's mum died a few years earlier, Lenny broke off contact with him totally. But he had understood that Lenny has sometimes secretly been to the cottage. In some ways that has made him hopeful. Now he is a bit happy but mainly worried. If everything goes all right then he'll never let go again. Now he is going to support Lenny. That, he'll promise.

There is a very serious atmosphere in the car.

CHAPTER 37

Party Prison

Titus blinks slowly when he tries to follow the course of the smoke ring on its way to the bunker ceiling. The ceiling is completely soft and slowly whirling around the cable that the light bulb is hanging in. Unpleasant. He turns his gaze away, looks down instead.

With clumsy fingers he squeezes the cigarette butt between the back of his thumb and the top of his index finger. With a comparatively nimble flick of his finger he sends the fag-end flying towards a large pool of cognac that he has spilt in the middle of the floor. When it lands there is a swoosh and a crackling and the pool burns up.

'Haha, what a suuuuperb floor flambé. Nice consissstency, without a doubt. Haha…'

Titus tries to roar with laughter.

'HAHA! Hahahaha! Haha…'

He can't get it right.

In a hoarse and leisurely voice he tries to talk himself into action again.

'Give me a P – P, give me an A – A, give me an aaaaR – aaaaR, give me a T – T, give me a Y – Y, and give me a P – P, give me an aaaaR – aaaaR, give me an I – I, give me an S – S, give me an O – O, give me an N – N. And what do you get: Paaarty prison. I can't hear you – wha'd'ya get? PaaaaRTY PRISON! Make an effort now, one more time…'

Jesus, what a fucking boring earth dugout.

He has tried everything. He has sung all the drinking songs he can remember. He has told all the jokes he can recall. He has roared and yelled, pulled all the funny faces and laughed. He is one hell of a party animal, one in a million.

But now he can't get it together.

He reels like an old heavyweight boxer that some greedy promoter has managed to resuscitate a final time with the promise of regaining his honour – if only he will allow himself to be knocked about just once more. But this vegetable has stopped defending himself years ago. He's taken knocks in many long rounds without so much as lifting his hand in defence.

Now all that remains is that final fall to the floor like a lump of lead. With his hands hanging loosely by his sides and with his nose as the bow door, Titus slops off the chair and down onto the floor.

Titus Jensen has gone quiet. Silence reigns now.

Dark red blood runs out of both nostrils and mixes with the dark earth colour of the floor.

A couple of minutes – that could just as well have been a couple of hours – pass.

The bundle on the floor moves.

He rolls onto his right hand side and first opens half of his left eye. Looks around. A half-empty bottle lies an arm's distance from him. With a final effort he stretches his left hand after it, gets hold of it and, with a shaky hand and considerable effort, manoeuvres it towards his mouth. He frees his right hand, which he has been lying on top of, and helps his left hand to get the bottle into his mouth. With their joint resources, the two hands manage to stick the neck of the bottle into Titus' throat. No more vomiting reflex; it's a long time since his muscles have tried to do battle. He hyperventilates through his nose since his mouth and throat are full of the bottle.

Then he turns on his back. The bottle sticks right up out of his mouth. A cross on a grave.

The contents gurgle slowly down his throat, into his stomach, bowels, lungs, blood, brain.

Gulp. Gulp. Gulp.

Active euthanasia. A suicide attempt. Help to self-help.

The hours are like minutes, which could be seconds.

He doesn't have a body any longer. Yet his back seems to be pushed against the ceiling. As if he had turned gravity upside down and was lying there resting on the ceiling. He can see himself lying down there on the cellar floor. Bloody and very much the worse for wear. But still with some respect, despite the cross in his mouth.

Still.

Not moving a muscle.

Not taking a breath.

A black iris circle closes in around the picture of the body on the floor. In the middle, the light gets all the stronger. The body gets slowly smaller and smaller and is mixed up with the white light. The white circle gradually disappears like the opening in the tunnel behind an underground train.

Titus feels the calm spread through his soul, the same almost euphoric calm that he has often experienced when he been sitting and writing this summer. He thinks about his old desk of mahogany, of the little airing window on the left beyond the computer screen which lets in the slight murmur from the city traffic and filters the chirping from the small birds in the trees outside.

He thinks of all the words that he has become friends with and all the favourite phrases he has tickled under the chin. How the work has made him realise that it is precisely work that separates him from decay and addiction.

Now, the white circle is only a little dot in the black tunnel. The last star in the universe is about to fade forever.

He found what he had been looking for.

A brief moment of balance between fortune and misfortune.

A short life.

His life.

He must settle for that.

Or not.

With a roar, Titus lifts up the upper part of his body. At an angle of 90 degrees he sits on the floor and stares straight ahead. Blurred, dizzy.

He challenges his reflexes a last time and forces almost all of his hand into his mouth. He manages to get his fingers part of the way down his throat. He wiggles his index finger. It works. His throat starts to twitch with muscle spasms.

Now.

It's happening now.

He vomits and vomits. Unbelievable amounts of putrid matter pour out of him. He sobs uncontrollably and the tears spray out of his eyes. The blood vessels on his eyelids rupture from the effort when the muscle contractions strike like lightning through his body. The small dots form a red eye shadow.

He wipes his mouth with the arm of his jacket and quakes from the effort when he laboriously clambers back up onto the chair. He puts his hands on the table top and stretches out his fingers. They have saved his life, yet again. They are dirty. They are trembling. But they are alive.

He straightens his back.

He sits in his writing pose. He is not going to abandon that one more time. Now he must empty himself of what is bad

so that he will be able to empty himself of something good.
He looks at his fingers. They have work to do.

Now.

Now is the turning point.

CHAPTER 38

The Contract

When Eddie and Lenny open the door to the earth cellar, they are almost knocked over by the stench and the smoke from Titus' party. Eddie holds his nose and pushes the door with his foot.

'Hello, Titus? Are you there?' he says, cautiously. He doesn't want Titus to be hiding just inside, ready to ambush him.

Titus hasn't answered for more than twenty-four hours when they have tried to call him on the walkie-talkie. Sometimes they have heard a violent yelling and singing at the other end. Other times it has been either completely silent or they have heard him snoring loudly. When he was awake, they have tried to talk to him, but it has been completely impossible to get any sense out of him.

'Hello? We're coming in now.'

When the fresh country autumn air dilutes the stinking cloud, the fug in the cellar is dispersed. Eddie and Lenny get the situation under control.

Titus Jensen is not about to ambush them.

He is sitting at the camping table and sleeping with one cheek resting on a heap of cheese puffs. He has vomited and all the vomit has run down from the table and over the pile of empty bottles, crisp packets and half-eaten salami sausages. The two empty wine bottles on the table are filled with cigarette ends. One of the fluorescent lamps is hanging loosely from the ceiling. There is some sparking from the loose electric cable.

Eddie and Lenny stare at the mess and the human wreck. Titus breathes heavily.

'Urgh! Jeeesus. Poor bastard,' Lenny whispers quietly.

'We're getting close now,' Eddie notes coldly.

'I really hope so. This is no way to treat people.'

Eddie goes up to Titus and shakes him.

'Titus! Wake up!'

He grabs the collar of Titus' jacket and pulls him up against the back of the chair. His face is all slack and his mouth open. Eddie takes a large plastic bottle of tonic from the shelf, which he shakes thoroughly. Then he unscrews the cork and sprays Titus' face with a hard and concentrated shower.

'Titus, damn you. Wake up!'

'Blaaah… Urrgh…'

'We're here now. You must confess. Sign the paper.'

Titus opens his eyes and stares at Eddie with a vacant look on his face. There is something friendly and accommodating deep inside that gaze. Not the slightest indication of hatred or anxiety. He raises his right hand somewhat listlessly.

'Erglsss… plshhh… schine…'

'What? What are you saying? Do you confess?'

'Mmmm… appsolllll…. mmm.'

'Good. Repeat after me.'

'… fffter mmmeeee'

'I, Titus Jensen…'

'Hiii, Titush Jenshen…'

' …do hereby certify that I have stolen ideas as well as texts from *The Best Book in the World* from Eddie X. I confess that I have made a break-in at Eddie X's. All the material that I have shown to my publishing house so far is nothing more than a completely plagiarised manuscript from works written by Eddie X. I hereby renounce all future claims to *The Best Book in the World*.'

'Shhure… Appsolllute…! Yepp.'

Eddie grabs hold of Titus' arm and drags it across the table a few times so that rubbish and dried-up vomit is wiped away. He places a sheet of paper on the table and puts a pen into Titus' hand.

'Sign here!'

Titus looks first at Eddie with a lazy gaze, and then at Lenny.

'C… cock in your ear…' says Lenny vacantly.

Titus puts the pen near the paper and the line on which he should sign. He hiccups before scratching his straggly signature.

'Yepp. Iiii'mmm Titusssh… Titush Jenshen.'

'Thank you.'

Eddie grabs the piece of paper off the table and with a few quick steps leaves the cellar. In the doorway, he turns round and looks at Titus and Lenny.

'The next time we see each other, everything will be back to normal, won't it?' he says in a low voice. 'Won't it?'

Lenny looks at him with dead eyes. He doesn't nod, but nor does he shake his head. He just stares at Eddie, his old friend whom he no longer knows. Titus' gaze has become a little bit clearer. His eyebrows are now high on his forehead, he looks as if he has just woken up, surprised. What's going on, he seems to be thinking. He looks first at Eddie, then at Lenny. His face gets some of its shape back and he breaks into a loving smile.

'Cheeeerssh?'

CHAPTER 39

To Gothenburg

By the time Astra and her companions approach the little Sörmland cottage, Eddie has long since left. He is on his way to the book fair in Gothenburg in his old Dupont-style Peugeot decorated with hand-painted hearts. There he will be cheered by the masses and he will show his new secret manuscript to his publisher. He is certain they will hit the roof with delight. For a long time they have been saying that he needs a vitamin injection for his future writing. To be on the safe side, he will always have the document with him too. He doesn't expect the drunkard Titus to make a fuss, but just in case.

Astra slams on the brakes and the car skids to a halt on the gravel. She leaps out and rushes up to Lenny, who is sitting on the porch steps. He looks calm as he sits there drinking coffee from an old china cup and saucer.

'Where is he? Where's Titus?'

Lenny holds up a silencing index finger to his lips and then puts the soles of his hands together and places them like a pillow against his head on one side. With his thumb he points over his shoulder into the inside of the cottage. With a sideward nod of his head, he invites her to enter. She runs in.

Now Malin and Lenny's dad get out of the car too. Lenny sees Malin first and smiles at her with a serious look. She runs up to Lenny, throws her arms around his neck and disappears into his arms. He looks at her and strokes her cheek.

'It's over now,' he says slowly.

Malin looks up at Lenny. She doesn't recognise him. There is something strange about him. He is not nearly as wound-up as usual. They haven't seen each other in quite a while but even so he isn't stuttering the slightest. Is he on tranquilisers? Is he ill?

First she nods slowly, as if to reassure Lenny. It doesn't matter if he is ill or weird or just high on whatever. She must be on his side now.

'It isn't over yet. But soon.'

Steps can be heard in the gravel in front of them. Lenny looks up.

'Dad!'

Lenny's dad stands with open arms just a couple of metres away. Tears run slowly down his cheeks. His chest heaves a little from his sobbing.

'I'm sorry, Lennart.'

Malin slips out of Lenny's hug and sits on the steps with her arms around her drawn-up knees. She looks expectant. This is not like anything she has ever experienced before. She knows that it will be a lovely scene, one of those you can live a whole life without experiencing in reality. A string orchestra is playing inside her and emotions are flowing over in her tear ducts. She takes a deep breath so that her sobs won't disturb the moving tableau.

Lenny gets up. He gives his father a serious look. It looks as if a million thoughts are passing through his head. He puts his hands up to his face and over his nose and mouth, and inhales with big and heavy breaths through his nose. He stares at his dad through his little fingers and ring fingers, all with rings on them. Then he runs his fingers through his hair and down over the back of his head, back and forth.

The seconds that pass feel like an eternity. Malin looks at them in turn, first one and then the other. She smiles, because it will soon come. Oh, how lovely it is.

Then Lenny holds out his right hand and takes a step towards his dad. Their hands meet in a handshake that immediately turns into a hug. When his dad puts his arms over Lenny's shoulders, then Lenny can't restrain himself either. He starts to cry and leans his face against his dad's shoulder. The tears run down the cheeks of both the well-built men. They look at each other and laugh through their tears.

Malin dries some tears with her large shawl. Her inner orchestra is now playing the most sorrowful music one can imagine. It is as if all the clouds are dispersed and the sun warms up the yard. If it had been a film, then little cherubs would come skipping out of the forest and throw confetti over Lenny and his dad. There is a glow and sparkle in their eyes. This is almost better than Malin had hoped for.

Astra sits on the edge of the big sofa-bed in the back room. The ceiling is low and the bed takes up most of the floor space. The old roller blinds are lowered and the light is weak. But here and there a few rays of sun break in through tears in the cloth and particles of dust dance in the cones of light. Titus is lying under a heavy old woollen feather duvet with an attractive upper side of gold-coloured silk. He is thin and looks like a little nestling that has fallen out of the nest too soon.

When he wakes up, Astra is holding his hand. With her other hand she is stroking him slowly on his forehead and his stubbly scalp.

He looks at her. Now he recognises her: she is the young woman on the reward picture. She disappeared but now she has evidently come back again.

He doesn't need her any longer. He still likes her, he feels that distinctly. But he doesn't need her to survive.

He almost died there in the earth cellar, he thinks. He was only a hair's breadth from drinking himself to death. A few more bottles and he would have had a major stroke. A few more cigarettes and he would have suffocated.

Miraculously, there in the cellar he had actually regained the will to live. He knows why. In the cellar there was time to think. Sure, he was sloshed when he thought over and over about his situation and analysed it. But the answer became all the clearer, the more time passed.

He had managed to write a book again.

Undeniably, the battle over *The Best Book in the World* was lost, but that didn't matter any more, he thinks. He can write some more novels, even better books. That's all that counts. As long as he can work, there is cause to live. It is the work itself that is the point, not the end product. Before, he always expected the publication of the finished book to give him joy and satisfaction. But the euphoria never came, and he had to deaden the growing rage within him with alcohol. Now he knows that it is the actual writing process that is the reward. That is when he is alive. He doesn't need any more cognitive therapy, no breathalyser locks or inflated personal vendettas on which to project his anxiety. He doesn't even need *The Best Book in the World*.

All he needs is himself. Sober and in good working order.

The final hours before Eddie and Lenny came and released him, he hadn't drunk a drop of alcohol or smoked a single cigarette. He had just been sitting there and waiting to sober up and become the new re-born Titus. The turning point was just as clear as the mushroom cloud after an atomic bomb. From this point on, he would heal.

He has taken over his life again. Since he – excepting a few short periods – hadn't been sober for thirty years, he must now define who Titus really is. Metaphorically, he is young again. He has all his choices before him.

Freedom is the understanding that you have a choice, he thinks. And as long as he has recourse to himself, he can do anything at all. Never again will he reject himself.

He looks at Astra, who is sitting on the stool next to his bed. She has let him wake up slowly and he is grateful for that.

'I'm free now,' he says.

She nods slowly.

'You are indeed free, Titus. Now we're going to Gothenburg.'

Astra comes out onto the porch steps with her arm around Titus' back. He sags like a little sack by her side.

Titus blinks in the sunlight and looks as if he has just woken up. He gives a smile of recognition to Lenny and Malin.

Then he sees a large smiling man in a white coat.

'Doctor Rolf? Ralf Rolf?'

What is that nutter doing here? He recognises the noisy and crazy multi-therapist that stubborn telephone seller had conned him into meeting. Who talked about placebo therapies and fell into a heavy sleep in the middle of the conversation. They are not going to con him into lots of daft multi-therapy now, are they? If this is one of Astra's new ideas, then she is way off…

'I'm Lennart's dad,' says Doctor Rolf and interrupts Titus' thoughts. 'Lenny's, I mean. I am Lenny's dad.' A big liberating laugh rolls out of his mouth. 'Call me Raffe, all my closest friends do that.'

Titus looks at Lenny and at Doctor Rolf. He can't believe his eyes. Are the two related?

'We'll sort it all out in the car,' says Astra. 'We've got to be in Gothenburg in five hours.'

Titus sits in the front seat and tells Astra about everything that Eddie has subjected him to in the earth cellar. That Lenny had only been a pawn in the game. That what had happened had, in some ways, been good because now he knows who he is and what we wants to do with his life. Astra stares hard at the road in front of her and mumbles quietly between clenched teeth: 'monster, odious loathsome repulsive monster'. She presses hard on the accelerator.

In the back seat, Lenny and Ralf are each sitting in their corner. Malin is sitting between them, leaning against Lenny. And Lenny has his arm around her.

'Eddie forced me,' says Lenny, in a serious tone.

'How? Why did you go along with it?' wonders Malin who hasn't really got over how blunted and weird Lenny has become.

'I don't have Tourette's…'

'What? You don't?' Malin shouts and looks up at Lenny. Now she understands nothing. Has he suddenly turned normal? Is that why he is so weird?

Ralf places his hand upon Lenny's. Lenny looks at his dad who nods silently as if asking Lenny to go on with what he was saying.

'He said he would reveal that I don't have Tourette's if I didn't help him to get hold of Titus' book. At first I thought he was kidding me, but then I realised he meant it for real. He was close to phoning the tabloids several times. So I did what he said, it didn't seem so bad. It was almost like a bit of a prank in the beginning. Then it sort of grew. He got totally obsessed by it. We never talked about anything other than the manuscript. The manuscript this… the manuscript that… It seems as if we hunted it all summer long, that we spied on Titus for every step he took. Broke into his flat and got him sloshed at Södra Teatern and lots of other crazy things. And then all this with the earth cellar…'

'But what d'you mean, I can't follow,' Malin interrupts him. 'Isn't it bloody good that you don't have Tourette's?'

'No… it's thanks to Tourette's that I have a public. Without Tourette's I wouldn't be anything, just an ordinary useless rocker-wannabe. I am Tourette's-Lenny, the guy who has had an incredibly tough handicap but who has nevertheless managed to do something with his life. But now I'm finished as an artiste. A rotten imposter. I have stolen sympathy and empathy from honest people. And as for all the people who have real compulsive syndromes, well, I've dragged them into dirt and dishonour. I have made a fool of them. As if Tourette's is something to joke about, like a false nose you put on to get a few quick laughs. You just shout out "Cock in your ear" and everyone gets happy and frightened at the same time. No, it doesn't work like that. But I'm pleased it's over now…'

'It's my fault,' Ralf interrupts in a loud and slightly grating voice.

'Why?' asks Malin and moves her gaze to him.

With almost a roaring sound, Ralf clears his throat. What he is going to say is deeply buried…

'I only cared about my patients when you were little. I never understood how much you needed me. That's right, isn't it?'

Lenny nods in silence.

'So your only recourse was to develop Tourette's in the hope that I would become interested in you and devote more time to you. You heard about my patients who had Tourette's. They seemed weird and you became curious. Then you started carefully with facial tics and soon moved on to mildly compulsive behaviour, avoiding lines on the kitchen floor and so on, swearing dreadful tirades with revolting expletives when your grandmother was visiting. Then you started with that damned body-blinking and suddenly everybody became terribly interested in you...'

Lenny looks out through the window and nods. A sad countenance.

Ralf goes on.

'But the whole thing was fake. I realised at once and could never reconcile myself to the idea that you just acted out what my patients suffered from for real. I demanded that you stop, that you got a grip of yourself. I wanted a healthy and normal kid. Even though many of my patients' problems were inside their heads, their afflictions were at least not a result of an active choice. They *imagined* they were ill, and they couldn't actually help it. But you, you *chose* to have Tourette's. And even though you got to try out all my therapies you never got better, just worse and worse. I put you through dreadful things and you were only a child. You became cynical because I never had any faith in you. I turned into a repulsive parent, a monster. And you refused to be cured, perhaps to punish me. Isn't that true?'

Tears run down Lenny's cheeks. Malin puts her hand on his stomach and pats him gently. He is still looking out of the window when he answers.

'I hated your patients. You gave them infinitely more therapy and attention. Then when they got better, they disappeared forever. You always wondered how things had gone for them. The sicker they had been, the more you cared. So I thought that the more Tourette's I got, the closer I would get to you. And at the same time I noticed that it led to attention at school and that people started to respect me. The more I swore, the greater the number of adults who wanted to talk to me. I was someone. I became someone.'

'But how did Eddie find out?' wonders Malin.

'He knew straight off. I have never been able to hide anything from him. But we haven't talked about it, never. Not until he suddenly started to threaten me a couple of months ago. It was horrid. Something had happened between him and Titus early in the summer, at that festival where we got pissed together with Eddie. We were boozing together all night long and the two of them were sort of holding back on each other. After that he was completely transformed. Angry and greedy, like. Even though I've known him all my life, I became afraid of him.'

'Forgive me, Lenny,' Ralf mumbles quietly with a large lump in his throat. 'I gave you too little love when you were small. I was obsessed with my theories and patients. I'm afraid I still am, I suppose. It didn't exactly get any better when I moved to Stockholm, everyone there is completely confused. But if you give me the chance, I'll never demand anything from you again. You can be whoever you want and I will love you unconditionally. Because I really do love you. I have missed you so much.'

Lenny looks at his dad, his eyes welling up.

'I love you too, dad.'

Malin's shawl is wet from all the tears. But the sadness isn't so sad any longer. Now the string orchestra is playing inside her again. Now the confetti is slowly falling over the back seat like pretend-snow in a fairy-tale film in the olden days. Now the angels are smiling; now the cherubs are playing their little trumpets. Everything grey has acquired the most beautiful of Technicolor pastel shades.

She will remember this moment for the rest of her life. She carefully dries the tears under her eyes so as not to smudge her mascara on her cheeks.

'I love you, Lenny. And you too, Ralf.'

Titus' body and soul have been through a purgatory, and half-way to Gothenburg he falls asleep.

Astra takes the opportunity to phone Evita and give her a rundown of the situation. Evita becomes radiantly happy and can't praise her enough for having found Titus so quickly. She says that the book fair seems to be a success. Everyone is there. Astra asks Evita to contact the Gothenburg police: Eddie X must be dealt with. What he has done to Titus is terrible. How many years do you get for kidnapping? Eddie has evidently forced Titus to sign a contract while he was imprisoned – Titus has relinquished the copyright of *The Best Book in the World*. He has 'confessed' that he has stolen both the ideas and the manuscript from Eddie. Such a contract can hardly be valid, can it? It would be good if the company's legal department could prepare for a match against both Babelfish and Eddie. Astra says that the police can question Titus at the fair before they arrest Eddie. Eddie is going to be at the Babelfish stand when everybody mingles at five o'clock and they ought to get there in time. Good, says Evita, and urges Astra to drive carefully.

Astra ends the call and breathes out. It's going to be all right. She has managed to get *The Best Book in the World* this far, so she will bloody well manage to get it that little bit further.

She looks at Titus snoozing against the window with the safety belt as a cushion. His black suit is grey with soil, cement dust and old, dried-up vomit. His face has lines of dirt. He stinks.

This isn't good enough, Astra thinks. We must tidy him up. Put him under a shower. She looks at the road signs to check if there is a hotel anywhere near. Where are we? Lake Vättern is down there on the right somewhere. She is lucky. The Golden Otter, two kilometres. She remembers that motel, her family used to stay there when she was little and they were on their way home from a motoring holiday down in Europe. They would eat salmon with dill in white sauce, buy a stick of peppermint rock and remember that it was nice to go abroad on holiday, but it was even better to be back in Sweden. They'd sit on the terrace and look out across the long narrow lake, talk about the mythical island – Visingsö – where her father believed that kings had lived in bygone ages. Run to the car to fetch warm sweaters. Brrrr. It is cool today, but it will probably be warmer tomorrow. Sweden, home sweet home.

When she parks the car and the sound of the engine stops, Titus wakes up. He looks around, then leans his head against the neck rest and closes his eyes again.

'I'll get a room so that Titus can have a wash,' she explains to the company in the back seat.

'Okay, we'll go in and get a cup of coffee and a Danish pastry. It's on me!' Doctor Rolf rumbles.

Astra goes round to the other side of the car and opens Titus' door.

'Titus, you need a shower. Come along!'

She helps Titus out of the car. He totters out and stretches his arms over his head, yawns widely and smiles.

Next to Astra's car on the parking area stands a car with an open bonnet and a man leaning over the engine. Something is evidently broken and his irritation can be felt in the air. He throws an oily rag onto the ground and mutters.

'Accursed vehicle!'

Titus recognises that voice. He bends down under the bonnet and looks.

'Christer!'

It is Christer Hermansson standing there swearing at his car. The zealous librarian from Stockholm City Library. Titus' fellow author, who writes laboured books about men on the verge of reality.

Christer Hermansson looks up at Titus.

'Titus!'

His eyes wander over Titus from top to toe.

'What have you been through?'

'It's a long story. This is Astra Larsson, my publisher.'

Christer looks at Astra. He wipes his hands on his trousers and pulls his ponytail tighter before holding out his hand.

'Christer Hermansson. How do you do?'

'Has your car broken down?' asks Astra.

'*Ich bin ein bibliothekar!*' exclaims Christer. 'Not a car mechanic…'

'I see. And are you on the way to the book fair too?' wonders Astra.

'Yes. But now I'm stranded here. I don't understand engines, and they don't understand me. We are not friends, I fear. A negative prognosis suggests this is a matter of lifelong enmity. I fear the worst.'

Titus smiles when he recognises Christer's austere tone. It is always hard to tell whether he is serious or is joking. An academic dryness with a humorous glint is always present.

'You can come with us!' says Titus, and turns to Astra. 'He can do that, can't he?'

'Of course!'

'Really? Most gracious of you!'

'Yes, but absolutely,' says Astra. 'Pack your things in the back. Incidentally, you don't have some extra clothes you can lend to Titus? And shaving gear?'

Christer Hermansson looks at Titus again. He nods understandingly.

'Indeed, I do have new clothes for the emperor. He can borrow one of my book-fair suits!'

The mood in the car couldn't be better when they set off on the final stretch. They have all eaten and been to the loo. Titus has stood under running water for half an hour and shaved his head and face. He has regained quite a lot of his former colour, and if you didn't know better you might think he had just returned from a holiday in the sun.

Malin huddles on Lenny's lap under the safety belt. They are purring like cats that have just had their favourite dinner. Christer Hermansson has found a space in the middle of the back seat. He looks small beside the large and jovial Doctor Rolf. Since he doesn't have any idea what has happened to this strange party in the car, he just sees the journey as divine intervention. He has escaped his wreck of a car and can chat with lots of amusing people who are also going to the book fair. Thanks to Astra and Titus, he will get there in time. He is as merry as a lark and starts up a sing-song.

'We're havin' fun sittin' in the back seat, kissin' and a'huggin with Fred.'

'Dee doody doom doom, dee doody doom doom, dee doody doom doom, DOOM,' answer Ralf, Lenny, Malin, Titus and Astra in a loud chorus.

They laugh as Christer guides them through some old popular classics. It is liberating to let something else take over, something from outside. There is still a world out there. They are on the way back now. They're having fun.

Then Astra's telephone rings.

Unknown number.

Astra hushes them with her finger on her lips. It could be news from the book fair. Has Eddie X disappeared? Has Evita got hold of the police? They might want to talk to Titus.

She presses the green button and answers in a proper tone:

'Yes, this is Astra Larsson.'

'Hello, Astra! This is Fabian Nadersson. Have you got a moment?'

Oh no! Not that dreadful telephone hawker again! He rings on the most unsuitable occasions. What a hopeless type. But Astra refuses to abandon her good mood. She switches to the loudspeaker and holds up the phone so that everybody can hear, turns the volume to maximum and shouts:

'Fabian, we are in the middle of a little conference here! Is it okay with you to sell to several people at the same time? We are me, Titus, Ralf, Christer, Malin and Lenny. Everybody – say hello to Fabian!'

'HELLO FABIAN!' The back-seat chorus shouts. Astra sets the tone by whirling the telephone in the air and whispering words to prompt the chorus.

'Hello everybody!' says Fabian. ' Great, several birds with one stone, we like that, haha. Well, the thing is, you understand, Astra and all the rest of you, that I am ringing on behalf of Seraphim Insurance. We offer a free meeting with one of our insurance experts.'

'THANK – YOU – SO – VERY – MUCH – FABIAN! The chorus yells in line with Astra's direction.

'It'll take an hour and during that hour he or she will go through your financial situation. Then you'll be given a proposal for a pension plan designed especially for you which will realise your old-age dreams. Does that sound good?'

'NO – IT – DOES – NOT!'

'I see. Perhaps your pension savings have been arranged some other way?'

'NO – THEY – HAVE – NOT!'

'Do you have any plans to think over your insurance policies in the near future?'

'NO – WE – DO – NOT!'

'I propose a meeting either on Tuesday, 10 October, at 11 a.m., or 1 November at 2 p.m. Which of those times would suit you best?'

'NEITHER – DON'T – YOU – LISTEN?'

'I see, well then, could you suggest another time when one of our experts can come to your office for a personal meeting?'

'NO – ABSOLUTELY – NOT!'

'Would you rather I phoned back another time?'

'NO – PREF – ER – AB – LY – NOT!'

'But you are interested in our services?'

'NO – NOT – ONE – TIIINY – BIT!'

'Well, thank you for giving me your time…

'YOU – ARE – WELCOME!'

'Okay, goodbye.'

'GOOD – BYE – FABIAN – NADERSSON!'

Astra ends the call and they all burst out laughing. There is nothing so liberating as when a telephone seller says goodbye.

They laugh and smile all the way to Gothenburg.

CHAPTER 40

The Book Fair Begins; the Book Ends

There are long winding queues outside the Book Fair. It is the wonderful first day when expectations are at their greatest. Professionals and the general public alike are welcome. Book lovers, teachers and librarians from the whole of Sweden have come. Publishers and authors from all over the world are there. Journalists are greedy for exciting interviews and compete to be the first to savour the 'buzz' of the day. The very heaviest titles are always released just in time for the fair. It is quite simply a paradise for those who delight in books in all their forms.

When the first day of the fair comes to a close, it turns into one great big party for mingling. The various publishing houses compete to arrange the most popular gatherings and clock up the most visitors. All are friends and all are happy.

Just in time for the first evening's big fair get-together, Astra brakes at the side of the main entry to the gigantic Swedish Exhibition and Congress Centre. There too is the entrance to Gothia Towers, the fancy fair hotel renowned for its stylish cocktail bar on the twenty-third floor. Over the years, Astra has bought a lot of Bloody Marys for thirsty authors. Several of them have even thought that the entire storey revolves on its own axis, which must be regarded as a compliment to the bartenders.

Down in the hotel foyer, there are two uniformed police officers together with Evita Winchester. They are waiting for Astra and her party. The two policemen look like twins: both of them have a trimmed chin beard partly shaved in a pattern and short ash-blond hair with lighter streaks. They look enormous compared to the little bundle of energy, Evita.

Evita who is wearing green boots, a green leather skirt and a very large white blouse that reveals a nicely tanned shoulder, hugs Titus and Astra and politely welcomes their fellow travellers.

One of the policemen stretches out his big hand to Titus and addresses him in the local accent.

'Hello there! My name is Glenn Johansson. This is my colleague Kevin Andersson. Evita Winchester here has given us some very interesting information about a certain Eddie X. Can we have a few words with you?'

'Yes, you can indeed,' says Titus grimly.

Winchester Publishing and Babelfish have – as usual – their gigantic stands next to each other: two explosions of red-hot books with colourful and flashy décor stretching from floor to ceiling. The two publishers are in the middle of the main hall as a symbol for their being the heart of the industry. Then, like rings on water, the smaller publishing houses, media companies, branch organisations and literary societies spread out. Hundreds of small and large stands populated by people of like mind.

When it is time for the big get-together for drinks, the security guards hang up thick ropes between the Winchester Publishing and Babelfish stands so that no unauthorised guests will get in and enjoy the free drinks. The ropes dangle loosely between smart brass posts. It looks very fancy, like an Oscar gala in miniature.

Every year the party at Babelfish starts up with Eddie X pumping up the mood with his warm poems about life and love. People inside as well as outside the ropes are welcome to listen. It is one of the highlights of the book fair and this year there are more people than ever in the premiere public. They are full of expectation.

Yes, Eddie X has also made his way to Gothenburg. He has driven fast and avoided the motorway as much as possible since he has had an unpleasant feeling of being followed. Now he has made his entry on the little stage in the middle of the Babelfish stand. He is barefoot and dressed in trousers, jacket and a buttoned-up shirt. His clothes are of super-creased cotton and the three items of clothing are batik-dyed in various shades of grey. It is different and very smart. His black hair is matted and the grey shades of his clothes are mirrored in his face. He has fist-size rings under his eyes, which stare right into the public. He is not his usual self at all. He must have planned a new exciting prank. You can see the public thinking: 'This is going to be cool!'

He sits on a high bar stool and grabs the mike.

'Hello. Everybody comfortable?'

'Yeees,' answer the public rather feebly.

'I said: EVERYBODY COMFORTABLE?'

'YEEES!'

'Good for you.'

The public laughs. It's amusing that he has switched perspectives. The loving one pretends to be grumpy. Hahaha.

'I'm going to read something for you.'

'YEEES!'

The people in the public look at each other. Now it's starting. It's going to be delightful and sincere.

'This is something that Titus Jensen has written. Do you remember him?'

Everybody laughs. Of course they have heard of Titus and his readings. The has-been who threw away his writing career. And now Eddie X is going to read Titus Jensen. A sort of meta-event. Hahaha.

Eddie produces a copy of *Treacherous Charades* and turns to the first page. He has seen Titus do this many a time and now he lays on the theatrical effects as best he can.

"'It is a daaark and stormy night. A high pressure area that has parked above the British Isles shows no tendency to divert to the north. The supercoooled sleet that has lashed Stockholm's windows for more than two weeks suddenly passed over Johannes Karlsson's attic flat. It rained into his little pad.'"

Pause for effect and a scattering of applause. The public smiles expectantly. It isn't funny and warm yet, but it soon will be.

"'In the glare of the lightning flashes Johannes could see that the floor was wet. It rained in even more and soon there were small waves on the floor and around the bed-legs. Johannes pulled the wet covers up over him, put on his goggles and observed the course of events. Pissing it down. How would he get to work now?'"

The public giggle. What a dreadful story.

They don't have time to find out more about Johannes Karlsson. Two police officers climb up onto the stage. Eddie looks at them and his gaze becomes wild. He throws the book at the policemen, screams at them to disappear. The public laughs. Hahaha, now it's starting for real. This is much funnier than the bedroom farces at the popular theatres. Eddie pushes the bar stool over when he tries to escape and the microphone smashes to the floor with a roaring echo in the loudspeaker. The grim-looking policemen have grabbed him each with a firm grip on one arm. They are a head taller than Eddie. His feet dangle freely between them.

'NOOOO!' he screams.

A man comes onto the stage. It is Titus Jensen! The man in black is now dressed completely in white. White buttoned-up frill shirt, white leather trousers, white leather jacket and white patent-leather shoes. He smiles like an American TV faith-healer. Somebody turns an extra spotlight on. The flood of white light almost dazzles the public. What's going on? Titus Jensen lifts up the microphone and taps it. Yep, it works.

'Hello?'

The public are now quiet. This is exciting. The police seem indifferent. Eddie looks desperate, dangling there between them. He stares at Titus with murder in his eyes.

'Hello. Hi, my name is Titus Jensen. I know you have come here to listen to Eddie X. But I want to borrow your ears for a minute. Is that okay?'

The public nod in silence. Mumble.

'I am sober,' says Titus in a low voice but close to the microphone. 'And I can work.'

The book-fair public has never encountered anything like this before. Is it an AA meeting?

Titus looks at Eddie dangling between the two policemen. His matted black hair hangs over his eyes and the blue and orange streaks look tired. He squirms like a worm.

'I have written a book that will be published in the spring. It is going to go well. But best of all is that more books will follow. And it is Eddie X who has made it possible for me to look ahead again. Eddie, your methods were unorthodox but they worked in the end. I am not a mess any longer. I am free, I want to work and I am grateful.'

Titus looks at Astra, Evita, Lenny, Malin, Ralf Rolf and Christer Hermansson, who are standing below the stage. They are watching him expectantly. Then he looks Eddie in the eye and takes a deep breath.

'Now I only want to say one thing to you…'

The public is extremely attentive. The air in the hall stands still. Eddie stares at Titus.

'Eddie, I am going to do everything in my power to ensure you come through this in one piece. I promise you that.'

The public don't know what it is about but they applaud cautiously because they think that what Titus is saying sounds good. Brotherly love, so to speak. Titus turns towards them and says in a serious tone:

'Love, that is the most noble form of energy in the universe. Love is the only source of energy that grows the more it is used. So if you want this planet to survive – love each other! EXPLOIT LOVE!'

Cheers and laughter. Warmth returns to the Book Fair once again.

There is more whispering than ever at the get-together party on the Winchester Publishing stand. The rumour about what has happened spreads rapidly and a lot of people sneak a look at Titus Jensen. Today he feels comfortable with those glances. It doesn't matter what they say. He knows who he is.

It is nice that it is all over. Sure, it is fun to be at the Book Fair, but most of all Titus longs to get home to his flat and his computer. His own computer, not the Winchester one with the breathalyser lock. He is looking forward to a long winter with hundreds of wonderful working days.

Evita puts her hand on Titus' arm. She leaves it there quite a while. Titus gets a tickling feeling in his tummy.

'Titus, I must tell you about a fantastic idea that the marketing department has come up with.'

'About *The Best Book in the World*? That sounds exciting…'

'We want the book to get on the bestseller lists in several categories, don't we?'

'Yeah, right… Fine by me…'

A waiter passes them and Evita snaps up a glass of champagne and a plate with cheese squares stuck on cocktail sticks. Titus takes a glass of juice.

'The content is just fine,' Evita goes on. She raises her glass in a sort of toast to the air and takes a sip of her bubbly. 'You have covered everything in the manuscript. It is exciting, useful, helps the reader develop, and all of that. But now they have come up with a brilliant idea for the cover.'

'Okay?'

Evita takes a bit of cheese and raises it to Titus' mouth. His mouth opens like a reflex. Evita smiles, pleased.

'Oh, it's such a great idea! Listen! This is how it goes: we're going to have two different covers. But on the same book. You see, the front and back covers are going to be upside down in relation to each other, so however you turn the book you will see a front cover. A stroke of genius, don't you think?'

'Err, yeah well,' says Titus not really understanding, and takes a gulp of juice. 'Tell me more.'

Evita takes a deep breath and adopts her sales-conference voice.

'First we have the thriller cover. Imagine a mysterious little girl in a white dress in a nasty hospital setting. The era is unclear, but it's in the past. Associations to ritual experiments, or possible trade in organs. And above the hospital scene hovers an unpleasant person in a gas mask, like an evil spirit. An all-seeing Dr Mabuse or Kaiszer Söze. In an old-fashioned mask against mustard gas.'

'But why, why that? There isn't any little girl or a gas mask mentioned in my book…' Titus attempts.

'That doesn't make any difference,' Evita interrupts him, irritated. 'There is surely nothing more unpleasant than small innocent girls and anonymous men in gas masks? No, that really is the most unpleasant combination one could imagine. We've checked that with focus groups. So people are going to buy it. And then perhaps we throw in a Gothic cross too, they can be really horrible.'

'But…'

'Ah-ah-ah! Sssh…'

Evita puts a finger over his mouth to silence Titus' protest. With her other hand she strokes the top of his hand. She puts a couple of fingers under his shirt cuff. A long way in. Caresses his arm quickly but soft as silk. Titus gives a start. He tries to think clearly and is just about to fire off one of many questions whirling around inside his head when Evita goes on with the unofficial sales conference.

'And then we have the other front cover. The self-help book. A beautiful couple running across a summer meadow. Slim, of course, thanks to your ABC Method. Perhaps we'll have a raised title in silver or golden foil to create associations to major prizes. Dazzling, fertile smiles. They look horny in a sort of jolly Danish lightweight porno way, but above all they are happy and successful. What do you think?'

'I don't know. I don't really understand. My covers don't usually have a picture, but just the title clearly visible. Black, grey, white, small print. Perhaps an edging. Slightly French literary cool… sort of…'

'Yes, exactly, that's why! We are launching a new Titus Jensen.'

She takes a cocktail stick with cheese and puts it into Titus' mouth.

'Tasty?'

'Mmmm…'

'The best part of this is that the bookshops won't know which cover to display on the shelves and in the window. That means they will place several copies side-by-side! So your book will get a lot of exposure. It will be the best visual effect in the world. *The Best Book in the World* plastered all over the bookshop. People will be falling over to buy it!'

'*The Best Book in the World* after *The Best Book in the World* after *The Best Book in the World…*' says Titus dreamily and paints the image before him with his hand.

'But, best of all… we're going to have some knockout blurbs.'

'Blurbs?'

'Yeah, you know, quotes from a celeb on the front cover. And you know what, I've got a really great hold on the permanent secretary of the Swedish Academy. And now it's time to make use of that!'

'You're kidding… you don't mean…?'

'Yeah, it's rather fun. But I'm not kidding. He'll do it. He coiled himself around my little finger some years ago. And did it all by himself. And now, I've only got to ask him nicely, my little permanent secretary. Isn't it wonderful?'

She puts another cube of cheese into Titus' mouth. Nice taste. Very nice. It is working out okay, this.

Evita leans over towards him. She breathes her warm breath into his ear. Blows out air down his neck.

Her décolletage approaches his eyes. He thinks he recognises that bosom. Is it her? Yes, indeed, it is!

A tremor runs through him.

She whispers into his ear. Snarls.

'You look good in white…'

The warm air from her nose is like a whirlpool inside his ear, like a fizzy tablet for his brain. Her hand rests on his arm. For a long time.

Snarl.

Growl.

'… but me, I look best nude.'

Doctor Rolf has never done the cocktail-party thing at a book fair before. Nor have Lenny and Malin. They think it's great and drink eagerly of everything that is served. Astra, who has had her hands full with greeting authors and book-sellers, comes by to exchange a few words.

'How are you getting on? Are you getting something to drink?'

'It's all great!' bellows Doctor Rolf. 'Tell me, are there lots of celebrities here?'

'One or two,' says Astra and looks around. 'Over there, for example, that's Pablo Blanco, the Mexican bestseller-author who writes self-help novels.'

She points towards a man, short of stature and wearing a black polo sweater. He has a little tuft of hair on his neck, the sort that the boldest little boys in day nursery tend to have nowadays, the ones who push little girls into the sand pit and have dads who play ice hockey. Standing a few feet behind him is a grumpy woman with a flowery old-lady dress. Despite it probably having cost a packet, it looks about as good on her as a moth-eaten curtain in an old barn. She is Blando's agent and manager. A number of pretty young girls have flocked around Blando. He has sold millions of books and his celebrity status is magnetic.

'The grey mouse behind him is his agent, Veronica Fuentes,' Astra goes on. 'The Bitch in Barcelona, that's what they call her in the branch.'

'What!' yells Doctor Rolf. His eyes grow dark. 'Is that Pablo Blando? Fucking... hell.'

Astra looks at him, surprised.

'What's the matter?'

'That bastard has destroyed many lives,' hisses Doctor Rolf. 'I've had loads of patients on account of him. First they read his books and then they think they have found the

"Path of Life". The worst book is *The Maker of Gold*. They read that and think they have seen the light. However, slowly but surely they bury themselves in gloomy pondering, start to imagine that they need to find more happiness in their lives. And in searching for that, they lose their foothold. And when the happiness doesn't materialise and liberate them, then they are going to feel unhappy, aren't they? They start looking for what's wrong with them, for symptoms. They read even more books about happiness, but no happiness results. In the end, they have acquired an affliction and they must somehow make their way out of that. If only they can become healthy again, then they will find happiness. But in actual fact they have never been ill! No, fucking hell! Years of multi-therapy can be necessary to make them whole again!'

'Oops, I had no idea…'

'No, nobody wants to admit it,' hisses Doctor Rolf aggressively. 'Everyone keeps mum about it. But lots of the people who read his books would feel a lot better if they read the telephone directory instead and didn't think so damned much. That is the truth! No, fucking hell, I am so damned tired of all the imaginary invalids who have read *The Maker of Gold*, I could throw up!'

'You don't say…?' Astra responds cautiously.

She does of course work for the publishing house which publishes all of Blando's books. They earn pots of money from them, and don't have any plans at all to stop. And from what she can tell, Doctor Rolf's intellectual wanderings are not exactly 'mainstream'. Has she ever heard of multi-therapy making anybody happy? Perhaps best to manoeuvre her way out of this subject. Ralf Rolf seems to be something of a powder keg. Astra adopts a diplomatic smile.

'You will have to tell him in person what you think.'

'Yep, um. Perhaps,' Doctor Rolf flares up. 'Good idea…'

Cocktail parties are the mother of all business deals.

Astra introduces one foreign publisher after the other to Titus. They have all heard of his story and now they want to say hello to the miracle from the earth cellar.

A distinguished elderly gentleman with an American accent introduces himself as Collin Harper. He claims that he wants to publish *The Best Book in the World* in fourteen countries. He has heard that it is 'amazing'.

Titus Jensen gives a slight bow.

Astra Larsson a little curtsy.

Evita Winchester laughs out loud.

After the drinks party, it is banquet time. The very most prominent guests at the book fair have been invited. A huge swathe of fair delegates gathers in the main hall ready to take the large escalator up to the party. Evita has quickly succeeded in conjuring forth tickets for all of Astra's fellow travellers. The singular group moves slowly towards the party like a little tail after the other guests. One by one they step onto the escalator.

Astra and Christer Hermansson go first. They are laughing and seem to be enjoying each other's company.

Then come Lenny and Malin. They are tightly entwined and can hardly believe this is true. Astra wants to publish a book about the story of Lenny's life. *Tourette's and Me – Not an Easy Journey*, by Lenny Rolf. She has offered him a juicy advance.

Then comes Doctor Rolf. He sneaks a grim look at the fairy-tale old man Pablo Blando who is a bit higher up on the escalator together with two young girls and his grumpy agent. Blando gesticulates and kisses the girls on their cheeks and hands. Doctor Rolf rolls up the arms of his white coat and mutters to himself with clenched teeth: 'I'm having an old friend for dinner.'

Last in the escalator come Evita and Titus, arm in arm. Flashes of lightning from her green eyes. He smiles roguishly with his blue eyes.

For a few seconds Titus turns his back on those who are above him on the escalator. He looks out across the wonderful mass of adventures and stories down in the hall. He loves what he sees. Fantasies, he thinks, mere fancies and fantasies. Dreams and illusions.

Titus is on the way up. He stretches out his arms. Extends all his fingers widely. Bends his neck backwards and closes his eyes. Fills his lungs. He is just about to shout out as loudly as he can. But he changes his mind and instead breaks into the biggest smile in the world. With a calm soul he whispers to his new-found best friend.

Better to be obsessed than dependent.

PART 3

In Which Reality Catches up with the Author and His Readers

Sometimes the final battle is not fought until as late as early October.

Walls of yellow and red foliage rise up among the trees while the high summer winds try to trick the course of nature. But even though the sun is warming, it is nevertheless too low in the sky to allow the leaves to reflect any green life. The struggle is doomed beforehand. The Indian summer has so far never beaten the autumn, but it does at least take its final breaths with a warm smile on its lips. To die a hero's death as a proud Indian, exhausted and in full warpaint, gives hope of reincarnation.

The cliffs, air and water. The long summer has allowed the elements of the archipelago to reach the same warm temperature. There are no contradictions and no strong winds blow up. The bays between Stockholm and the outer skerries have a mirror-like surface reminiscent of newly washed shop windows.

Astra's long narrow vessel cuts through the water with a whisper. Her hair is collected in a ponytail which sways in time with the movements of the boat. She holds the tiller in one hand, and has her other hand's index finger on the nautical chart. She has turned the GPS off. Navigating without electronics is freedom. Making way slowly with a super-fast boat is relaxation.

She glances behind her to see how her passenger is managing. He is sitting right at the back on the leather-clad cushions on the stern thwart. His arms outstretched and his hands with a firm grip on both the port and starboard railings. His shirt is unbuttoned almost down to his navel. His taut chest is brown and newly shaved, with a shiny glow. His long black hair waves in the air in keeping with the proud Swedish flag in the stern. A few dyed strands decorate his hair, rather like speed stripes.He is the very image of a handsome young man.

Astra smiles and eases on the throttle. They are almost there now. They're going to have all of Stora Nassa to themselves.

She lets the boat slowly glide in towards the old jetty on Stora Bonden. This is the largest island among the old crown harbours where the fishermen used to spend the night during the most intensive herring-fishing periods. The first settlers came as early as the eighteenth century, and at most about ten poor families lived in small cottages on the cliff. Nowadays the whole area is a nature reserve and a protected area for birds. But when the nestlings have flown their way at the end of the summer, then you can visit again.

Astra turns the engine off, steps nimbly over the wind-screen and jumps out onto the jetty. With just one hand she quickly secures the boat fore and aft. The silence that arises when you have turned off an engine in the outer skerries is paralysing.

'Now do you see?' she whispers with pretended irritation out of the corner of her mouth. 'I'm not as unfamiliar with boats as you seem to think.'

'Sorry,' he laughs, and gets up on unsteady legs to try to go ashore. 'Sorry, but I have only written a novel. It isn't the truth.'

She stretches out her hand and helps him off the boat.

'Get a look at this. It is a paradise.'

After having meandered around on small paths among stonecrops and heather amidst the cracks in the rocky surfaces, they sit down at the highest point on the island and look out across the bays to the west. Nassa is so far out that even the inner skerries disappear beyond the horizon. Far, far away in the glitter above thousands of invisible islands lies Stockholm. A white-tailed eagle hovers like a wide plank high up in the sky searching for shoals of fish in the evening sun which is slowly crawling down from the sky. Soon darkness will come, soon the last battle will be fought.

Astra strokes her hands over her thighs to straighten the creases in her short summer dress. She then pulls out a couple of glasses from a little cooler in padded beaver nylon, and a beautiful bottle which looks deliciously chilled with its drops of condensation running along the narrow body.

'May I tempt you with this summer's last glass of rosé?' says Astra, and unscrews the bottle.

'I need to talk to you,' he says and lifts a strand of orange hair off his face. He looks worried. Pained.

'Yes, that's what we're going to do. We shall celebrate and talk. That's why we are here.'

'I… I want to talk about the book,' he says quietly in his leisurely northern accent.

'Yes, Titus. That's why we are doing this. We're going to celebrate that you have finished editing the manuscript. And talk. About the book.'

Titus' dark velvet eyes don't look as if they are in a party mood. They are sad.

'I don't know, Astra. It feels as if I've committed suicide.'

'What are you saying? Why?'

'Well, using their names…' he says and scratches his neck inside the black collar. He twists his loose hair half a turn and lets it fall onto his back.

'Yes?'

'I don't know... is it really going to work? People know who I am and what I stand for. Is it wise to do this? I'm smashing everything with this book. Besides, Eddie X is going to go bananas.'

Astra puts her hand on his arm.

'Now listen to me. It isn't the end of the world if he does. Who cares about bald old men in batik clothes? Don't bother about him, we must think about what is best for you now.'

'But what I mean is: is it really necessary? Do I go too far? Why can't I be the young guy in the book too? Perhaps all it needs is to change clothes on the characters? I've only got to "find and replace" and change all the names in the manuscript to make it all more credible. Not quite so utterly barmy.'

'You know what I've said all the time. Poetry and collections of short stories are a cul-de-sac, Titus. You are young. You have a large public who love what you do. This is your debut as a novelist and you must be prepared to take a few risks. You are an artiste, remember that. Besides, it was your idea from the very first. It was you who wanted to explore more sides of yourself.'

'Yes, I know. But it's all so bloody weird... will the readers really understand? There are so bloody many meta-levels... It is almost as if I myself get confused. An author writes a book about an author who in actual fact is another author. And that author is also writing a book and competing with another author who wants to write the same book. And the last author is really the first author. That is... me. Or however it is. What the hell do I mean anyway?'

'But Titus, what is the alternative? That we use a pseudonym instead of your real name? That would be even worse: an author pseudonym writes a book about an author who is writing a book about an author who is competing against another author. And the last two both think they have written the best book in the world. No, it wouldn't make it any better.'

'Don't you think… But… We could think about it, couldn't we?'

Astra raises her hand as a stop sign. A serious wrinkle appears between her eyebrows.

'No! Remember one thing, Titus. You already have the best readers in the world. They love to be misled. And now you'll get lots more. You have invited them to join you on a fun journey, but you are not their cicerone. They themselves are the ones who create their experiences and memories. I think that they like that everything isn't fixed like the worst sort of package holiday. I promise you. Besides, most of them are going to laugh maliciously when they think about Eddie X in reality. Sitting there half-sloshed in former colourful silk rags and sitting in a rage at his regular table at the Association Bar. Talking about *Baroque in Their Blood* from '95 and similar bombastic nonsense. Trying to pick up cultured ladies and supporting himself by reading weird old books at pop festivals. No, in the long term I think you're doing him a service. Perhaps he might pull himself together and write a good book again.'

'Do you think so?'

'Well think and think…' says Astra, a big smile appearing on her face. 'You can use your imagination a bit, can't you? Makes life a bit more fun.'

They remain sitting a while on the rocks, talking about the book and about each other and following the course of a belated flock of geese flying in plough formation over the archipelago. Astra puts her arm around Titus. They watch the sun against the horizon. Titus buries his cheeks in Astra's hair. It turns to evening.

'Now it's time to gorge ourselves on prawns!'

Astra comes up out of the cabin with a large bowl of fresh prawns. They have put up a little camping table in the middle of the cockpit, laid with china plates, oil lamps and linen serviettes, fresh bread, wine and aioli.

'Ho, ho, wonderful!' laughs Titus. 'When fiction turns into reality, so to speak!'

'You can bet on that,' says Astra and blinks her long lashes a couple of times. 'This is only the beginning.'

They eat the prawns and throw the shells into the sea one by one. Small and medium-size fish come and gobble those delicacies in the dark water and disappear down among the clumps of seaweed with their catch.

'Cheers to the summer!' says Astra and raises her crystal glass.

'Cheers to the autumn! That is nice too,' Titus responds.

'Cheers to the book and because it is finished!'

'Cheers to the publisher!'

They clink their glasses together.

'So how does it feel now?' asks Astra with eyes that encourage total honesty.

Titus sighs.

'Fine, thank you, but I am starved and dried up. I am empty and a bit down. I'm jiggered. I just want to eat, drink and be myself. I am so incredibly tired of Eddie X. I must start thinking about something new soon.'

'You can take it easy, Titus. You have done a good job, a great job. I am pleased to have been a part of that journey. And extremely curious as to what is going to happen with you and me. We have shared so very much more that just work during this period. Plus that in between the lines of the manuscript I read a hidden declaration of love.'

A glow comes to Titus' eyes.

'Hidden, uhmm hidden…'

'But I can't fathom how you could know that my middle name is Evita. It isn't exactly something one likes to make a show of. Yes, there is something new between us. A bit ticklish, I like it. But now let's eat! And then we can have a dip. If you dare – there is a full moon.'

No more wine bottles left, the coffee cups have been emptied and the schnapps glasses are empty. The last summer night has now settled like a comfy rug over Stora Nassa and Astra's boat.

They have moved into the cabin. The oil lamps are struggling to dry the dampness from the wet towels lying across the floor. Not with much success. The windows have misted over.

Steam rises up from the bodies of Astra and Titus entwined under the covers in the wide berth in the forepeak. They kiss each other gently, stroking each other's wet hair, caressing each other's damp bodies. Feeling their way forward.

It is the calm before the last panting minute of the final battle, when the summer's death rattle meets the first breaths of autumn. Molten lead will be poured over those who can't keep their cool. The cowardly ones will drown in their own blood. Now they are blowing on the trumpets, now the battle calls are starting to ring out. Now shining swords are being unsheathed, now rifles are being filled with powder, now the guns are being rolled towards the fortress and millions of brave soldiers are running towards the raised drawbridge to make the leap of their life – to life or death.

Soon the battle will be underway.

There is shaking and rocking in the cabin, everything is wet and stiff.

It is shining all shiny.

Astra's telephone rings. For a couple of seconds, the sound waves from the phone are the only thing moving in the whole world.

In a reflex action she reaches for the phone. But before she answers, she looks at the display to see who it is.

'What? It can't be true!'

Astra looks at the phone with uncertain eyes. It doesn't care about her unwillingness, but just goes on ringing. The seconds march with ant-steps through the cabin. Hundreds of uniformed drummer boys hitting their hickory sticks against the taut skin of the drums.

Derre-dumm.

Titus stares at Astra without blinking.

Derre-dumm. Derre-dumm. Derre-dumm.

It is a fateful moment. Everything will be decided here and now.

Derre-dumm. Derre-dumm-dumm-dumm.

The will to live conquers the will to try to please people. Astra clicks on the 'Don't answer' button. She turns her phone off and without looking around throws it over her shoulder. It lands softly on the pile of wet towels on the floor.

Dark angels blow fanfares on their trumpets. The warriors on the battlefield bang their steel against the flint. The gunpowder in the fuses starts to hiss again. Attack. Forward!

'Who was that?' Titus asks while simultaneously greedily licking Astra's earlobe.

'You wouldn't believe it anyway.'

'Yes, please, I want to know.'

Astra rolls Titus over onto his back. She holds his arms against the mattress and boards him slowly while simultaneously painting his chest with her wet hair.

'You… you don't need to know everything. Mmmm… you should live in your fantasies instead. Life is much more fun then.'

When Peter Stjernström got tired of his career in the financial industry a few years ago, the only thing to do was to sit down and start writing. The suit was changed for more comfortable attire and the computer became his constant companion. His first novel, *Enn Mann*, was released 2003. He also works as a copywriter and entrepreneur. He lives in Stockholm.

Cold Courage
by Pekka Hiltunen

When Lia witnesses a disturbing scene on her way to work, she, like the rest of the City of London, is captivated and horrified. As details unfurl in the media, the brutal truth emerges – a Latvian prostitute has been killed, her body run over by a steamroller and then placed in the boot of a car to be found.

As the weeks pass and no leads are found, the news story dies but Lia finds herself unable to forget. When she meets Mari, another Finn living in London, she thinks it fortuitous, but Mari has engineered the meeting for her own advantage. There is much more to Mari than meets the eye: she possesses an unnatural ability to 'read' people, to see into their innermost thoughts and pre-empt their actions. Mari heads up a mysterious unit she calls the 'Studio'.

Mari and Lia strike up a firm friendship and when Lia shares the thoughts plaguing her about the murder, Mari thinks she and the members of the Studio can help where the police have failed. But Mari and Lia are about to set foot into extremely dangerous territory, especially as Mari is not above using the Studio to unscrupulous ends.

'Rich in details, sure in its descriptions of London and smoothly written, this novel is a stylish debut.'
Turun Sanomat, Finland

'Confident, unique and captivating thriller.' *Kaleva*, Finland

NOW AVAILABLE

The Merman
by Carl-Johan Vallgren

Nella and her brother Robert live a difficult life with their mother and father in a small town on the west coast of Sweden. Robert is bullied at school, and Nella has to resort to debt and petty crime to pay off his tormentors.

When she turns to her friend Tommy for help, her suspicions are aroused by the mysterious comings and goings of his brothers at their dilapidated boat house. But when she uncovers the reason behind their enigmatic behaviour, her life is opened to the realities of a mindboggling secret.

The Merman is an exhilarating and beautiful book about sibling love and betrayal – and what happens when the mundane collides with the strange and wonderful.

'An intense little gem' *Dagens Nyheter*, Sweden

'Worthy of Stephen King on a good day' *Expressen*, Sweden

'Bitterly harsh and beautiful' *Svenska Dagbladet*, Sweden

PRAISE FOR CARL-JOHAN VALLGREN:

'Charged, atmospheric, thought-provoking' *Daily Telegraph*

'Challenging and shocking' *The Guardian*

NOW AVAILABLE

The Hundred-Year-Old-Man Who Climbed out of the Window and Disappeared
by Jonas Jonasson

Sitting quietly in his room in an old people's home, Allan Karlsson is waiting for a party he doesn't want to begin. His one-hundredth birthday party to be precise. The Mayor will be there. The press will be there. But, as it turns out, Allan will not...

Escaping (in his slippers) through his bedroom window, into the flowerbed, Allan makes his getaway. And so begins his picaresque and unlikely journey involving criminals, several murders, a suitcase full of cash, and incompetent police. As his escapades unfold, Allan's earlier life is revealed. A life in which – remarkably – he played a key role behind the scenes in some of the momentous events of the twentieth century.

'Arguably the biggest word-of-mouth literary sensation of the decade'
The Independent

'Imaginative, laugh-out-loud bestseller'
Daily Telegraph

'Should carry a health warning for spouses or partners who are easily irritated by the sounds of helpless chortling'
The Irish Times

NOW AVAILABLE

HESPERUS PRESS

—◄○►—

Under our three imprints, Hesperus Press publishes over 300 books by many of the greatest figures in worldwide literary history, as well as contemporary and debut authors well worth discovering.

HESPERUS CLASSICS

handpicks the best of worldwide and translated literature, introducing forgotten and neglected books to new generations.

HESPERUS NOVA

showcases quality contemporary fiction and non-fiction designed to entertain and inspire.

HESPERUS MINOR

rediscovers well-loved children's books from the past – these are books which will bring back fond memories for adults, which they will want to share with their children and loved ones.

To find out more visit www.hesperuspress.com
@HesperusPress